<u>D E A D</u>

<u>W I N N E R S</u>

DAVE McDONALD

For
Natasha and Al
for showing me the trees in the woods

PROLOGUE

Indianapolis, Indiana

"Is this Jim Smith?" The deep male voice on the phone rumbled like a Harley Hog in a mountain tunnel.

He peered through his efficiency's window, a few feet from the only chair in the room. A late January snow fell on the small visible section of highway near his apartment. Early morning commuters and trucks jostled for openings on the white bordered section of the I-465 loop around Indianapolis, the road noise constant and tiring.

"Is that your real name?"

Jim squinted, strange question for a telemarketer. "Tell me who you are and what you want, or I'm hangin' up." He eased back into the ugly brown cloth-cover chair.

"A friend of mine said he knew ... well, that you have some rather unique skills."

He slumped his thin body in the worn chair and channel-surfed the small television. "What are you talkin' about?"

"He ah, he said you liked to kill people," said the phone voice.

Jim dropped the remote and bolted upright. "Who is this?"

"He also said you were currently unemployed and ... he said you needed money. I've got plenty of money and a job for you. You'll find

1

notes and an airplane ticket in your mailbox. Use them. Just remember, none of this is free." A click terminated the call.

By the time the plane's wheels touched down in Florida, Jim Smith's nerves and fear of the unknown had him primed for taking the next flight home. When he stepped off the airplane, though the sun had set, the tropical January air caressed him, calming his nerves. At that moment, he knew he wasn't going back to cold, dreary Indy, at least for a while.

The car was in the West Palm Airport's long term parking lot right where the printed note said it would be; the keys under the mat. The directions to an address in "The Cascades," a retirement community in Port Saint Lucie, were in the glove compartment.

Jim took a tire gauge out of his carry-on and placed it in the glove box. He never drove a car without having a tire gauge with him, never, a painful lesson scarred on his body from a former foster-father.

Driving with the driver's window down, he let the warm wind flutter his hair. He couldn't believe he was here, as if he were a trained animal reacting to stimuli. Although, for as long as Jim could remember, he'd had an obsession with taking a person's life; he had never killed a human, just animals, domesticated animals.

Someone, however, must have believed his attention-gaining war stories, 'I killed a dozen people, maybe more … in the war.' Jim had told that story to everyone he knew.

Yeah, he'd been to Afghanistan, but as a truck engine mechanic, not a ground pounder or as the sniper he claimed to have been. The only action he'd seen was a mongoose fighting a cobra. The ringside seat had cost him twenty rupees. Watching the cobra die had been worth much more. He regretted not making a video of it. A film of the cobra's death would have been a great addition to his collection of death videos.

But the lies, the war stories, were all he had. His life was a zero, void of anything of interest, no women, no sports, no college, and no jobs worth mentioning; not even any beer-slopping sexual conquest tales. The only thing that separated Jim from oblivion and gained him respect was his war fiction. When he told his fibs, people looked at him differently, especially when he embellished his tales with vivid details of hand-to-hand fighting.

Someone had believed him. His mailbox had more than a ticket and instructions, much more, twenty thousand dollars more. All hundreds wrapped by a rubber band in an envelope, with a note that eighty thousand more would be waiting for him after he completed the job.

He'd never seen, touched, held, or smelled twenty thousand dollars before, let alone eighty thousand. It was like a ticket to a new life.

The least Jim could do was go to the residence and check it out, maybe take a cell phone picture for proof. He could always claim nobody was home. But he would have to give the money back, the caller had ended his call with, "Just remember, none of this is free." And how could he return the money? He had no idea how to get in touch with this mystery employer.

His free hand slid into his pocket and touched the banded bills, so many. He could keep the money, buy a trailer, and start over somewhere in the south where it was warm year round, that'd be good.

But this unknown person, this phone caller, had found him once, what would keep the caller from finding him again? In this electronic age, could anyone actually get off the grid? He had no idea. Ignorance, not stupidity, was one of his problems. Maybe if he knew how the system worked, he could beat it. But he couldn't run or hide without knowing how someone found other people.

He was here. He had twenty thousand dollars in his pocket. What would it hurt to take a look? Maybe for once in his life he'd get lucky and catch a break, like maybe these people would die some other way today, like a car wreck or a house fire; nah. But he was here; just a car drive away.

The community was secured with an eight-foot wall and a guarded entrance. But the directions led him to an unguarded, walk-in gate with no security cameras. He parked his car, and pen light and directions in hand, entered the portal. By the time he'd wove his way through the many streets, hid from passing cars, and found the specified address, it was almost ten p.m. Most of the homes were dark.

He stood across the street from the lit house of Catie and Ed Mahoney and for the first time since leaving the plane, he thought about what he was being paid to do. His hand touched the knurled grips of the twenty-two automatic he had stuck in his waistband under his pulled out shirt. The silencer made the gun too long to fit in his pants pocket. Like everything else, the loaded gun had been in the glove box with the note, where the mailbox instructions had stated they would be.

Touching the gun made him taller, stronger. The weapon offered him something his empty, pathetic life lacked, power and control.

The note said he should knock on the door and introduce himself. The elderly Mahoney couple expected him. All he had to do was walk in, close the door, and start shooting. Simple.

So why were his hands trembling and sweating? It'd be like shooting a couple of old dogs that needed to be put down. How many dogs had he killed? He couldn't remember. He'd lost count years ago.

Another eighty thousand dollars after completing the job, he couldn't imagine that much money.

Jim glanced at his cell phone, it was after ten. The old farts would be going to bed soon. If he was going to do anything, it had to be soon. He had one hundred thousand reasons to at least knock on the door, and let things run their course. He would have killed a couple of old dogs for nothing more than the thrill. Why wouldn't killing a couple of old defenseless people be any less exciting? Surely he'd be empowered by taking their lives, plus rich.

Jim had nothing. He was nothing. Tonight he could be someone; someone to fear, someone who controlled others' destinies. And tomorrow he could have whatever he wanted. Jim'd have women-buying money. More importantly, he'd have attention-getting, respect-demanding money.

Energized, he jogged across the street and up the driveway. His feet slowed to a walk when they got on the brick pavers leading to the front door.

In the blackness of the home's portico, he pulled the gun, flipped the safety off, and chambered a round. The heavy, cool-to-the-touch gun fit his hand like it was custom-made for him. This weapon represented the brawny superiority he'd never had, but always wanted.

Jim glanced around at the houses across the street, nothing stirred. He'd come this far, he had money in his pocket, and a gun in his hand. All he had to do was ring a door bell and go from there; just a door bell away from a new life.

Returning the gun to his waistband in the middle of his back, Jim dropped his hands to his sides, shaking them and wiggling his fingers. He focused his mind on one-hundred-thousand dollars, took a deep breath, and rang the door bell.

A dog started yapping.

"Now who would be calling at this hour?" a high-pitched woman's voice yelled from within. "Eddie, you be sure to check who's there before you open the door. Cuddles, shut up!"

Several foot-clomps approached the door. "Who's there?" a male voice cracked by age asked.

Jim cleared his throat. He had to push the words out. "Jim Smith."

The security chain rattled as the man yelled, "Honey, it's the man from the lottery. He's here just like that fella said he'd be."

The door opened, spreading light over Jim. A tall, thin, bald old man wearing a sleeveless white tee shirt, blue and white polka dot pajama bottoms, and fluffy blue slippers motioned him inside.

"Come in, come in, young man, we've been expecting you," Ed Mahoney said, a smile adding to the lines on his drawn cheeks.

As Ed closed the door, a short, overweight woman appeared in a ratty white robe and fluffy pink slippers with a white towel wrapped around her head. She cradled a brown, snarling Yorkshire terrier in her arms.

"Ed and Catie Mahoney?" Jim asked.

"That's us," Ed said, as he walked over and took his wife's arm. "We wire transferred the money like you told us. That was a whole lot of money to send away." He shook his head. "How much cash you got for us? After seeing the check for all that money, I'm thinkin' it'd better be more than what we asked for."

Greedy bastard, everyone seemed to be greedy anymore. How stupid was this old man, trying to negotiate with absolutely the wrong person?

Jim knew the longer he waited the harder this would be, just like dogs, old dogs at that. With one hundred thousand dollars, maybe he could live in

Florida too. He reached behind him, grabbed the gun grips, and in one motioned aimed and fired.

A picture exploded to the right and behind the man.

The woman screamed and the man raised his hands.

Jim wrapped his other hand on the gun and corrected his aim. He shot the blabbering man in the chest, then the mouth-gaped woman just above the cuddled dog, and then the dog, when she dropped it. After the couple fell, he stepped close and shot them each in the forehead as specified in the instructions.

The adrenaline rush made him raise his hands in jubilation. Jim had to restrain himself from shouting. He'd done it. He'd be rich. And killing these old people had been easier than killing old dogs. They had just stood there.

But he wasn't done. As ordered, he donned his surgical gloves and ransacked the place, stuffing anything of value in a pillow case. The only thing that excited him in his booty was the man's diamond pinky ring; the stone had to be at least two carats.

After he left the house, making sure no one saw him; he wanted to run all the way to the car. But he didn't. He walked like an old man on a can't-sleep-walk. A borrowed hat pulled down, the pillow case of goodies stuffed inside his shirt making him seem fat; he strolled to his car.

Once inside his car, he released a long sigh, the release of a lifetime of pent-up frustration. He was a changed man. His crappy life would never be the same; a good thing.

Jim drove the speed limit even after he got on I-95 heading north. He would have to drive all night to get to Charleston, South Carolina. The further he drove, the more excited he became. But his excitement wasn't induced by the prospect of his earnings, it was the power. For the first time in his life, he had taken not one but two human lives. He had liked watching them die. How bizarre and yet how wonderful. The novice killer wanted more.

He tossed the fingerprint-cleaned gun and scattered everything he'd stolen along the highway, except about two hundred dollars in cash and the ring. Jim left the car, wiped clean of prints, in long-term parking. The next morning, he took the first flight to Indianapolis.

$$\bigodot_{1}$$

Beaufort, South Carolina
Two Weeks Later

I hated the hair net, but I loved the job, if you call volunteering with no pay a job. My first recollection of a hair net was my grandma wearing one, and that was forever ago. I remembered how she looked; I didn't want to imagine how I looked. Ever since I'd put the damn thing on this morning about an hour earlier, my hand kept drifting up to touch the soft pouched-out weave. My fingers were trying to tell me how I looked with my in-need-of-a-haircut long brown hair stuffed into the elastic restraint. Did I look like a six-foot-three grandma? If my ol' Marine boot camp DI, Gunnery Sergeant Joe Paul, could see me now, he wouldn't have been able to conjure up enough expletives to emphasize his ridicule. But what difference did it make? No one in this soup kitchen cared how I looked. The recipients were always glad to see me, and all I really cared about was giving them a little nourishment and maybe some joy.

All my life, I had never been a morning person. Though active, I wasn't normally conversant. It took me awhile to assimilate. My mind slid back into the blank void it had occupied most of the morning as I tilted the stock pot and scooped out the last ladle of potato soup. Somewhere during the process of dishing out three pots of soup, I had become a mindless robot; bowl, ladle, scoop, fill; a garbage-dumpster-smelling recipient's grunt or nod, maybe an exchange of smiles; bowl, ladle, scoop, fill.

Another volunteer and I heaved a fourth steaming pot onto the table.

"Hey, Mister Layne," a gruff voice from across the four-by-eight table snapped me into reality. "Semper Fi. How you doin'? Find a job yet?"

I looked down at the short man, whose long matted gray hair, tangled with leaves and twigs, nested on his shoulders.

"Charlie." Despite his condition I couldn't help but smile. The man always awoke my interest and empathy. I glanced at my watch. "You're late. And my name is Brent."

I had to think to disrupt my muscle memory in order to give the frail man an extra scoop of the steamy soup, I always gave Charlie more.

"I'm doin' fine," I said. "And no, I haven't found a job yet. Couple more weeks and I'll lose my unemployment." I handed him the heaping bowl, and since he'd awoken my mind, I decided to tease him a little. I needed to do something to offset the tedium. To emphasize my words, I leaned my large frame on the table, dwarfing him, and scowled. "My loss of unemployment pay won't be good for either of us." I paused, letting my words divert his attention from warming his cupped hands over the bowl. "'Cause when that happens, I'll be taking both your park bench and that coat I gave you."

Charlie held his blank expression as his capillary-radiating brown pupils focused on me. "I done lived in Beaufort all my life. January's never been colder. And February ain't startin' out any bedder. Someone forgot to tell South Carolina 'bout global warmin'." His dirt-smudged face crinkled into a smile exposing a dark void where his front upper teeth used to be. The oral vacancy was flanked by yellow and black stained teeth whose days had to be numbered. "This here-ah coat," a red, weathered hand laced with blue-green veins rubbed the black sleeve of the dirty, wrinkled Pea Coat, "though it's a might large, saved my ass this winter. All's I can say is you'd bedder find a job." The smile faded into an arched brow glare.

"Are you saying I won't be able to take my coat back?" I chuckled. "My shadow outweighs you."

"Bigger 'n needier men than you have tried." The smile, this time unsupported by emotion, returned.

I laughed and reached across the table and patted his shoulder.

"You are something else, my man. Tougher than a"—my cell phone played the Casinos' *Then You Can Tell Me Goodbye.* I motioned Charlie on his way as I fumbled with my apron to find my pants pocket and the phone. Three rings later, I had the phone on and at my ear. "Bean, if you're checking on me, yes, I mailed all three resumes this morning."

"Forget that." Her sultry radio voice was elevated with excitement. "Brent, I—you've got a job, a good job … that is if you want it."

2

I slouched in my desk chair wearing jockey shorts and a sleeveless tee shirt, my office work attire. The computer back-lighting, along with the morning sun's rays slicing through the blind slats, dimly lit the small second bedroom converted into an office.

My girlfriend and I had bought this condo almost two years ago when I was working. At the time, we'd both felt confident enough about our relationship to co-sign for this property.

My desk was clean except for the computer, the morning paper, and those damned five, word-heavy, government manuals. The manuals I kept re-positioning on the desktop and hadn't completely read yet. I had a scheduled meeting with the boss in a few days, and I had a ton of things to do before that meeting. But I just sat there, in a mental nap. After years of data gathering, I had come to the conclusion that my mother was right, I was allergic to morning. At least that was my excuse.

At some point during my almost year-long state of unemployment, I had succumbed to depression. I didn't want to be there, but I was. Day after day of wallpapering cyberspace with resumes only to get a few phone interviews, followed by head-bowing rejections had pushed me down, way down, with the whale shit.

I knew there were millions unemployed, but few had my credentials. I was an Annapolis graduate, defensive captain of the football team, a decorated Marine officer who had led men in combat in both Iraq and

Afghanistan, and I had successful work experience. So why didn't anyone want me?

I had a job. I should be happy and clawing my way up and out of my self-pity pit. But no, I just sat here, afraid, a man who had overcame the fear of failing most of his life was afraid.

Nothing had ever been given to me before; I had to earn all my prior accomplishments. This job was given to me. I hadn't applied, interviewed, or competed in any way to get this position. That bothered me along with the fact I had no idea what was expected of me. All I had been told was when and where to report. These bureaucratic manuals, which were about as much fun to read as a phone book, were a list of 'do's and don'ts', not a job description.

Right in the middle of a yawn and a groin scratch, my office door flew open and Robin "Beanie" Hays glided in wearing her pajamas, nothing but one of my extra large tee shirts. Today was President's Day, and like most teachers in America, she had the day off.

I had nicknamed her "Bean" or "Beanie" because of her love of jelly beans.

She had a steaming cup of coffee in each hand.

I wasn't sure whether the coffee aroma or the flesh moving under Beanie's shirt awoke my mind.

"Mornin', sunshine." She had an attention-grabbing voice, a soft, sultry tone laced with enthusiasm, a dreaded morning person.

If the petite, pony-tailed blonde had a wand in her hand instead of my coffee, she'd made a perfect Tinker Bell.

She sat one of the mugs on my small, three drawer metal desk. "Is this your business attire today? I've got to give you credit, your apparel has been consistent since you took this new job. However, I think the plain black Jockeys are more formal than the striped ones. What do you think?"

I picked up the cup of coffee and mocked a toast. Any response would be wrong.

Her free hand, palm out, jerked skyward over her canted head like she was a kid in school trying to get her teacher's attention. "Excuse me. Hello? I know better than to ask you any questions before ten o'clock in the morning, which, by the way, is only fifteen minutes from now."

I needed a diversion from her ridicule, something, anything, to prevent a flare-up. So I improvised. The pestering itch had leaped from my crotch to my head. As my fingers dug through my thinning, pillow-combed long brown hair, another itch-stimulated yawn sought release.

I caught the yawn in my fist. "Where do you hide your batteries?"

"What?"

I took a sip of the hot, void of milk or sugar, coffee. "I want to pull them out."

"What would Andrew think if he walked in here?"

Our relationship had deteriorated since I'd lost my almost two-year job as an Investment Manager at the Beaufort Bank. The bank manager told me, though I had exceeded his goals and objectives, he had to let me go because of the economy. My take was he was afraid of the competition.

I'd hoped things would improve between Bean and me with my new employment. I loved her. Or at least I thought I did, except in the predawn hours. Obviously, she had once again failed to realize that I needed a little time to acclimate to mornings.

Pushing back against the chair, I straightened my posture. "Let me remind you, your brother, Andrew, is Pro Tempore of the South Carolina Senate. He ain't gonna walk in here."

"'Ain't gonna?' You think that's how the newly appointed Vice Chairman of the South Carolina Lottery Commission is supposed to talk?"

"Beanie, I'm tired."

"No, Brent, you were tired when you sat here for months and months drawing unemployment. Andrew gave you a job, a damned good paying three-year job. And you need to get out of that funk you're in and get to work. You owe him that much." She crossed her arms over her chest.

Her arm-crossing wasn't a good thing.

"What did you call that guy in the Marines, the one you liked and respected so much?" Bean asked. "The one who reported to you when you were in Afghanistan?"

"You mean my Gunny Sergeant, Carl Thompson?"

"Yeah, that's the one. What'd you always say he called you?"

"Granite with a heart," I answered, trying not to grin as I thought about Carl Thompson, one of the best men and Marines I had ever known.

"Well, I've experienced your heart, and you've got a great one," Bean said. "But now it's time for the granite."

I shook my head. Our ratio of fighting versus making-love had been beyond lopsided since the banking gig went away. "Are we going to fight today?" I looked up into her dark brown, almost black, eyes, wrapped my arm around her tiny waist, and drew her hip against my shoulder.

She twisted free. "Maybe you should move to Columbia where you'd be with the rest of the commission and have an office in the capital building. Maybe that would motivate you."

"Bean, we're in a recession. I can't sell this condo. We'd be supporting two residences if I moved there. We can't afford that."

"And you can't afford to lose this job either. Are you ready for the meeting my brother set up with the rest of the commission ... including the governor?"

I placed my coffee mug on the desk, stood, and stretched. Then I pulled her into my arms, dwarfing her five-foot-nothing with my softened ex-college linebacker mass. Her tiny but warm body erased almost all the irritation her nagging had created.

I rubbed away the tension in her back.

Tilting her head, with the point of her chin rested on my breastbone, she looked up into my face. Though she shook her head, her eyes said she loved me.

"You're right, as usual," I said. "You know how much I've wanted a job. I should be elated." I shook my head. "I don't know why I'm in this funk. Maybe it's the nepotism, or it could be I'm not used to handouts. Charity can destroy a person's pride, I see it every day at the soup kitchen."

"Brent, if you had any pride, you'd be dressed before ten o'clock." She pushed to arms' length and looked down. "And please clip those soon-to-be sheet slicing toe nails, or I'm gonna haul your ass down to the spa and get you a pedicure." She looked up at me, canted her head, and smiled. "I'll even treat."

My immediate reaction was to go on the offensive and find something about her person to attack. But that would just start World War III. That was the last thing either of us needed. Though her criticism was ego-bruising, she was right. And she had ended her attack with a smiling offer.

I shrugged. "I don't know where my clippers are."

She shook her head. "That's not all you've lost."

I watched her purse her puffy pink lips and blow on the coffee before she took a sip. She was cuter than my first puppy, and I loved her more, despite her button pushing.

"What'd you mean by that?" I dropped my hands from her trim waist, picked up my coffee, and took a big gulp. I coughed and sputtered, "Haaa—hot."

"How many people worked for you at the Beaufort Bank, Brent?"

She wasn't done. My eyebrows sought my hairline. "Come on, you know that no one worked for me."

"And how many work for you now?"

I looked down. "A hundred and fifty." My voice trailed away. I wanted to remind her that as a platoon commander I'd had much more responsibility in the service, more people whose lives depended on my leadership skills. But I knew where this was going, and I wasn't going to win. She was right, damn it.

"So let's push Andrew aside for the moment. Don't you think you are obligated to try to do a good ... no, a great job for those people?"

I studied Beanie for a moment. My mom, who had manipulated my dad and me forever, could learn a few things from Gunny Bean.

I grabbed a pair of pants hanging on the back of my chair, pulled them on, and sat. A sigh escaped my lips as I picked up a manual.

"You sigh," Bean said. "Am I pushing you too hard?" She flicked her long nails together. "Did you know the governor is a woman?"

3

As I climbed the South Carolina State House steps, my legs got weaker and weaker, and it wasn't due to the unbelievable number of steps, the early morning hour, or the neck-choking collar and tie. Anxiety had a mountain climber's grip on my balls. All of the bureaucratic bullshit in those endless manuals had flowed into a glob of lawyer-lingo in my mind. I couldn't remember any of the material. I was going to engineer a record setting, briefest career train wreck in the history of American government.

Almost to the top of the climb, I stopped and took a deep breath. I couldn't fail; I wouldn't fail, for me, or Bean, or … for me.

Though February mornings in Columbia were cool, I wiped perspiration off my forehead as I entered the polished marble lobby of the building. Andrew Hays, Bean's brother, was there to meet me. The average-looking short and slender blond man looked like he belonged in his tailored black-pin-striped gray business suit; like it was his everyday, even play, garb. His suit made me wonder how my old, outdated, college graduation black suit compared.

He stepped forward and extended his right hand.

"Brent. It's good to see you. Welcome to my world."

I shook his polite grip. "Thanks, Andrew, for ah, for everything. I don't know what to say, except … well, you saved me."

One of his eyebrows arched. "Don't be too quick to thank me. There's been a change of plans. Did you read the material I sent you?"

Oh fuck! My heart skipped two or twenty beats and some organ, I never knew which one it was, deposited a train-car load of acid in my stomach.

"Ah, yeah, sure … every page." At least that was true.

"Then you know that as Vice Chairman, you are in charge of the Audit Committee. Right?"

"Yes, it's part of my title, as well," I said, with false assuredness. So far, I was two-for-two in question answering.

"Did you happen to catch the news last week about the elderly couple in Florida; the ones who presumably won seventy-five million bucks on the South Carolina managed Powerball Jackpot?"

My confidence faltered. Was watching the nightly news a job requirement? Since I lost the investment job, I rarely watched the news or read the paper, except for the job listings. I was burned out. Plus, people would tell you if something major had happened.

All excuses aside, the world's sadness just didn't interest me; I'd had my own problems to deal with for too long.

"No, I didn't." Now my answering skills had waned to two out of three.

"They were found shot to death in their home, gangland style. The money they'd won is missing, and the Feds are investigating the crime. The governor has canceled our committee meeting and has opted to meet with just the two of us. Because South Carolina just took over the management of the multi-state Powerball, and the feds are investigating, she wants assurance our lottery controls haven't been compromised."

My stomach rumbled. What assurance could she expect from a first-day-on-the-job guy?

He glanced at his watch. "We're due in her office in five minutes." He pointed a finger at me. "Don't let her looks deceive you. Katharine Franklin can be a real ball-buster when she wants to. She didn't get to her position without leaving a bunch of broken careers in her dust." He fidgeted with his shirt cuffs. "Oh, and don't forget to address her as Governor Franklin; never, ever, call her Mrs. Franklin, or God-forbid, Katharine. Okay?"

I nodded and wondered why he was nervous; whatever I had read in those manuals about lottery controls had been lost in the mountain of words. I'd be the one looking for another job by the end of the day.

People getting killed over millions of bucks shouldn't surprise anyone. And the money had crossed state lines, so the FBI was involved, so what? That was their job, let them do it. Why did the governor want to meet with me about a murder-robbery? If the lottery system had been compromised, the FBI would find out how, why, and by whom, long before I could. At the risk of sounding stupid, I had to ask, besides, new people always ask dumb questions.

"Andrew, this sounds like a job for the FBI, not a Lottery Commissioner. Why does she want to see me? If there was something she wants me to do, this is my first day. She had a first day a year or so ago, she has to understand. I don't know anything about government protocol, or how do get anything done in this bureaucracy. What'll I do or say I'll do?"

"Don't say anything, just listen."

Great, I'd sit in a chair and nod my head like one of those bobble-head dolls on the back deck of a car.

When we got off the elevator at the top floor, facing double ten-foot high walnut doors, Andrew leaned close and whispered, "The fun begins now with Ms. Jeanette Cummins, Governor Franklin's receptionist, the gate-keeper from hell."

Andrew Hays opened one of the tall doors to the receptionist's office. We entered a large, cold room, not just cold because of the twelve-foot high stone walls or the air temperature, but chilling due to another person's presence, something I could sense more than feel.

'Ms. Jeanette Cummins,' an inlaid brass lettered wooden name plate declared. The name sign sat on a large oak desk beneath a gigantic oil portrait of the handsome, rather young though stoic, female governor. The portrait hung above a mounted, carved wooden State Seal of South Carolina, a crescent moon over a palm tree.

Ms. Cummins sat at her desk. It only took me a few minutes to realize this short, thin, bespectacled, perfectly-in-place gray-haired woman dressed to the conservative high-collar nines, had become a product of her environment, a job witch.

She reminded me of a chow someone bet me I couldn't pet when I was a kid. Ms. Cummins sorted through papers and acted like we weren't there. When we attempted to approach her, she emitted a deep, vicious "I will call you when it is time," forcing us back to chairs against the wall.

Having been a former Marine Officer, I respected position and rank. But there were always some people who abused it; normally insecure, little, weak people who loved to muscle-flex.

When she snarled at me, I wanted to snatch her by her high-collared blouse and ask her what had she done for her country other than be a bitch.

How many times had she had to wipe the blood of her comrades off her hands and continue to fight? Or how many letters had she written to the families of the men and women who had made the ultimate sacrifice? Now that would've been interesting, but job hunting wasn't.

Power and position had its advantages, and, unfortunately, liking the person in charge wasn't a factor. In the service, I had always stressed to my reports that I didn't care if they liked me, but they would respect my rank.

Ten long minutes later, Ms. Cummins' phone buzzed. She rose, straightened her almost floor-touching pencil skirt, and walked to the double doors just to the side of the governor's portrait. She looked over her shoulder as if she were looking at someone vomiting and said, "You may enter now." Then a smile burst through her sneer, like sunshine appearing during a sky-blackened violent storm, and she opened the door. "Governor Franklin, Senate Pro Tempore Andrew Hays and Lottery Vice Chairman Brent Layne to see you."

If my job came with an assistant, I'd have to have them do what she did, because I was horrible about remembering people's names.

My stomach gurgled as I rose to my feet. It was my first start in a college football game all over again. Brent Layne, a kid from a village, not a city or town, but a small village in southern Ohio, was meeting a state governor, his new boss.

5

I followed Andrew Hays into the Governor of South Carolina's office. He stepped aside and swept his extended arm at me.

"Governor Franklin, may I introduce Brent Layne, your new Lottery Commissioner and Vice Chairman."

I stopped in the doorway. My mouth gaped open. A mid-thirties female-surprise in a business suit had risen to greet me. I had assumed the portrait of the governor I'd seen outside her office had been doctored to cover imperfections and to subtract some years. Not so. The Katharine Franklin who stood behind a gigantic walnut desk across twenty-feet of Persian rug should have had the artist beheaded for incompetence. Her shoulder-length black hair framed a high cheek-bone face, with sea-blue sparkling eyes, a slender turned up nose, and full red lips spread over whiter–than-white perfect teeth. I guessed her to be at least five-foot-eight and her grey tailor-made suit flowed over curves everywhere they were supposed to be. The very sight of her jacked my pulse.

This lovely stateswoman stepped from around her desk and approached, or more like floated toward me, with an extended hand. "Mr. Layne, I hope you're as smart as you are handsome."

I had to command my rigid legs to move. Liz Taylor, in her prime, would have been jealous of the governor, and Frankenstein would have envied the stiff steps I took to meet her. My huge paw swallowed her soft, warm, slender hand. Her grip was firm and lingered for a tad longer than customary, while her sapphire eyes captured mine.

"I, ah … it is an honor and pleasure to meet you, Governor Franklin."

She released my hand. "Please have a seat," she motioned at several leather-padded walnut chairs fronting her desk. Then she swiveled on heel-and-toe and glided back to her high-backed black leather chair, wafting me in a soft bouquet of magnolia.

Seated in front of a flagstone facade fireplace, she glanced at a folder open on her desk. "I assume Andrew has briefed you about the purpose of this meeting, Mr. Layne." Her magnetic eyes rose from the paper requesting a response.

I glanced at Andrew and then back to her. "Yes, he did."

"You and I will be meeting again this week, Mr. Layne, maybe more than once. So, is it okay if I call you Brent?"

"That'll be fine, Governor Franklin." My words and my thoughts weren't quite in synch. My limited knowledge would definitely be exposed in several meetings.

"Ah, how old are you, Brent?" she asked followed by a smile. She tapped the file with a slender red-nail finger. "I read your paperwork, a math major and football player at Annapolis, an ex-Marine Captain who served a tour in Iraq and one in Afghanistan, recipient of a Bronze Star and a Purple Heart, but I can't recall your age."

She flattered me with her personal knowledge, but her odd question, a little too personal and irrelevant, made me scoot forward on the wooden chair. "I'm a few months shy of what everyone tells me is the downhill side of life, thirty."

She flipped a hand at me. "Whoever told you that is wrong. Thirty is just the beginning. Anyway," she focused on Andrew, "I think you're old enough not to need an escort any longer. Thanks, Andrew, for bringing Brent here. I'll have to let you know later if I approve of your choice. Please leave us." Her piercing blue eyes returned to me. "Brent and I have some rather delicate matters to discuss."

My first play of my first game and a gigantic, muscle-bulging fullback with an intense bone-breaking demeanor had just broken through the line and was hauling ass right at me.

6

When Andrew Hays closed the door behind him leaving me with the Governor of South Carolina, I hadn't felt as vulnerable since when I disembarked from the plane in Kabul for the first time.

I sat facing Katharine Franklin in front of her huge walnut desk. How ridiculous, a bloodied war veteran, who didn't know what to do with his hands.

Governor Franklin rose from her desk, reminding me of how I envisioned Cleopatra rising from her unrolled carpet to captivate Caesar. She motioned to a small round table in the corner. "Let's talk over there," she said, her voice soft and yet firm, a woman used to being in control. "It's less ah … I want to get to know you better and that gargantuan desk prohibits that."

Her words caused all kinds of images to frolic in my brain. But the one that lingered was of me sleeping on Charlie's park bench.

After I sat down next to her, well within scent range of her alluring magnolia fragrance, she asked, "Would you care for something to drink, coffee, tea, juice?"

Though I loved my morning coffee, curiosity overwhelmed any of my physical needs. "I'm fine."

"An Annapolis graduate, honor codes; a 'Simper Fi' Marine, always faithful; so I assume I can trust you." Her blue eyes studied mine.

I wanted to blurt out though I'd read all those boring manuals I hadn't retained ten percent, and I knew nothing about government and not much more about the state lottery. But why make a total idiot of myself? The woman obviously had an agenda. So I just nodded.

Her eyes scanned the room. "You'd think, being the top dog, I'd know everything about this place, I'd be in control. Well, even after two years, I hate to say this, but I'm not. Accountable, yes, in control, no … not a good combination." When her eyes returned to me, her voice dropped to a whisper. "The lottery is a black hole to me; a black hole full of millions and millions of dollars. Though there are nine different, selected people serving staggered terms on the Commission, it would only take one insider to steal. The dollar amounts are mind-boggling. So hiding a few million missing dollars here or there would probably be easy." She scanned her long red nails as if she were bothered by what she was about to say. "And some strange things have happened of late. Frankly, I'm more than concerned, I'm paranoid." Her voice rose when her eyes again fixed on me. "I need someone like you, someone who is not embedded in the system; someone I can trust." She hesitated, placed a fisted hand under her chin, glanced away, and then back. She sighed. "Tell me, why should I trust you?"

One of my eyebrows leaped skyward and my head subtly tilted downward. "I, ah, I've never been asked that question before." Strangely, I found myself whispering as well. I cleared my throat and spoke in a normal tone. "The old cliché is trust must be earned, and it must. I guess you'll have to test me somehow." I shrugged my shoulders. "I don't know."

"Exactly, a test." She smiled and pulled a cell phone out of her jacket pocket. After tapping the screen with her long nails, she handed me the phone. "Put your cell number into my phone. The FBI is supposed to visit me about this mess in Florida sometime this week, and I'll need you in attendance. As soon as I know the timing, I'll have Ms. Cummins call you." Then she whispered again, "Is it possible for you to meet me later this evening?"

What the hell had I gotten myself into? None of the dozens of questions, ripping through my head, seemed proper to ask at the moment. The Governor of South Carolina wanted to meet me, a total stranger, later, outside of her office, at an inferred private or even secret meeting. What could I do other than nod my head? A damned bobble-head.

I touched my number into her phone. "Sure. I'm scheduled to be here for a week or two, depending on how long the orientation and training take. You're the boss, ah, I mean the governor."

When I handed her phone back to her, her fingers wrapped around mine. Her warm hand trembled.

There was no way I had made this beautiful and powerful woman nervous. She was scared.

Her intense eyes bore into mine. "The Governor of ... who am I fooling, *I* need to see you, Brent," she murmured. "I'll call you, after six."

She pocketed her phone, rose, and offered her hand.

I stood and again softly clasped her fingers.

"Welcome on board, Mister Layne," she said, voice at a standard level. "May this be the beginning of a strong relationship between you and the state of South Carolina."

"Thank you, Governor Franklin." And I was shown the door.

Confused didn't come close to defining my state of mind.

From the governor's office, I was directed to another room in the bowels of the capital building where I went through six hours of state government orientation. And I thought the manuals were boring. And this was just the first of five days of training. At least now I knew the organizational structure of the state government, all the governing bodies, and their responsibilities. I wondered if our forefathers, the authors of the Constitution, would be happy or befuddled by our evolved bureaucracy.

By the time I got back to my hotel room, I was data numb. Thinking hurt. I had two goals, to wash away the day with a martini and then call Bean.

I made it to the hotel bar just in time for the end of "happy-hour." Halfway through the first gin martini with 'all the olives you can get in the glass,' I pulled out my cell phone. The phone in my hand reminded me; the governor was supposed to call me after six. I glanced at my watch; it was five forty-five. I needed to unwind first. I wanted to close my eyes with Bean's sultry voice in my ear, as if she were there, naked, laying next to me in my room.

I hadn't been away from Bean a whole day. Could I be homesick, or just wishing to be?

I touched my speed dial for Bean and immediately got diverted to her voicemail. Though her voice always induced images of our best times together, the memory-spawning sound of her recording wasn't enough to offset my disappointment.

Then I recalled she had an "open house" at school for her third-graders and their relatives this evening. Sitting around with a bunch of nine-year-olds and their doting parents wasn't my idea of an exciting evening. But I did enjoy witnessing the creativity Bean used to entice kids to learn. I would've loved having her for a teacher.

Bean and I used to be so close, so happy. Those days had slipped away. Maybe our love was nothing more than infatuation. I didn't know. One thing was for sure, my unemployment had damaged our relationship. I hoped this new job would resurrect the good old days.

I didn't leave a message. What was I going to tell her, that I was going to have a private meeting with the 'wow' looking Governor? That'd be like playing toss with a live grenade.

I stared at the empty martini glass in my one hand and my cell phone in the other. Choices. Have another martini or wait for the governor's call? Though tempted, I didn't want to meet her after two martinis. Despite my disgust with the systematic-overkill of government, I needed this job. I decided to snack on some hors d'oeuvres and wait.

My fried brain didn't want to dwell on why the beautiful governor wanted to meet me. I'd deal with that when the time came.

A bite into my second spring roll, with some sinus-opening mustard, and my phone trumpeted; a tone I had selected for an unknown caller. The screen depicted a 'Private Number.'

"Hello," I said, wondering if I should have added 'Governor' to my greeting. No one else called me from a 'Private Number.'

"Brent, this is Katharine." The governor's soft voice faded my surroundings.

"Katharine?" After Andrew's lecture I couldn't believe she was using her first name.

"Ah, Governor Franklin. I, ah, I thought since I called you Brent, we should both be on a first name basis."

"Oh. It's just that … well, I was told never to call you anything but Governor."

She chuckled. "I guess Andrew's wrists are still red. Please call me Kitty, when we're alone. I'd like that. That's what my friends call me. Plus I think it adds to this trust thing we're trying to establish."

26

"Okay … Kitty." I didn't like being used, manipulated, or not knowing what was going on. And I was afraid all the above applied. Either Andrew didn't know this lady, or she was playing me.

"Have you eaten?"

I glanced at the remnants of the spring roll in my hand. I could say 'yes' and maybe find out how badly she wanted to meet and maybe why. And why would she want to meet me privately? She'd read my file. She knew I didn't know anything about government, the lottery, or investigating a possible crime. Could this be about more than dinner?

If she were just looking for a roll in the hay, I didn't need the temptation. She was gorgeous, and I was vulnerable. I hadn't punched fur with Bean in a long time, way too long.

For certain, Miss Kitty had an agenda, and I needed this job. Would I sleep with the governor to keep this job? I didn't want to, but what if I weren't given a choice?

What was I thinking? It was a dinner meeting at a restaurant. It wasn't as if we were meeting at a hotel. This new job, the pressure, my ignorance, I wasn't thinking clearly. This had to be about something else. I couldn't turn down the Governor of South Carolina, my boss. "Ah, no, I haven't eaten."

"Would you like to meet me for dinner at the Seven Gables Inn? They have a private dining room reserved for me anytime I want it, a perk of the office."

'A private dining room,' made me feel more vulnerable than being ordered to take the lead into a 'hot' zone.

It was too late, I couldn't renege now. "I'd enjoy that, ah, Kitty."

"Are you at your hotel?"

"Yes, I'm staying at the—"

"My driver will pick you up in fifteen minutes, okay?"

"Fine."

"And Brent, lose the tie."

I looked down. The tie was the first thing I'd taken off when I got to my room, followed by my jacket. I'd need the jacket.

I wondered what Bean would say if she knew I was going to dinner with the governor, and not just the governor, but a gorgeous woman who wanted me to call her Kitty while just she and I dined in a private room?

8

The extended limo was everything plus more than I expected my tax dollars to provide a governor, but one thing was missing, the governor. The driver informed me she would meet me at the restaurant within the next half-hour. She had suggested I have a drink and some hors d'oeuvres while I wait. She was buying.

The Seven Gables Inn was an old, wood-siding white house, resembling an ante-bellum mansion. Per its name, seven gables jutted out of the roof and round columns supported a balcony over a sprawling front porch.

I entered through one of two towering, weathered oak doors. As soon as I told them who I was, I was whisked down the entry hall and sequestered in a backroom. I didn't have an opportunity to tour the interior of the converted home-to-restaurant.

Like the hallway, and most turn-of-the-century homes, the private room had several oil paintings of people dressed in clothing from long ago covering a majority of one plastered side. A dormant stone fireplace covered most of another. Windows with closed plantation shutters disrupted the two remaining walls.

An eight-place, rectangular oak table with ornate legs with lions' feet was centered in the room and adorned with a white table cloth. A large, lit, crystal chandelier hung from the twelve–foot ceiling over the table. A single place setting with a menu was positioned on the opposing table ends.

Under a pair of the shuttered windows sat a brown leather couch, across the room from the fireplace.

I didn't need another drink or any more hors d'oeuvres, so I passed the time by reading the back page of the menu. The original house, a two-story structure with sixteen rooms and detached buildings including a kitchen and originally servant quarters, was built in the 1840's by a doctor and burned during Sherman's occupation. The original home was duplicated on the old foundation in the late 1860's, though the slave quarters were not rebuilt after the war.

Using my phone, I was in the middle of researching the controversy of who had set the fire that destroyed most of Columbia during Sherman's invasion when I got a low battery light. I had just turned off my phone when the door opened and Kitty entered, posture perfect with the airs of royalty.

She wore a slightly above the knee beige skirt exposing shapely legs, accentuated by high heels, and a brown leather jacket with a white silk scarf wrapped around her neck.

I rose and helped her remove her jacket, a lesson from my mother. I hung the coat on a hall tree standing in a corner. When I turned to face her, the governor, or probably more appropriately Kitty, had removed her scarf exposing a pale yellow sweater with a vee-neck that plunged way below government standards., I knew it would be difficult to control my eyes for the rest of the evening. What the hell; she wore it, so I'd adore it.

If I were being used, so be it.

⑨

Governor Kitty and I sat at opposites ends of the long table in a private dining room of The Seven Gables Inn. I had to think of her as 'Governor' Kitty. My mental repetition of the two names helped me keep my eyes from exploring, most of the time.

Governor Kitty raised her glass. "Here's to your new job, Brent, may you be successful."

I honored the toast and took a sip of the Bombay Sapphire Gin martini 'up' with olives she had ordered for both of us. At least we had one thing in common, good gin.

She sat her glass down, folded her arms under her chest, and leaned forward onto her tabled arms. Her bulging breasts both captured my eyes and erased the 'Governor' from my mental compounded name for her, now she was just Kitty, or more like umm-umm Kitty.

"I have a problem," she said, taking a dangerously deep breath and sighing.

If she were looking for a response, I had none. To me, her problem was the containment battle waging inside her yellow sweater.

Why would she dress like this and then sit like she was sitting? Was the Governor of South Carolina or umm-umm Kitty trying to tempt me? If her intent were to command my full attention with her words, she had failed. Though confused, I really didn't care. I was enjoying the entertainment.

Her bluebird blue eyes fixed on mine and following my stare dropped to her chest where her boobs were close to winning their insurrection for freedom. She bolted upright and adjusted her sweater.

There went my temptation theory and my stroked ego. My next, less exciting, assumption was this aggressive woman had jumped into a man's world and fought her way to the top. Along the way, she had picked up manly physical traits, like how she had been sitting, but had forgotten the effect on her feminine assets in a low-cut sweater bolstered by push-up forearms.

Her arched brow eyes gazed at the ceiling and she rubbed her chin with her thumb and index finger.

"I, ah … I wonder," she said. Her gaze remained fixed and skyward, while her body language implied she was on the verge of action.

I shelved my inquisitiveness about whether she was embarrassed or puzzled. "Wonder?" I asked.

Her bluer-than-blue eyes returned to mine, blazing in the chandelier light with intensity. She spread her arms. "Never mind." Her elbows dropped onto the table, hands clasped in front of her. "Ah, you've never been married have you?"

"No." For a governor, she had a lot of strange questions.

"I have, once, years ago, my college sweetheart. Five years into the marriage, I caught him cheating. That cost me more tears than he was worth." Head canted, she chewed on her bottom lip while she studied me. "It's not a good thing to be a single woman in politics. You're constantly under a microscope."

"I can't imagine." This woman loved to keep me in a state of confusion.

"About tonight … this meeting, after serving as governor for just over two years, I've never had any worries professionally or personally until—" a knock on the door brought her to her feet, facing the door. "Come in," she said.

The door opened and a young man dressed in black slacks and a white shirt, with the restaurant's logo sewn on the breast pocket, entered. He had an order pad in one hand and a pen in the other.

"Ah, Sedgwick," Kitty said, with a hand covering her chest. "You're here for our dinner orders."

"Yes, Governor," he said, his eyes never getting above shoe-top level.

She looked over her shoulder at me. "Brent, what would you like?" Her tone teased more than asked.

Though I wanted to, I couldn't take my eyes off hers. "I, ah, I haven't looked. What would you recommend?"

Her head swiveled to face Sedgwick. "He'll have the filet, with those delightful onion straws and your garden-fresh green beans with the tasty chunks of bacon." She eyed me again as if assessing me. "And I'd say he was a medium-rare man."

I nodded, though I preferred medium.

Her hand dropped from her chest and glided over her flat abdomen. "And, though I'd love to order the same thing, I'll just have the house salad." Her hand flashed up and she snapped her fingers. "Oh, and bring us a bottle of your best Merlot."

Sedgwick scribbled on the pad as he backed toward the door. "Yes, Governor."

In a blink, he was gone, the door closed behind him.

She kept her eyes on me as sat down in her chair. I had seen that look many times before, at the soup kitchen. It was the way Charlie and most of the others eyed a steaming bowl of soup.

She took a sip of her martini, and then picked a skewered olive out of the drink. "Their service is very fast here." Her expression morphed from the informative teacher to a lusty streetwalker. "While we wait, why don't you tell me about Robin Hays?" Her tongue slid out and licked the olive. "Or should I refer to her as 'Bean'?"

⑩

The dinner plates had been cleared along with the empty bottle of Merlot. And although I craved a cup of coffee, I stared at a full glass of Drambuie liquor Kitty had ordered. She was in control, total control, she had sent a car for me, reserved the restaurant, ordered martinis, the meal, the after-dinner drinks, and knew everything about me, everything, Bean and all. I knew nothing about her. She had everything on her side, power, knowledge, beauty, and the low-cut sweater.

As for me, I wasn't sure why I was here, and I wasn't sure I cared anymore.

The more I drank, the more thankful I was that Kitty was at the other end of the eight-place table. A couple of martinis and most of the bottle of wine had done major damage to my self-control. Like the ol' country song said, "the girls always look prettier at closin' time,' and Kitty was damned pretty and sexy from the onset.

Kitty raised her glass. "Here's to you." Two swallows and she had emptied her glass. "I normally don't trust first impressions, but I've got this … call it intuition, I don't know, but I think we'll make a good team." Her voice was as clear as when I had first met her earlier. The booze seemed to have no affect on her.

I raised my glass and took a sip of the golden liquor; it was like drinking Napalm. My ego coughed over a gasp, but there was nothing I could do to stop my eyes from watering. What the hell, I chugged the rest of the liquid fire and put the empty cordial glass on the table.

She nodded at the glass. "Would you like another?" she asked.

"No, no." I wiped excessive moisture from an eye. "I could use a tanker truck full of coffee, though."

"You sound like my gramps. He loves his coffee. There's a great little all-night diner that has the best coffee this side of Brazil on the way to your hotel. We can stop there if you'd like."

"Yeah, I'd like that." I couldn't help but smile. My first little morsel of knowledge about her, and I liked it. She obviously had required the services of an all-night coffee house in her past.

She smiled in return. Her whole being seemed to pump life into her smile. "What are you thinking right now?" Her face continued to gleam.

I shook my head and looked away.

"Don't be shy." She leaned toward me. "Tell me."

Her soft imploring words and her movement drew my eyes back to her. I watched the reflection of the chandelier light flicker in her sapphire eyes. "I, ah … well I really never paid much attention to politics. Up until a few days ago, I couldn't have told you who the US Congressmen or Senators are from South Carolina, let alone who was Governor. I didn't care. If someone would've asked me a couple of weeks ago where I'd be tonight, the last thing I would've guessed is that I'd be sitting here, alone with the Governor of South Carolina, having drinks and dinner. Although I knew you were a woman, I didn't know your name let alone that … that you were so lovely."

She grinned. "That's very sweet of you." She pushed back in her chair. "Maybe we should go get some coffee before we start talking business."

Eddie's Bean Barn was on the other end of the spectrum from The Seven Gables Inn. From the outside, I wasn't sure there was enough room in the place for me to change my mind. But Kitty was right; their house brand coffee had a deep robust flavor that made having only one cup impossible.

We sat at a tiny round table in a corner. We were almost touching close. Her magnolia perfume was like a harbinger of spring. Thank God she had looped her scarf over her exposed chest before we left the restaurant.

Kitty took a sip of her steaming coffee. Her brow furrowed. "Have you ever heard of Joshua Franklin?"

"Sure. The paper-mill mogul, a multi-billionaire. My father briefly worked for the son-of-a ... your ex-husband?"

"Heavens no."

"Franklin, it's your maiden name." My cheeks burned, I knew I had to be red-faced. "Is Joshua your father?"

"My grandfather." She flipped a hand. "Don't worry; I've called the domineering, arrogant asshole much worse." Her warming smile returned. "But I do love him very much, and I think you would too if you ever got to know him."

I wanted to say how much I trusted my father's judgment of people, and how much he didn't like her grandfather. But what good would that do me? But I couldn't help parroting a recent memory. "Wasn't he recently accused of insider trading?"

Her face scrunched together like she had mistakenly taken a big bite of a shit sandwich. "That's untrue; a chain linked by lies and conjured up by some vindictive bastard who couldn't compete with Gramps on a level playing field."

Her blazing cheeks and trembling lower lip conveyed it was time for a subject change. "How old is your grandfather?"

"He's a young seventy-eight." She pressed her stiff arms on her knees, flexing the tension from her shoulders and then relaxed, reducing her facial redness. "And although my father is now the CEO, he's just a puppet. Gramps is Chairman of the Board and still controls the business." She took another sip. "He's the reason I'm Governor. I'm his only heir. Throughout my childhood, my father told me how much his father wanted one of his heirs to be President of the country. Obviously, my father didn't qualify." She stirred her coffee with a plastic spoon; there was nothing special in Eddie's, except her. "Gramp's aspirations are contagious, or at least he makes you think so."

She looked away as if to collect her thoughts. "I'm telling you this because ... well because I owe you an explanation for this rather strange meeting." She glanced away as if organizing her thoughts and then faced me. "Having mega-bucks helps a political career immensely, but when you're a woman trying to aspire in a man's world, particularly their no-holds-barred quest-for-power world, you need more than money. I've had to do a lot of things to get this far; things I'd never dreamed of doing, let alone thought I could do. Things I'd like to forget. Things I'm … I'm not proud of." She closed her eyes and shook her head as if to erase memories. When she reopened her eyes, they were fixed on me.

She finished her coffee and dabbed her red, full lips with a napkin. Silence prolonged the moment.

I had to say something to fill the void. "If you're waiting for me to ask what you've done, I won't. That's your business. I always assumed that in order to get to the upper levels of politics, you had to leave your scruples behind."

She fisted her hands on her hips; I had crossed a line.

"Oh, I still have morals and scruples … I don't know why I'm telling you my history?" She chuckled, a not-funny chuckle.

She picked up her coffee cup and rolled it between her hands as if she needed to warm them. Her eyes scanned the small diner. "I don't feel comfortable here. Can we finish this conversation in the car?"

⑪

Kitty and I sat next to each other in the stretch limo. As the chauffer had done on the trip to the coffee house, he raised the blackened privacy window between his compartment and ours before he moved the car.

"Pardon my bluntness, but you wanted to leave the restaurant to come here to talk 'business'," Brent said. "And now you don't feel comfortable in the coffee shop. I don't rattle easily, but you've got me looking over my shoulder."

She gave me a sideways glance. "You think I'm paranoid." Kitty took a deep breath and released it. She opened a panel on a small bench between us and the facing seats and removed a bottle of Bombay Sapphire Gin.

"How about a nightcap?" she asked. "The compartment is a freezer so the gin is nice and cold."

I raised my hands palms out. "I don't—"

"You've had your coffee, come on, placate me."

When your new boss tells you to drink, what else can you do? I decided I had to be 'politically correct,' a term I loathed. I'd accept the drink, and maybe take a sip, but not drink it. The two cups of coffee I had in Eddie's Bean Barn were just beginning their battle to make me a wide-awake drunk. I wouldn't want to be asked to say Eddie's Bean Barn three times as fast as I could.

"Okay, but just one," I said and dropped my hands. I had never been a 'yes' man before, but I had never been unemployed for over a year either.

I watched her pour a couple of shots each into martini glasses she had retrieved from the refrigerated compartment. I couldn't help but wonder if the woman had a drinking problem.

After adding skewered olives, she handed me a glass. "I've enjoyed your company tonight, Brent Layne." And she clinked her glass to mine.

"Well, thank you, Kitty." She wanted me to placate her, so I did. "I never would've thought I'd feel this at ease in the presence of a governor." So I elongated the truth a smidge, she seemed happy.

She drank and with her free hand she pulled off the white scarf and tossed it onto the seats across from us. She sat her glass down and turned to face me. Wave after wave of passing street lights washed over her exposed cleavage.

A little Tinker Bell blonde in Beaufort made me look away.

Kitty took a breath and sighed. "And now I'll answer your question as to why I wanted to leave the coffee shop." She straightened her torso accentuating her bosom. "You are a sexy man, Brent Layne, much more so than your pictures give justice to."

Sexy? Pictures? She had pictures? What kind of research had she done on me? This scenario was more than leaning toward my first impression; it was crashing down on my original assumption, with her being a vamp.

A bent finger pulled my chin to face her.

My eyes were drawn to the gaping sweater. I quit trying to figure out the reasons for her provocative actions and let her magnolia perfumed cleavage work its spell.

She reached down and took my hand and pressed it against one of her soft breasts.

Mouth open, brows arched, I had to look like a teenager touching his first boob. Totally off balance, my eyes sought hers. A sweeping band of light later and I knew something was amiss. Her words and actions portrayed a seductress, but her facial expression betrayed a hint of reticence, maybe even guilt.

"Would you be my lover, Brent, at least for the night?" her whispered words more a demand than a question. "I desperately need a man."

I shook my head. "I, ah … there's Bean, we have a—"

"Trust me. She'll never know. No one will ever know. I have much more to lose than you, so I have taken more than the necessary precautions.

No one will know, and you won't regret it, not a second of it." She squeezed my breast-cupped hand.

Her soft breast, her sweet smell, her unequaled beauty, her promised precautions, all coupled with her seductive words. My aroused groin begged me to scream, "Yes, hell yes," and lean into her and smash her red pouting lips with my mouth. But the roar of my conscience blaring, "How would you feel if Bean cheated on you?" muted my lust. Plus I didn't want to face tomorrow if I cheated tonight.

I pulled my hand away. "I can't tell you how tempted I am. You're everything a man could want, smart, powerful, beautiful, and heart-pounding sexy; but I can't. I'm committed to Robin. We're living together, and we ... I can't."

She gave me a cold look, leaned away, and straightened her sweater.

I wanted to say something, anything, to quench my rejection of her beyond-tempting offer. But no matter what I said, words wouldn't undo the damage to her ego.

Head lowered, like a recipient of horrifying personal news, she turned sober-faced to glare at me.

I knew what was next, back to the job market.

And then to my chagrin, she smiled a teeth-gleaming 'I got you' smile in the pulsing light.

"To paraphrase your words, Mr. Layne, trust must be earned."

$$\textbf{(12)}$$

My emotional roller-coaster ride was over, or at least I hoped it was. I sat in the State-owned limo an arm's length away from my manipulator, Governor Franklin, a.k.a. umm-umm Kitty. Percolating, untrustworthy emotions led me to stay quiet. Anything I said would most probably be wrong. I needed time to think while my pride and my financial needs debated what it would take to keep this job and if the job was worth it.

Hand over her exposed cleavage, she stooped forward and retrieved her scarf and again concealed her fleshy weapons before returning to her seat. Then she picked up her martini.

Screw thinking, I'd drink with her. I didn't need to worry about self-control anymore.

She squeezed my arm, a gentle reconciliation. "My little game to test your trust had nothing to do with politics … well almost nothing."

My martini glass stopped en route to my lips.

"This governorship is a lower tier stepping stone to me. It's one of many punches in my ticket to get to bigger and better things. So I can't screw this up."

She slid an olive between her glossy lips and chewed.

I sat my glass down, my patience on life-support. "And?"

She spoke while she chewed. "Last year, out of forty-two states plus the U.S. Virgin Islands, South Carolina was selected to do the Powerball drawings for the first time in our lottery history. Columbia will do the drawing for the next three years. And … well things aren't right."

I eased forward to the edge of the seat. Could this day get any worse? "What do you mean, 'aren't right?'"

"My daddy and Gramps didn't raise any dummies. Since being in this job, I've made sure everything I'm responsible for is working as it's supposed to. So I delved into the Powerball data shortly after we took it over. Prior to us controlling the drawing, over the past nine years in which South Carolina has been involved in the Lottery, there has been an average of thirteen Powerball Jackpot winners per year. In that same nine-year period, there have only been five Powerball Jackpot winners from South Carolina. In the past six months, there have been ten Jackpot winners, four of which are from South Carolina." She raised her arms, palms up. "From four percent to forty percent in half-a-year; a tenfold increase in a twentieth of the prior time period. Totally unbelievable."

She shook her head. "Luck is one thing, statistics are another."

I spread my arms to emphasize my confusion-coated frustration. "So why don't you let the FBI handle it? Why do you need me?"

"Why you versus the FBI? Four out of these ten winners had mysterious deaths within days after cashing in their winnings; three of those were from South Carolina. Not a penny of their winnings was found. Due to these crimes along with the statistics, the first place the FBI will investigate is the South Carolina Lottery program. Therefore, to keep my slate clean, I've got to take the lead, not the FBI, me. This cannot even smell like a cover-up. You'll be holding a press conference tomorrow."

"What?" My heart rate accelerated. I could visualize standing before a bunch of screaming reporters with cameras. They'd rip me open and expose my ignorance. "I don't know what to say. I haven't even finished orientation yet."

She held up a hand. "And why do I need to trust you? One concern is that there is close to a half of a billion dollars missing."

"Wow. That's a whole bunch of trust there."

A smirk creased her lovely face. "My primary need to trust you is there are many very powerful people out there who want me to fail. And they would do anything, and I mean anything, to bring me down. If you'd been hired by one of them, you wouldn't have hesitated to get me into bed. They'd love to have those pictures."

I didn't want to think about picturing her naked. I had to concentrate. "This press conference," I shook my head, "I'm not ready."

She patted my arm. "You will be by tomorrow."

$$\textcircled{13}$$

I was in bed. The lights were out. Perspiration beaded on my forehead and the only thing faster than my panting was my pounding heart.

Kitty's sultry voice whispered close to me, very close, "God, you were remarkable. That was—" her hand squeezed mine—"incredible. Aren't you glad you stayed? There was no comparison with the first time. We were both too horny. It was over before it really got started. But this time ... the way you—"

The door to the room burst open silhouetting in the light from the hotel suite's living room a petite blonde, a Tinker Bell.

"Screech ... screech ... screech." The alarm on the nightstand forced me into semi-consciousness. I flailed in the dark searching for the clock's off button.

I punched off the alarm, switched on the light, sat up, and scanned the hotel room. I was alone and sweating. A pile of scribbled notes sat on the small round table by the curtain-closed window, the product of a long evening of word-smithing with the governor. An evening spent in her office, ending as it had started, with the governor's chauffer bringing me home, alone.

I yawned away my mental fog and each memory of the dinner meeting produced another. I needed to get up, I had assignments to complete.

Today, I had four chores. Set up a press meeting for late in the day. Buy, with the state's money clothes, from top to bottom, from inside out, at a men's store whose name and address Kitty had jotted down. 'Get handsome' as she put it, in my new duds. And then recite to the news media the final version of the press release we—er—she had dictated and edited, at least thirty-seven times, last night.

After that, all I had to do was finish orientation, and then act like I was investigating the lottery system until the FBI figured out what really happened and who did it. I was Miss Kitty's boy, pawn, interface, or as Bean would proudly say, the governor's Vice-Chairman of the Lottery Commission responsible for auditing.

My first assignment, a real ball buster, was to look good and speak slowly and clearly in front of a frenzied school of politician-eating land sharks. I had zero experience with public speaking, unless barking out orders to a bunch of jarhead grunts was considered speech-making.

Of course Kitty, whose gramps probably had her giving speeches at age two, told me how easy the press conference would be. All I had to do was blandly read notes and afterwards wave off any questions as I walked away.

To me, on the fun scale, this was barely a step above reading those damned manuals.

(14)

I have to admit, the new clothes positively affected my attitude, for a while. But then, I had to walk out on the steps of the capital building to a podium sprouting microphones. God was apparently trying to help me, for it was a cold overcast day and nobody wanted to be there for long.

Wearing a gray suit, white shirt, blue tie, and shiny black tie-shoes, with notes in hand, I treaded out the front doors to the podium. The cool air offset my rising body temperature created by the boiler in my gut. To my surprise, there was no one near the podium. But as I approached the stand on numb legs, I became a people-magnet, drawing the many clusters of people on the steps into a single mass pressed in a semi-circle fronting the podium.

Between last night and today, I had read this damned speech too many times. I'd probably be able to recite it to my grandkids, but at the moment I reached the bank of microphones, I couldn't remember any of it, and wasn't sure I could talk if I did.

Cameras, red lights alive, hand-held, shoulder-mounted, tripod supported, sprung out of nowhere all around me.

I stood for a moment, acting like I was sorting through the papers I had placed on the stand. I prayed no one could see my trembling hands or my quivering spine.

Kitty had advised me last night that just before I started to talk to think about something that made this seem trivial. Hell, I was an Annapolis graduated, war-bloodied, decorated Marine officer. A microphone was shoved in my face, and I almost dropped some of the papers. I glared at the mike and then saw that it was in the hand of a lovely woman with a big smile. Her beauty made me think of the pale yellow sweater, and the trembling stopped. I took a deep breath and exhaled. Then I focused on the words seemingly printed on the shaped, pink skin inside the yellow sweater.

"Ah, my name is, ah Brent Layne. I am the newly appointed Vice-Chairman and Chief Auditor of the South Carolina Lottery Commission. Governor Franklin asked me to call this press conference.

"The governor conducts monthly reviews of each and every State managed program. During her review of the Lottery statistics this past week, a skewed data trend caused her to request me to perform an audit of the program.

"Recent associated felonious events caused the governor to request the FBI's assistance in this matter as well.

"Although there is currently no positive information of misappropriations of Lottery funds, to preclude the possibility of any future injustices, every precaution will be taken to ensure that the existing fault-proof system for the Mega-Millions and Powerball drawings is in place.

"As the State Commissioner in charge of auditing, I am here to attest that these measures are in place, and to inform the public the drawings will continue as scheduled."

It was over. I could breathe normally again. I folded the papers and stuffed them in my inside coat pocket.

The crowd erupted with a cacophony of undistinguishable questions. And as instructed, I turned and walked back into the building.

I stood before the bank of elevators; my words 'I am here to attest that these measures are in place' echoing in my head. My system returning to almost normal as the adrenaline dissolved. My cell phone trumpeted a 'Private Number.'

My fingers squeezed the phone in anticipation of a grade on my press release. "Hello, Kitty," I said.

"Kitty?" a deep male voice asked, sounding like a computer-generated response. "Sorry about your luck, but this isn't 'Kitty.' But it's interesting that you've gotten to a more than first name basis with the governor.

"This is your newly appointed health advisor. They say the truth will

set you free, but in your case, it can either make you very rich or very dead."
The connection terminated.

I looked around frantically to see if the caller was nearby. Of the few people in the lobby, no one held a phone. I ran outside. The crowd was gone. The steps to the Capital Building were barren.

(15)

At five p.m., in my hotel room at the Barstow Inn, I paced, wondering if I should call the governor, the police, the FBI, or do nothing. I had just held a press conference, something important people do. And there are some sick bastards who like to mess with important people. The call was probably just a prank. Any iPhone or computer geek could probably find my cell phone number. Personal information was brought and sold in cyberspace. Privacy had become a thing of the past, something the ol' folks had in the good ol' days.

I needed to refocus, think about other things, so I checked my phone for places to eat. Just as I entered a search engine, my phone played the Casinos' *Then You Can Tell Me Goodbye*.

"Hello, sweetheart," I said.

"When was the last time you checked your messages?" Her tone was like coarse sandpaper rubbing on my skin.

"Well, hello to you too. What a greeting."

"I'm sorry, but I called and texted you several times last night. What's the deal? Why didn't you call me back? Where were you? What were you doing?"

She could ask more questions in one breath then I could answer in an hour. And I wasn't in the mood to be interrogated. I wouldn't have all this mental anguish if Bean and I had parted on good terms. I wouldn't have had second thoughts when the governor put my hand on her breast. My guilt plate would be clean. It was my turn to ask some questions, and her turn to have some second thoughts.

"Do I detect a tinge of jealousy? Is the ice queen just now becoming concerned about having sent a horny man away on an extended trip?"

She paused, which was good news, pre-empting bad news. I had found her 'my fault' button, but, I had been here before, she was preparing a much more abrasive response.

"Sex doesn't fix our problems." Her tone implied shared knowledge I couldn't refute. "As a matter of fact, it makes them worse. Sex makes you think everything is back to normal, and you stop trying to resolve anything. And we and our problems stay in limbo." She cleared her throat, paused again, and then said, "Why … should I be worried?" Concern dripped off her words.

Women don't play fair. She had dropped me into one of her verbal minefields, no matter which direction I went, I'd most likely lose. If I told her the truth, she'd probably detonate the entire minefield with me in it. And if I told her not to worry, she'd either think I was lying, or I didn't care.

But she actually sounded worried. Her love for me had never been an issue. I was our problem.

After I lost my job, with each passing week of failing to find work, I had grown more and more depressed. I felt useless. My pride was wounded, more than wounded, near death. I had become dependent on her, and I had been raised to not be dependent on anyone, and never had been. The weeks became months, and I morphed into a low self-esteem, lazy, uncaring funk. Despite my character decay, her love for me never faltered. Had the tables been reversed, I wondered if my love for her would have been as strong.

Bean was special, and I didn't need to make her worry or have second thoughts.

"My phone's battery went dead. And I was too busy to go back to the hotel and charge it. I was at a meeting to prepare for a press conference I gave today. I was told the six o'clock news was going to broadcast it across the state. Watch it and let me know what you now think of your man."

"You held a—"

"Bean, I know I've been a load. I know I'm the problem. But that's behind us now. And believe me, if I lose this job tomorrow, I won't slide back down with the whale shit. I've been there, and once was enough. I'm sorry for what I put you through. In retrospect, I can't believe you stayed. I don't think anyone's ever loved me that much. And no, you don't need to worry. I love you, and, God, I wish you were here right now. I have so much making up to do."

"You held a press conference in your first week? Wow. I'll glue myself to the TV. I'm so proud of you. And I know you've suffered. I, I tried to help you but I couldn't. I ... baby, I miss you too. Every night I roll over to cold emptiness. And you're right; I should've never sent you away horny. That was stupid. I want you so bad. Why don't I come up this weekend? You and I can start over again."

"Tomorrow's Friday, why don't you call in sick and come up to Columbia tonight?"

16

Bean and I lay on the hotel bed, side-by-side, naked, her blonde head rested on my arm. I struggled to stabilize my breathing. My eyes were glued to her body as if this was the first time I'd seen her naked and had made love to her. She was so petite and yet wonderfully proportioned. I was a lucky man.

Though I was shocked she'd made the two-plus-hour drive in record time, I was so glad she was with me. Dinner had been a rushed requirement. And it had been a miracle we were both still dressed after a six-floor elevator ride.

She turned on her side and kissed me on the cheek. "I know I've already said this at dinner, but I'm so proud of you. I saw the newscast on my phone on the way here. You looked so good on TV at your press conference, so handsome in your new clothes. And you were so calm and … and professional. I was enamored with how good you looked and how well you did; I forgot to ask you about a bunch of things."

Her words drew my eyes from her shapely body to her almost black, squinted eyes.

"What things?" I asked.

"We never talked about what you said. You announced you are the newly appointed Vice Chairman of the lottery, and the governor has selected you to investigate the lottery. Why you? You're a neophyte. You don't know anything about government or the lottery. And what's going on with the lottery?"

I edged toward her, cupped one of her butt cheeks, and pulled her body against mine. She was warm and damp from our coupled exercise. Her queries were melted into a mental void by my rising body heat.

"Too many questions," I said and nuzzled her neck making her gasp.

Hands on my chest, she pushed away. "Brent, I'm exhausted. Can we just talk?"

I eased my arm out from under her head and pushed up on an elbow. "Okay, but could you ask me just one question at a time? Your machinegun interrogations riddle my mind."

"Sorry." She sat up, stacked up several pillows against the headboard, and rolled onto her side facing me with an arm under her head.

I wished she hadn't done that. Now, not only was her nude body fronting me, she was watching me. I was having enough problems concentrating, let alone keeping my eyes from roaming over her nakedness.

"So why you?" she asked.

"She, ah ... the governor needed someone she could trust." As soon as the words left my lips I knew I had made a mistake.

I took her free hand and played with her fingers. She always liked me to do that. She said it relaxed her.

Bean pulled her hand away. "Trust?" One of her thin eyebrows arched. "Why would she trust you? She doesn't know you."

My mind ran around in circles chasing its tail like a puppy; going nowhere and returning again. "Ah, I guess ... she had a file, she'd researched me. She knew everything about me, including you."

She pushed up on a stiff arm, causing her breasts to jiggle, and me to lose my concentration.

"She knows about me?" Her voice jumped up an octave. "What does she know about me?"

I forced my eyes back to hers. "She knew your name, and that I called you Bean."

"What else?"

"That was all she said ... about you. But she knew everything about me."

She eased down onto her pillows. "Including how you talk in your sleep?"

My blood turned to wet concrete. I couldn't move or think beyond what I assumed Bean was implying. I had come so close to sleeping with Kitty. Was my mind an open book? Women, they weren't human, no way.

"Ah, of course not. Even though she's a gorgeous woman, I haven't slept with her." Damn, what was wrong with me? My flapping mouth was supplying Bean with ammunition to shoot me over and over. "I barely know Kitty—ah, her." I needed to just shut up. The implication that I was going to get to know first-name-Kitty better had to bury me a little deeper.

Bean sat up, reached down, and pulled the sheet up to her chin. Great.

"So, what's going on with the lottery?" she asked.

Her aggressiveness during our sex had screamed how much she had missed me, almost as loud as her decision now to change the subject and not attack me. Thank God.

The defensive tension drained from my body. "Six months ago, South Carolina was awarded control of the drawings for Powerball and Mega-Millions. Since then, the Powerball statistics have changed radically, beyond belief; both the number of winners and, more specifically, the number of South Carolina winners. Ka—er—" I sucked some air, damn my mouth— "Governor Franklin wants assurance the State controlled drawing system hasn't been compromised on her watch. But it's worse than just a possible lottery fraud, several of the recent winners have died mysteriously after collecting their winnings, and all the money they won is missing, over a half-a-billion dollars."

"Wow." She shook her head. "So what're you going to do about it?"

"Me? Not much. I'm supposed to act like I'm auditing the system while the FBI catches the crooks."

She rubbed her chin with her forefinger. "So, this *gorgeous* Governor has made you her sacrificial lamb for anyone concerned about an investigation."

Son-of-a-bitch, I hadn't thought about it that way. Kitty had said she wanted this to look like she was in charge. But her words in the press release had put me in the lead. She had said she was scared. Now I knew why, the phone call ... son-of-a-bitch.

(17)

I stepped out of the bedroom of my hotel suite while Bean slept. She had to be exhausted from the drive to Columbia and the sex after she arrived. I eased the door closed.

My fingers swept over the face of my phone dialing Kitty's number.

"I can't talk to you right now, Brent." Her words separated by puffs of her strained breathing. "I'm walking into a convention of Ohio teachers where I'm going to give an after-dinner speech. Maybe later."

"Kitty, I—"the line went dead.

I wanted to throw the damned phone through the wall. Politics and politicians. She ranked my importance relative to who was next on her agenda. As soon as she had set me up to be the target versus her, she had better things to do, other favors to either collect or repay.

How bad did I want this job? My wandering eyes stopped at the bedroom door. That pretty, little woman nude on the bed in that room, my sensuous Tinker Bell, had gone out of her way to get this job for me. I couldn't let her down, not unless I wanted to end our relationship and, although we had some issues, I didn't want to do that. I would have to figure out how to pass the buck like all the other politicians did. Maybe if I really audited the lottery, primarily the structure more so than the system, I'd find a way to cast the blame, another lamb. Hold another press release and feed them a different goat.

That's what I'd do. I had a plan. I sucked in a long breath and let my tension flow away with my expelled air. Something for tomorrow's agenda, tonight I had other plans.

I walked over to a coffee table fronting the flowered cloth-covered couch. I plopped onto the couch. Sorting through the hotel pamphlets stacked on the table, I found a wine list and a movie guide. Maybe after Bean woke up, we could watch a movie, snuggle up to a bottle of wine, and hopefully get naked again. A few glasses of wine always made her frisky.

I was waffling between a Merlot and a Shiraz, when my phone trumpeted.

"Kitty, I thought you said you couldn't talk?" I asked, pleased that I had moved up her priority list.

"She can't," said the deep, too familiar male voice.

⑱

This was like déjà vu, when I'd returned to the hotel after work earlier, I'd paced the living room wondering who I should call because of the malicious call. And now, close to nine p.m., almost four hours later, I was pacing the same rug. But this time I was on the phone with the man who had threatened my life earlier.

"Let's put Kitty on hold for the moment," the deep male voice said. "Let's talk about your sassy little Robin Hays, or should I call her Bean? She's damned cute in a sexy way. Even though I'd love to snatch her and enjoy her, is that really what you want?"

This man knew everything, both the governor's and Robin's nicknames. He knew too much. And now he was threatening to kidnap and rape Bean. I squeezed the phone until my fingers ached to keep from screaming into the phone.

"What do you want?" My controlled, monotone words surprised me.

"First of all, if you tell anyone about this call or what you're doing for me, I'll know. And I will take her and enjoy her to the point she will never want you again. Do you understand me?"

A slug of rage slammed against my thin wall of control; bulging and stretching my will power to its limits. My nostrils flared taking in as much air as I could to fortify my anger barrier against the assault. "Yes ... I understand." I cleared my throat. "I assume you've done your homework, and you know who I am. I'm not just an ex-two-Afghan-tours Marine officer. I was Special Ops. So you need to understand something as well. If you ever touch her, I will spend the rest of my life searching for you. And I've been trained to find people who don't want to be found, and I will find you. And that will be the day you curse your mother for giving you life. Do *you* understand?"

"Yes, I do. But none of that will be necessary as long as you do what I want and keep silent about it. I think you'd be doing the same thing I am if you were in my place."

"I doubt it. I'll ask once again, what do you want?"

"I want you to tell me how Governor Franklin is fixing the Lottery drawings."

⑲

I stood at the window in the living room of my hotel suite and sipped Scotch; I needed something to settle my mind. The clear liquid seared a path down my throat. I stared into the blackness outside my window. Vehicle head and tail lights streaked the darkness below, through the intersecting canyons between lit buildings.

The caller said he'd call me back in a few days for a status check and then disconnected. He had threatened to kidnap and rape Bean in order to force me to investigate how the governor was cheating the lottery. And the governor had held a private session with me, during which she had tried to seduce me to test my trust, in order to get me to investigate the lottery. Two separate sources plying me to do the same task. I was confused, totally.

Was the bad guy really a good guy and the luscious Governor crooked?

I didn't have a clue.

I needed to quit this job; just walk away, go back to unemployment and a soup kitchen ladle. At least Bean and I were safe then. But Bean wouldn't accept that. She had used her brother, Andrew to—or had she? I sat the glass of Scotch down. Andrew ... had Andrew set me up? Was my new job totally Andrew's idea? Did he think he could manipulate a job-hungry man? Did he and the governor need a government-ignorant scapegoat?

I didn't know. I didn't know Andrew very well. Apparently I didn't know Kitty at all? I didn't know anything.

All I knew was I couldn't quit for Bean's sake, and yet she was at risk if I stayed. I was pinched.

Regardless of who had gotten me the job, Bean or Andrew, if either Andrew or the governor were criminally involved, the guilty one would use me or my replacement to take the fall. If that were the case, the stealing and killing had to be stopped, and so did the man who threatened Bean. I had to stay.

I eyed the glass of booze and took a swig. Who was I fooling? I was letting my emotions take charge. I wasn't an investigator, and I was government-stupid. I should tell the FBI everything and walk, and let the Feds do their job. They were trained for this. If someone were crooked, they'd find out, and if they didn't, at least they were more capable of finding the truth than I was.

But the caller had warned me not to talk to anyone. Should I risk Bean's safety by involving the FBI? Did I have any other options?

I sat down in one of the flowered-cloth arm chairs and traced the top of the glass with a finger. I was a Commissioner, a Vice-Chairman Commissioner. The title alone should wield some clout. Why not stick around for a few more weeks and nose around a bit? Maybe then, if I found something, I could involve the FBI. Then, hopefully, the FBI could help me catch both the crook, if there was one, and the caller. Plus, if I quit after a week, Bean would never believe any reason I gave her.

All I had to do was watch my back.

⟨20⟩

The bottle of Scotch had been my only companion last night, and not much of one, one lonely glass. Drinking alone didn't suit a social drinker like me.

Bean never left the bedroom. She had slept through the night. Nothing disturbed her, not even me, when I crawled into bed next to her.

The next morning, I had to wake her to tell her I had a meeting and wouldn't be long. Then, she sat in her underwear and yawned over a cup of coffee and the breakfast I had ordered her. When I leaned down to give her a goodbye kiss, she turned away and raised her hands as if repulsed.

"Whoa. I thought you were the morning person. Why so grumpy?"

She scrunched her shoulders. "I don't know. Maybe too much sleep."

"So how about a kiss?" I asked, leaning closer.

She acted as if it took all the energy she could summon to give me a peck on the cheek. Now I knew how she had to feel about me just a few days ago.

Fifteen minutes later, I walked through a maze of cubicles on the third floor of a rental office building in an industrial park. The complex was about three or four miles from the State Capitol Building on the east side of Columbia near I-77.

Following the directions given to me by a third floor security officer stationed by the elevators, I knocked on the open door of an office on the periphery of a 'bull pen' of partitioned desks. A woman with brown hair, cut short like a man's, sat at a metal desk, head down behind a computer monitor. She raised her head. Green eyes, magnified by her Sarah Palin glasses, looked at me. My eyes were drawn to her throat. There was no demarcation between her chin and neck, just loose skin.

"Are you Sally Kellerman, the Drawing manager?" I asked.

"Yes. I manage the drawing procedures for all lottery numbered-ball games conducted by the State, including Cash Five, Pick 4, Keno, Powerball, and Mega-millions." Her words sounded like a memorized response that had been said too many times. "How can I help you?"

I entered the windowed, fifteen-foot by fifteen-foot office, squared my shoulders, and extended my hand. "I'm Brent Layne, the new Lottery Vice Chairman and Commissioner of Auditing. I apologize for being a little late. I hope I didn't screw up your schedule. I got lost. I'm not familiar with Columbia, yet."

She rose from her high-backed, leather chair, a tall woman, probably five-nine or ten. She was dressed in a black pants suit with a buttoned vest covering most of a white cotton blouse. She took my hand, a strong grasp. Her squinted eyes scanned me from top to bottom and back. "So you're the new commissioner, Mr. Layne. You're only twenty minutes late."

Her sharpened words shredded the effect I had hoped my title would have.

She waved at her paper-strewn metal desk. "Don't worry about my schedule, I can always find things to do. Have a seat." She flipped a hand at the three wooden chairs fronting her desk.

I glanced around her office. The window and doorway were the only areas of the office walls not covered by either filing cabinets or five-foot high bookshelves. All of the shelves were jammed either with manuals, what looked to be textbooks, or just stacks of paper. If she wasn't a hoarder, she was overwhelmed with information.

I sat in one of the straight-back, unpadded, wooden chairs. If I were to guess, I'd conclude she had purposely picked these uncomfortable chairs to limit the duration of visits.

She folded her arms across her chest and stared at me.

Now I knew how a roach must feel when the lights were turned on.

I cleared my throat and pushed up to my tallest seated height. "I am here to audit the drawing procedures."

Her head turned sideways and sagged along with her shoulders.

"What's wrong?" I asked.

She braced her hands on her desk and pushed upright. "I've been in this job for almost ten years, and every time someone appoints a new Commissioner, they come here." She shook her head causing the flap of skin that used to be neck to wiggle. "And that happens every year." She leaned forward, her glasses-enlarged eyes hardened. "We have spent years of people effort writing and revising those manuals." She waved an arm at a bookshelf. "Have you read them?"

Her posture and tone reminded me of my first Gunny Sergeant when I was a green First Lieutenant in Afghanistan.

I rubbed my hands together. "Ah, yes, I have."

She leaned back and folded her arms across her chest again. "Really?" Her expression painted the word smug. "Then you should know that the procedure is so laden with mandatory, documented, checks and balances that an audit is a waste of time."

My experiences with arrogant Gunnies had taught me the privileges of rank. I put an elbow on an armrest, cupped my chin on a fist, and took a long second to study her.

"I've seen this before," I said.

Her no-neck-no-chin pulled inward. "Seen what?"

I flipped both hands palms up. "Stagnation."

She canted her head like she was having trouble hearing me.

"When people stay in a job too long, they have a tendency to become, ah ... complacent," I said. "They need a new challenge, new surroundings; sometimes a new career."

Her posture straightened, jerking to military attention. "That won't be necessary, sir. How may I help you?"

I got back to the hotel in time to take Bean to lunch. I figured she was probably bored out of her mind from sitting in the room waiting for me. So, I mentally prepared for the worst.

When I entered the room I was surprised to find her dressed in snug black slacks and a tight beige blouse. Her make-up was light, but complimentary, and her hair perfect. But that wasn't nearly as shocking as her smile, the rush into my unprepared arms, and the full tongue-probing kiss she gave me.

Arms wrapped around the small of her back, I came up for air. "Wow. That was nice and ... well, unexpected. I thought you'd be bored to aggravation after sitting here all morning."

She canted her head, and her enticing smile returned. "I would've been if it hadn't been for the room service masseur."

"The ma—what?" I asked, shaking my head.

"A man who gives massages, Larry to be exact," she said with too much gleeful recollection in her voice and eyes. "And to make a glorious story way too short, I treated myself to an absolutely marvelous massage. Larry, ah I mean the masseur had the hands of an angel. I cannot recall ever feeling as good as I do now."

She had lit my Bunsen burner of concern and placed it under my stored jealousy. I stepped back, out of her embrace, and extended my arms sideways.

"Did you say room service masseur? This man came here, into our room?"

She looked at me like I was crazy. "Well sure, that's the nice part, I didn't have to get dressed and go anywhere."

"You mean to tell me you let a strange man come into your room when you were alone and," I widened my eyes, "and put his hands on you? Have you lost your mind?"

As I had done too many times in the past, I caused her smile to vanish; Brent the smile eraser; the joy blocker; that was me.

Her hands fisted on her hips. Her face morphed into squinted eyes and pressed together lips, as if she were holding her breath making her face redder and redder.

If there had been a bomb shelter close by, I would have been in it.

"I can't believe you're gonna stand there and scold me like I was a dumb child. You, the man I disrupted my schedule for, the man I drove at breakneck speeds for over two hours to be with, the man I made love to last night like it was our home-from-the-war reunion, the same man who left me in a hotel room by myself this morning." She flipped her hands, palms up, outward. "He wore a uniform ... a white uniform. He was lugging all this stuff, a basket full of towels and oils and a portable bed. He knew I was in the room because of his housekeeper friend. Daaah ... he works for the hotel. Plus he told me if I got a second massage tomorrow, the first was complimentary." One of her hands returned to a pushed-to-the-side hip which seemed to tilt her head in that direction. "And even if he'd been the Boston Strangler, the massage would have been worth whatever he would've done to me."

My hands rose as if I were holding a basketball. "And ... and what were you wearing during this ... this 'marvelous' massage?"

Hip, hand, and head locked in place, she released a sigh. "A towel ... like everyone else wears when getting a massage."

"A towel? Nothing but a towel? You got naked for a strange man and let him touch you?" I shook my head as if I didn't know her.

"Brent. He was a masseur. Nothing happened. Except I got a once-in-a-lifetime rubdown. I'd think you'd be glad I was happy for Pete's sake."

My arms fell, letting my hands slap my thighs. "Honey, I am happy for you. It's just that ... I couldn't stand it if something bad happened to you.

There were these … never mind." What good would it do to tell her about the threatening phone calls? She couldn't defend herself if she were expecting an attack. And living in a vacuum wouldn't help. She'd probably leave and go back to Beaufort where'd she'd be alone, an easier target.

"'There were these' what?" she asked.

"Nothing. I'm just a little … no, I'm a whole bunch jealous, and … I'm sorry."

Her smile half returned. She stepped forward, reached up, and pinched my chin. "Well, I guess I should be flattered. But, Baby, you don't need to worry. I'm all yours." Then she eased back a step and looked up at me out of the tops of her almost black eyes. "But there was a moment, when his hands were—" her little smile broke into a grin—"just kidding you. Let's go eat. Those full body massages make a girl hungry."

"Full body?"

She punched my arm. "You're so easy." She laughed all the way to the elevator.

We stepped from the elevator into the lobby and she grabbed my arm. "I'm not kidding you anymore, Larry was good, and when he told me the massage was free, I forgot to tip him. Do you mind if we go to the desk so I can leave him a tip?"

"I'm not goin' back into that minefield. But, I'll go with you."

We walked over to the front desk and waited while the only clerk on duty, a female clerk, finished checking a couple into the hotel.

"Yes, may I help you?" she asked accompanied by a pleasant look.

Bean nudged me.

"My, ah … my companion received a massage in her room from a Larry, and she'd like to leave him a tip. Can you make sure he gets it?"

The clerk's head tilted and dropped a fraction of an inch. Her pleasant expression changed to confused. "Let me see if I got this right. A masseur named Larry gave you," her head nodded at Bean, "a massage in your room and you want to tip him?"

"Yes," Bean said. "Aren't tips allowed?"

"I'm the manager, the hotel doesn't employ a masseur, let alone anyone named Larry."

(22)

An elevator ride of unanswered Bean-questions later, we were back in our hotel room. I was somewhere between pissed off and scared. I could give Bean answers, but not solutions, so why bother. But there were professional people involved in this mess who got paid to find solutions. So, I had Bean call her brother, Andrew. I wanted the name and phone number of a FBI agent investigating the associated lottery crimes. After exchanging brother-sister stuff, Bean, sitting on the bed with pen in hand, asked for the information.

Her black eyes rolled from a hotel note pad by the nightstand phone to me. "Brent asked for it. I don't know why. He just asked me to call you and get it. Well, you'll have to ask him that. I don't know; I'm just a messenger. Okay, thanks." She scribbled on the note pad. A few pleasantries later, she hung up the phone.

"Okay." She jabbed the note pad at me. "I did it. Now tell me what's going on. An imposter comes into my room and ... and now you ask for a number for the FBI." She hugged herself. "I'm scared."

I had no choice. Possibly my threatening caller had touched Bean, physically, to show me he could. She needed to know, all of it, every detail, well not everything. My touching the governor's boob really wasn't pertinent, at least not in my judgment. I had made sure my physical encounter with Kitty had gone nowhere. So why destroy my relationship with Bean over nothing?

I pointed an index finger upward. "In a minute, sweetheart. Please try to relax and be patient." I sighed. "I should've told you this earlier, but … you'll know as much as I do shortly."

I sat down on the bed across from Bean and punched the number Andrew had given her into the hotel phone. I probably should tell her everything before the call, but why put her through the details twice. It was going to be hard enough for her.

I wasn't sure why, maybe paranoia, but I didn't want this agent to have my cell phone number, not yet anyway.

Two rings later, a deep male voice said, "Hello."

I was expecting something more formal, like, I glanced at the pad, 'Agent Nicholas Sanders of the Federal Bureau of Investigation, how may I help you?' And I had this image of Melvin Pervis in my head, the geeky FBI agent who bagged Pretty Boy Floyd and Baby Face Nelson back in the day.

"Is this FBI Agent, Nick Sanders?"

"Who wants to know?" the baritone asked.

Another strange response, maybe I'd watched too much television. It was time for a little title leverage. "Brent Layne, Vice Chairman of the Ohio Lottery Commission."

"Ah, Mr. Layne. Yes, this is Agent Sanders. I saw your press conference yesterday. I can't tell you how much my colleagues and I appreciated the fact that you are taking the lead on a *Federal* investigation."

I glanced at Bean and realized how she felt as a message carrier. "Ah, this is my first week on the job. I'm not a politician … neither am I an investigator. At this point, I'm just a presenter, a mouth-piece for the governor."

"I see. So why the call, are you going to tell the FBI what the governor wants us to do next?"

Another button pusher, just what I needed. "No." I looked into Bean's questioning eyes, and reached out and took her hand. Then I told Agent Sanders everything that had happened, what the governor had told me about the lottery numbers, the associated deaths, the threatening phone calls, the caller's demand to have me tell him how the governor was fixing the Lottery, and the phony masseur.

In between my words about the phone calls and the masseur, Bean's grip on my hand tightened. I looked at her, her eyes were wide, and her free hand covered her mouth, as she slowly shook her head.

"Is your girlfriend still with you?"

"Yes, she's sitting here listening to every word."

"Keep her there." His words were firm, an order, not a request. "What's your room number?"

"Six-thirty-two," I said. "At the—"

"Barstow Inn, I know. I'll be there in fifteen minutes. Stay in your room and don't let anyone in except me." He disconnected.

Everyone, the governor, the masseur, and now the FBI, knew where I was staying. Kitty's gate-keeping secretary probably had made the reservation and had told her. My mystery caller was like my shadow, he knew way too much. But how did Sanders know, caller ID, or had the FBI been watching me also? Why would the FBI be watching me? I looked around. Maybe there were cameras in the room. Then I thought about last night and wondered if there were possibly cameras in the bedroom as well? My eyes roamed the room. I felt like someone forced to streak at a televised NFL football game.

Our location was one thing I could fix.

Bean released my hand and clutched her chest, bringing me back to the present. Her face was white. "Tha-that man, La-Larry, you think he's the-the man who threatened to—" she clutched her chest with her free hand—"oh, my God. I … nothing but a towel and … oh my God."

I slid off the bed onto my knees and took her into my arms. I rubbed her back with both hands, hoping to erase her visions. "Shh. Don't go there. Nothing happened, thank God. And we really don't know if Larry and my caller are the same people. The masseur could just be an imposter, a man who —" I was heading toward a thousand-foot-high drop off. "Nothing happened. I won't let anything bad happen to you. I promise."

She pushed away. Her features scrunched together. "How are you going to do that?"

Almost exactly fifteen minutes later, there was a knock on the door to Bean's and my hotel suite. And I recognized Nick Sander's deep voice when he yelled his name through the door.

Bean, whose head top came to about my armpit, stood behind me and to one side as I opened the door.

Nick Sanders was a tall, slender man with brown close-cropped hair. He had a long, thin face with a proportionally long flat nose, the kind of face that blends into a crowd. His black suit hung on his large fat-free frame.

I couldn't help but wonder what kind of gun he carried.

"Mr. Layne, Nick Sanders." He extended his right hand.

His hand was thin, but his grasp firm.

"Call me Brent." I stepped to one side and motioned at Bean. "And this is Robin Hays."

Nick stepped into the room and took Bean's hand. "Miss Hays."

"I've never met an FBI agent before," Bean said. "Do I call you Agent Sanders or Mr. Sanders?"

"I'd prefer Jim." His eyebrows arched as if he had said something wrong.

"Jim?" I asked, turning from closing the door. "I thought your name was Nick?"

"Ah, Jim is a nickname I picked up in grade school. It's a long, stupid story." He swept his splayed fingers over his head as if to push his hair back, the habit of a man who once had long hair. His eyes swept over Bean. "And may I call you Robin?"

"That'd be fine, ah, Jim."

The FBI agent reached into a coat pocket and retrieved a small notepad and pen. "Robin, can you describe the man who gave you the massage?" Sanders asked.

Bean's eyes looked to the side and up. "Let's see … he said his name was Larry, no last name. He was a little taller than you, but shorter than Brent. He was stocky, muscular, like a weight lifter, big shoulders and a small waist. Seemed in great shape. He had long blond hair and wore it in a ponytail. Blue eyes, and a strong, square face," she wagged her head, "almost a nice face, except for his nose … his nose was crooked, like it had been broken and not set properly, like a boxer's nose. And he had very white, perfect teeth. He was articulate with no accent; I'd guess a northerner from the Midwest."

I watched Bean's face as she described this imposter who had put his hands on her bare skin, all over her skin, or at least I assumed as much. Her concentration was frequently disrupted by a grimace or a small body quake. I slid my arm around her and pulled her to me. I couldn't fix the past, but I could add comfort to the present.

"That's very detailed. Good job." Sanders nodded at Bean and finished his scribbling. "I'll have to get you with one of our computer artists Monday, so you can recreate his face."

Bean bit her lower lip, glanced at me, and then at Sanders. "Ah, I won't be here Monday. I'm going back to Beaufort, South Carolina, tomorrow," she gave me a questioning look, "or maybe Sunday, but no later."

"Is there someone there you can stay with, someone capable of protecting you?" Sanders asked.

Bean's brow furrowed with concern. Her black eyes fixed on me, and she shook her head.

"Until we unravel these threats, being alone is not a good idea," Sanders said, looking at me for support.

"He's right, you can't—"

"I've got a job," Bean said. "There are twenty-three third graders depending on me to teach them multiplication and division and … and why South Carolina seceded from the Union."

Agent Sanders bent at the waist, tilting his head toward her, and spread his arms. "Someone has made you his target, Bean."

Like being on a hot desert and getting struck by a snowball, my focus was diverted. How did he know her name was Bean? Had I referred to Robin as 'Bean' during my phone call with him? I don't remember using either of her names. I was pretty sure I had referred to her as my 'girlfriend.'

(24)

After promising Nick or Jim or whatever his name was we'd call him before Bean left for home, I opened the hotel room door and motioned to him. He walked out looking at me like he hadn't completed his business.

And I didn't care. I wanted him gone.

I closed the door and locked it.

Bean sat on the corner of the bed, her fingers intertwining, linking, twisting, over and over, as she chewed on her lower lip.

The only thing I'd gained from Agent Sanders's visit was more doubt. I should've asked him for identification, whatever good that would've done. With today's computer technology, anyone could make false I.D.'s, and I wouldn't know an authentic FBI badge from a phony one.

If Sanders were a phony, then Andrew had set me up. And if Andrew was dirty, the governor probably was too.

Over a half billion dollars had been stolen, the FBI was investigating, and it was time for the bad guys to cut and run with the money. But to get away clean, they required a fall guy, me. They needed to keep track of what I knew, how better than to set me up with a phony agent. And that made my caller a pseudo-hero except for his threats.

But what if this Nick-Jim guy was really a FBI agent and Kitty and Andrew weren't dirty, who was the caller? Was he the thief using me to cast blame elsewhere so he could get away with the money?

I needed to talk this though with Bean. Because of this stupid job, because of her brother, we were in this jam together, and it would take both of us to find a solution. But she didn't look fit to talk about anything. And what was I going to do with her? She couldn't go home, not by herself.

I walked over and sat down next to her and put my arm around her. I pulled her close and took one of her fidgeting hands in mine.

She leaned her head on my shoulder. "What are we going to do, Brent? I can't stay here. I, ah, I'd lose my job. And even if I could stay, you'd have to leave me to go to work. I don't want to be alone either here. I'd be better off back home." A shudder rippled through her body. "I'm … I'm scared."

She wasn't alone there, I was scared too. But what good would my admitting that do?

I kissed her forehead. "We've got a couple of days to figure out what to do. Don't be scared. And don't worry. We'll be okay."

I tilted her head up and kissed her soft, sweet, lips.

She put her arms around my neck and kissed me back, more of a tongue-searching desperate kiss than a passionate one. She broke the kiss, buried her face against my neck and clung to me. "I'm so sorry I got you this job." Her words slightly muffled by her lips brushing my skin.

"None of this is your fault." I stroked her hair.

She snuggled closer. "I … I need you, Brent."

I was tempted to enjoy her dependency on me, to take advantage of her desperation. She was vulnerable and seeking companionship. And how much closer can two people become than when they physically, intimately bond? I shook off the selfish thought. This wasn't the time. We both required time to think.

"We've got to get out of here … find a different hotel, one where no one knows we're there," I said.

"That's for sure. But I need some time before we go anyplace." She pulled away and looked down. "I'd like to … to take another shower. I, I feel dirty. Right now, I'm not certain I'll ever feel clean again. I'm sorry, can we wait 'til it gets dark to leave?"

I couldn't imagine how she felt. And I wasn't sure what I could do about it.

"Sure, whatever you want."

She got up and walked into the bedroom without an endearment or a look back.

This was all our relationship needed, another wedge.

25

The sun had disappeared leaving a soft glow in the sky by the time we got to our destination. Charley and Annie's Bed & Breakfast, west of Columbia, was on the wrong side of quaint, the 'hillbilly' side. The weeds outnumbered the flowers ten to one and the external décor of the two-story farmhouse had to be called peeled and chipped.

Bean took one look, folded her arms across her chest and said, "I may have to go home tomorrow or maybe tonight." She sat in my old Ford Taurus and shook her head. "First you make me turn off my cell phone, separating me from my text world, and then you expect me to sleep with bugs. I think I'd be more comfortable in my own bed even though I was alone."

Based on her quips and attitude, my old Bean was back. "No one will find us here." I opened the car door.

"Yeah, not even the bug exterminator."

I motioned at her. "Come on, we'll check the place out before we commit. But you have to think 'tolerable' versus 'classy.' Okay?"

She pushed her car door open like a child going to the dentist. "Okay, but if I don't like it, you have to promise me we'll go someplace else."

I raised one hand. "I promise."

Charley and Annie, cotton mill retirees, were both pleasant and neat freaks, thank God. The inside was clean and fresh, and the whole second story had been remodeled into an apartment, latest-appliances kitchen, walk-in shower, satellite TV, the works.

Bean smiled and we rented it through the weekend, paying cash.

After I signed the papers, and we returned to the car for our things, she asked, "Now what?"

"I think we should talk to your brother, together."

She nodded. "I most definitely agree."

We drove toward town around seven p.m. and halfway there it started to drizzle rain. At the outskirts of the city, she called Andrew with her phone speaker turned on at my request.

"Andrew," her black eyes glanced up at me, "don't say anything bad about Brent, he's listening. Your sister and her beau are on our way to your house."

"You're what?" he asked.

"We're coming to see you. We need to talk."

"You, ah, you can't come here. It's Friday night. I've got … an appointment." His tone was filled with more rejection than his words.

"My brother the workaholic has a date? Tell her you're going to be a little late. This won't take long. Besides, you need to keep a girl a little off balance at the beginning."

Bean's commanding tone was way too familiar to me.

"I don't have a date. I'm, ah … hold on a second." A long pause followed, the background interspersed with what sounded like muffled voices, maybe a TV. Then Andrew said, "I *cannot* see you." He sighed. "Robin, I know we haven't seen each other in a while, but you can't just barge in uninvited. I wouldn't do that to you. How about tomorrow? I'm open most of the day."

"We're here, minutes away, and we won't be there long. When is your appointment?" Bean asked.

"Not tonight, Sis. I can't. Call me tomorrow." He disconnected.

Eyes wide, she glared at the phone. "He hung up on me. I don't believe it."

"Sounded like he may already have company," I said, trying to express my empathy for him. "So what do you want to do now?"

"I want to talk to him face to face. I don't care who's there."

Even in the rolling streetlights, I could tell her cheeks were inflamed. There was no turning back now.

Ten to fifteen minutes later, we pulled into a densely wooded suburb with at least five-acre lots. Two mistakes and two turn-a-rounds, and we found his driveway. His large ranch house sat several hundred yards from the road, concealed by trees.

"The state government must pay senators well." I parked in the visitors' pad just off the circular drive in front of the house. "Bean, look, the front door is open."

"Oh God, what if he's doing what you used to do when you invited me over, door opened and lying in bed naked?" She smiled and winked.

"I hope not." Erotic memories flashed. "Maybe we should come back, tomorrow."

"No way." A blink later, she was out of the car.

We jogged through the drizzle to the front door.

Bean pushed the door fully open. "Andrew! It's me, Robin. We're here. You should've known I'd come after you hung-up on me."

Seconds ticked with no response.

She took a step into the house.

I grabbed her arm and stopped her. I didn't like the vibration in my spine or the hairs standing at attention on my neck. I stepped in front of her and motioned for her to wait.

I walked through the foyer into a large great room and froze. Andrew was there to my left, sitting in a leather armchair, facing me. Half of his head was missing.

26

"Brent?" Bean summoned from the entryway around the corner behind me.

"Bean, just stay there. I'll, ah, I'll be right out."

Rain pelted the night blackened windows of Andrew Hays' great room, but my focus remained locked. My eyes, my mind, my whole being was drawn to Andrew's lifeless body.

I had seen a lot of dead people in my life. Most of my encounters with death, too many, had been in the war. And those men and women had been killed in many ways, generally gruesome. Most of them I didn't know, but there had been a few, friends, buddies. Regardless, each of them had left an indelible memory, a vivid, Technicolor picture of carnage.

Death had such an allure, no one could look away without at least an imprinting glance. The morbid attraction was probably because we all had to encounter our own end to life. The inevitable loss of life was a common bond to all the living. The cold, stiff state of the lifeless, the termination of being, challenged our blind faith in the hereafter. These people were dead, just like the many mosquitoes or flies we had squashed, there was no tomorrow. Like the insects, were we just dust to dust? These were thoughts for another time, not today as I stood looking at what was left of Bean's brother.

Viewing Andrew's lifeless body bothered me above and beyond my prior experiences with dead bodies. My reaction wasn't because Andrew and I were close. We weren't. And, even though half of his head was splattered across the wall behind his chair, I had seen worse. My insides churned because Andrew's murder slammed me with the reality of Bean's and my situation. Someone was damned serious about this Lottery business. I was scared, for both Bean and myself. And fear was such a dominating master.

Brent, don't leave me standing here, what's going on?" Bean's tone conveyed her concern and impatience. "Brent, talk to me."

I scanned the room looking for a weapon and clues. There was no sign of a struggle. Someone Andrew must have known, walked up to him sitting in this chair, and blew his brains out. Andrew hadn't tried to run, or fight, or even shield himself. He had been totally surprised. This had to have just happened; the flowing blood splatter on the walls had only migrated halfway to the floor molding. We had just talked less than twenty minutes ago. The call, the background voices, the killer was probably the person Andrew was talking to during our phone conversation.

"Brent, if you don't talk to me, I'm coming in." Patience wasn't one of her strengths.

"I'm coming," I said in a flat, unemotional voice. That's all I could think of saying. I couldn't convey any concern. She would run in here. And she didn't need to see anyone, let alone her brother, disfigured and dead.

I backed out of the room, continuing to scan. Then I saw something, the tip of a piece of paper protruding from Andrew's shirt pocket.

I glanced at Bean standing in the doorway with her hands on her hips. I gave her one of my stern looks I'd learned to use to get young men to follow orders in combat. "Stay right there. I'll explain everything in a minute."

I stepped over and remembering all the TV crime shows I had watched, I pinched the corner of the paper between my thumb and forefinger and slid the paper out. It was a small three-by-five memo card made of thick, heavy stock paper. There were numbers written on it, five spaced numbers followed by a dash and a sixth number; and below those numbers were three numbers separated by slashes, like a date, this coming Wednesday's date. Five numbers followed by a sixth … Powerball numbers. The Powerball drawings were every Wednesday and Saturday. These were the Powerball numbers for next Wednesday's drawing. Could these possibly be the numbers that would be drawn?

I don't know why, but I carefully put the evidence in my shirt pocket.

(27)

The earlier, sprinkling rain had changed to a heavy, deluge. I took Bean by the arm and ran to the car. In the twenty or so feet, we both got soaked.

The pounding torrent on the roof of my Ford created a deep hum like a den of disturbed rattlesnakes.

Bean pushed her wet hair off her face. "What took you so long?" She spoke loud over the hum. "Why would Andrew leave home with his front door open? He would never do that, unless he wanted us to come in and wait for him."

We couldn't sit here without calling the police. There would never be a good time to tell her Andrew was dead. The dark interior of the car, the dense patter of the raindrops on the roof, all befitted the depression of the moment.

I took a deep breath and blew it out. I reached out, put my arm around her wet shoulders and pulled her as close as the seat-dividing console would allow.

"Andrew ... he didn't leave. He's in there."

"What? Then why are—"

"Someone shot him ... I'm so sorry, he's dead."

"What?" She tried to pull free, tried to reach for the door handle.

I held her firm against me.

"What are you saying? Let me go!" She twisted and dug her nails into the flesh of my constraining arm.

Her violent struggling subsided in futility, and she relaxed.

I could sense her eyes searching the darkness for mine, seeking visual confirmation.

"No, Brent. No."

I wrapped both arms around her and rested my cheek on top of her shaking, soaked head.

"Let me go. Andrew's dead? That's crazy. Brent, tell me you're kidding. That can't be, I just talked to him. Brent?"

"He's gone, Baby. Someone killed him. We've got to call the police. Now."

"Oh my God, no." Her voice faltered, like someone admitting defeat. "Brent, tell me it's not true. Andrew's my big brother, my—he can't be dead. No." She sobbed and tried to choke back the tears, but couldn't. Her sobs turned to moans.

I was useless, totally useless. I could think of nothing to say or do except hold her, press against her, and maybe absorb some of her pain.

She sniffed. "Brent, please let me go." She gently touched my arm. "I want to see Andrew. I need to see him."

"You don't want to see him, Bean, not like he is now. Later, you can see him later. Not now."

I held her with one arm and dialed '911' with my free hand.

The note card was like a brick in my shirt pocket. Maybe I should put it back where I found it before the police came. But if these were next Wednesday's Powerball numbers, Andrew would be deemed dirty. And what if the killer planted the card in Andrew's pocket to implicate him?

Bean had enough on her plate. She didn't need to have her dead defenseless brother labeled a crook and maybe a murderer as well.

For Bean's sake, I had to find the truth.

(28)

After I had called the police, it didn't take long for them to arrive, and then they just kept coming, one car or van after another. The station house had to be empty. A couple of detectives wanted to talk to Bean and me, and there wasn't anywhere to talk because of the rain except in Andrew's house, not a good idea. I finally suggested the garage where two detectives and I sat on some fold-out lawn chairs. Two other investigators took Bean to a squad car to interrogate her.

In retrospect, it seemed like we were in the garage for a year. The concealed, lied-about, three-by-five card in my pocket made the time pass like overflowed lava, slow and heavy and too hot to try to force past.

I told the detectives everything, the same story I had told the FBI agent, Larry or Jim Sanders. Then, I told them about Bean's phone call to Andrew, the noises in the background, and why we had decided to visit Andrew. The only things I left out were our move to the B&B and the index card.

When Bean and I finally got back to Charley and Annie's Bed & Breakfast, it was almost midnight, and we were emotionally and physically spent. Only absolutely necessary words were spoken, terse, and to the point. We changed into dry clothes and went to bed, as if we thought we'd sleep.

The night crawled by, slower than the time-carrying lava that had oozed by Andrew's garage door earlier. The events of the week accompanied by the same unanswered questions repeated over and over in my mind. After several iterations of leaving the bedroom and sitting in a chair in the small living room, I was able to focus on just one question, what to do about Bean. As the dim light of dawn ate into the surrounding darkness outside our bedroom window, I decided I'd try to convince Bean to take a leave from work and go stay with her best friend, her college roommate, Doreen, in Wichita, Kansas. The sadistic caller would never find her there, not in Kansas with Toto and Dorothy's red shoe.

29

Sunday morning, swollen-eyed Bean awoke late.

I had gotten up three cups of coffee earlier. Dressed in a pair of dark jeans and a light blue, short-sleeved buttoned shirt, I sat in the living room eyeing the plastic-baggy-covered card when she entered. I slid it into my shirt pocket.

Wearing a tattered grey USC sweatshirt and sweatpants, she staggered by me like I was a piece of furniture.

After a half pot of coffee, sitting at the small kitchen table, she found the strength to call her parents and tell them about Andrew. Not a pleasant experience to witness. During the call she committed to her mother to return home that afternoon. She'd take bereavement leave from work and stay with her parents at least a few days beyond Andrew's funeral. Her retired parents lived in Walterboro, South Carolina, about halfway between our home in Beaufort and Columbia.

After she disconnected, she turned to me. "I didn't get much sleep last night," she said followed by a mouth-stretching yawn. "I had a lot of time to think … about too many things. I, ah, I want you to quit your lottery job. I don't want to lose you too. When you come to Walterboro for Andrew's"—her head dropped and she took a big breath. "After the burial, let's go home; to Beaufort." She raised her head and looked up, her puffy eyes scanning my face. "You'll find another job." Her pleading eyes fixed on mine. "Promise me you'll quit tomorrow."

She was right. I should quit. It made no sense to stay. No job was worth dying over.

What would I accomplish by staying, other than an above-average income, health insurance, and a possible future in some government job with a great pension? All the things I had been seeking since getting out of the Marines, a dream come true.

'You'll find another job;' words, filler, but not reality. If only she knew how hard I had tried before. I'd be back in that soup kitchen fighting depression daily, a rejection or two away from becoming one of those I was feeding.

There had to be a way to keep this job and stop the madness, the death threatening insanity. There had to be.

I stood and went to her and pulled her to her feet. I took her into my arms and hugged her. I couldn't imagine her pain. Now wasn't the time to make promises. Neither of us was thinking normally. Right now, all I could do was assure her how much I loved her.

"I'm so sorry," I said and rubbed her tense back. "In your condition, maybe I should drive you to Walterboro."

"Brent, promise me." She looked up, a look of exasperation.

Anything I would say other than a promise wouldn't be acceptable. So I said what I was thinking. "Now is not the time to be making promises. We're both mentally and physically exhausted. I'll talk to the governor and the FBI tomorrow and see what I can do to eliminate any threats to either of us. I'm sure the FBI will send someone to Walterboro to watch over you and your parents. If there is no other way to stop this madness, I will quit."

She pushed out of my arms, looked away and shook her head. "I can't take much more. If you don't end this soon, it won't take much to push me over the edge. One little thing, one more call, or a little note, like the one you keep touching in your shirt pocket, and I'm through."

My hand jerked to my pocket. Had I been touching the note during my interview with the detectives?

"What is that in your pocket?" She nodded at my shirt.

A blood serge of panic had to have turned my cheeks crimson. "Ah, oh that, it's ah," my hand patted my chest, "it's a meeting reminder, ah, for ah … next Wednesday." Not exactly a lie.

"A meeting next Wednesday, it must be important the way you keep touching it."

"It could be." I pulled her little body against mine trying to squeeze her into another subject. "I think I should drive you home."

"That won't be necessary. I'll be fine. Plus I'll need my car; I can't drive that tank Dad calls a car. And my parents and I," she sighed, "we must have some time together, just us three … to grieve and … just to hold each other."

She packed. Then I drove her back to the Barstow Inn where we had left her Pontiac Solstice, her Master's degree present from her parents and her prized possession.

We got out and hugged. She gave me a peck on the lips.

I held her at arms' length. "You shouldn't be alone right now."

"I got a full tank of gas, and I won't stop 'til I get there. I'll call you as soon as I'm there." She reached up and pinched my chin, her way of commanding my attention. "And tomorrow, Brent, I want you to quit that damned job."

"Tomorrow's another day," I said. I knew she had to be with her parents, but I didn't want her to leave. I needed her to be with me, where I could protect her. I pulled her to me, and kissed her like there would be no tomorrows.

30

I was back at Charley and Annie's B&B wondering what I would do with the rest of Sunday, when my phone trumpeted. Each and every nerve and hair on my skin had a Viagra moment. I prayed it wasn't my tormentor, not with Bean being on the road, alone.

I forced out a "Hello."

"Brent ... Kitty." The sound of her soft voice was a relief though she sounded stressed. "Andrew—" she sobbed.

"I know. I was there."

"I," sniff, sniff, "I read the report." She blew her nose. "Poor Robin, I can't imagine. How is she?"

"She's—" I started to tell her Bean was on her way home, but I had more than a touch-my-boob trust issue with Kitty—"she's coping."

"Brent, I'm scared ... scared for all of us."

This woman knew a lot more than she was telling. And she hadn't called me on a Sunday just to express her condolences. "You were scared before Andrew's murder. Why? Why are you afraid? What were you and Andrew involved in that would get him killed?"

"Camden said—"

"Camden, Senator Camden Sparks, our US Senator?" A vision of an ugly, fat, balding man with three chins and an unlit cigar stuffed in the corner of his mouth popped into my head.

"Yes." One spoken word, just one, but overflowing with venom.

She paused.

For a second I thought I had lost the connection. And then whatever had taken her away brought her back.

"You have been listening during your indoctrination," she said, like a teacher praising a student.

"I don't know anyone else named Camden."

"Can you meet me this evening, another private dinner, please?"

Visions of a yellow, low-cut sweater flooded my mind. "Why me? How can I be of any help?"

"I'm not sure. But Andrew thought you could help. That's why he chose you."

My stomach flipped. So my job skills, my work experience, my education; none of the normal criteria for hiring someone had meant nothing. I was chosen to 'help'; whatever that meant. "That's why he chose me, to help? Andrew chose me because you and he were in trouble, and he thought I could be a savior?"

"Yes."

I didn't have a clue. What did Andrew know about me that I didn't? What unique skill did I have? My mind was blank. Another dinner was the only way to the answers. "When do you want to meet?"

"Is six o'clock too early?"

"No."

"I'll send my driver."

A little voice told me not to be dependent on her for transportation or to let her know where I was staying. Tonight would be my turn to test her for trust. "No, I'll just meet you."

(31)

I walked into the Seven Gables Inn for the second time in my life; this time on wobbly knees. The old historic mansion had lost some of its allure.

The inn's staff had been trained well. This time there were no questions, just a "Welcome, Mr. Layne," followed by an escort to the back room.

Kitty was already there. She rose from her chair dressed in snug designer jeans and an oversized blue sweatshirt stenciled with 'USMC'.

I couldn't believe I had forgotten how pretty she was.

The hotel's escort left, closing the door. Kitty took several quick steps toward me, wrapped me in her arms, and hugged me. Her soft breasts to my chest, her thighs to my thighs, coupled with her soft magnolia perfume, caused me to want to engulf her in my arms and return her embrace. But above and beyond my concern for more of her trust games, was my commitment to Bean. So I just stood there, arms to my sides, a mannequin with noticeable serge in pulse.

Although the tension remained, the extended hug dulled some of my concerns. I took the comfort she offered. I wanted to stay in her arms and let her soft, scented body shield me from the dangerous world around us. I didn't want to know anything bad about her or Andrew, or why I had been chosen, or used. And I sensed she wanted the same thing as she wrapped her arms around my neck and snuggled further into me, burying her face into the crevice of my neck. Her warm breath lapped my skin.

When my never-to-be-monogamous groin began to stir, I eased my arms to her waist and tried to push her away.

She held firm. She raised her head, gazed at me with her unlawfully blue eyes, and then gave me the softest kiss I had ever received, two sweet-tasting, silk-soft lips on mine. I didn't pull away. I should have, but I didn't. To claim I was shocked and therefore unmoving would probably have been acceptable to any observer. But the truth was, I liked her passionate and yet non-intrusive, rather formal kiss.

She eased her lips from mine and slid them to my cheek.

"We need to talk," I said, trying to assert control, although my breathing had become a little ragged.

"Shhh," she said with her lips against my skin.

She kissed my cheek, my nose, the other cheek, and then returned to my mouth. This time her tongue wedged past my lips and danced in my mouth.

Was this a kiss from a liar and user or from a woman desperate and scared? She had rushed into my arms liked a fear-driven child. And her tenderness seemed genuine.

But this was wrong, crazy. I didn't have an excuse for kissing another woman. Bean had trimmed my horns. I tried to gently pull away, but Kitty's arms held me and my lips prisoner.

It would take some force to break her hold on my neck, but I could do it. I may have to hurt her, but——her mouth was so soft.

I'd give her this kiss, and I'd pull away.

Kitty's lips and tongue teased and lured, touched and probed, and nibbled and licked, exuding bliss.

All my tension and stress accrued over the last couple of days were being consumed by Kitty's hungry mouth, lips, and tongue. Both my mind and body craved the relief from fear-generated pressures. It was like the physical and mental release I had so often experienced after the many fire-fights in Iraq and Afghanistan. There was an overwhelming release from fear that grew with each moment of silenced guns. All the external horror-filled elements that had affected your mental state disappeared, erased along with your surroundings. My entire being would become enraptured by the freedom-from-fear ecstasy. Nothing else existed, only total, untainted joy. This state was a self-feeding euphoria, once you took a bite you had to have more. And at this point in time, I wanted more of Miss 'umm-umm' Kitty's lips and tongue.

A breath-seeking moment later, my tongue involuntarily joined the game of tag. The quietly beating pulse coursing through my temples had sped to a pounding kettle drum. And soft was no longer a descriptive adjective for my groin.

I had become so focused on her tongue that I didn't realize she had removed one of her arms from my neck. Not until her hand took mine and guided it under her sweatshirt and up to one of her warm, breasts. The now moaning Governor of South Carolina had come braless to a private meeting with me. Her premeditative lack of attire should have been a warning beacon to me, but for the moment, the thought excited me. Her soft, breast more than filled my hand and her nipple, like me, was hard and erect.

Her hand left mine and went south. I knew I was seconds from losing all control. Her fingers found my belt buckle and opened it faster than I could and then deftly unbuttoned the waistline of my pants. I knew if she wrapped those skilled digits around my conscience-blocking penis, we were going to fuck.

I grabbed her hand and pulled my mouth from hers. "What are we doing?" I gulped a much needed breath. "Many people we know are being either murdered or threatened; and we're groping each other like a stranded couple on a deserted island."

Gasping, she cupped my chin. Her intense blue eyes conveyed the same message I had seen countless times at the soup kitchen when the hungry eyed a bowl of soup. "Not now, please, not now." She smashed her mouth to mine, wedged her tongue into my mouth, and pulled her hand free from my halting grip and finger-walked south.

And then my heterosexual cravings, my male weakness took over. Possibly I was just a hollow, easy man. Or maybe she was too beautiful and too sexy to shun. Or maybe it was her unbelievable fingers stroking away any logic, commitments, or purpose for this meeting. Nothing mattered except I wanted what she was offering, and I took it.

Kitty and I sat at opposite ends of the table, dinner had been served.

Guilt ate at my insides. I felt dirty, both physically and morally. I couldn't justify my actions, and I wasn't sure I could live with the memories. But I knew regrets had never fixed anything. Done was done.

I pointed at her bust line. "Nice shirt." My words sounded so empty and pointless.

Kitty eyed a forked asparagus spear. "A gift from an old friend that I thought appropriate for the company I was keeping."

My efforts to cut the tension fell short, so I tried again. I cut away a rib bone from the pork rack. "An old boyfriend?"

She spoke between chews. Etiquette had left this room a while ago. "Donny, a cousin, my age, more like a brother … he never came back from Afghanistan."

Great, that eased the tension about as much as a gun at a fist fight.

"I'm sorry." I hacked on the ribs, though I had no desire to eat any of them, I needed something to do.

She scooped a load of mashed potatoes onto a spoon and raised it in front of her lipstick smeared mouth. Obviously she hadn't lost her appetite. "What was Afghanistan like?"

I watched the potatoes disappear into her wonderfully skilled mouth. I had to force my mind back to her question, a non-instigated question I really didn't want to answer. I blew out a deep breath. "The 'Ghan' is the ultimate survival test." I had never been able to totally push aside the sleep-robbing memories. Visions flashed. "Everything opposes you, the terrain, the climate extremes, and the brutal Taliban. No invader has ever totally conquered the 'Ghan', and no one ever will."

She whittled on her rare steak, and then stuffed a large chunk of the blood-dripping meat into her mouth. Not a waist-watching salad tonight, she was having a full course meal. I wondered what had induced her hunger, the sex, her fears, or the after-sex tension.

She had wanted me to cuddle afterwards, to lay naked and hold each other while our bodies returned from the mountain top. But that was what Bean and I did. And I was overwhelmed with guilt. I almost sprang from the leather couch into my clothing. And I would've left if she hadn't stopped me and insisted we talk.

But the talk hadn't happened, at least not until now.

Her loaded fork stopped midway to her mouth. A long table away, her seductress blue eyes searched my face. "Have you ever killed anyone?"

(32)

The sex clung to me, on my face, my hands, and my genitals, spawning more guilt. I wanted to get up and run out of the private dining room in the Seven Gables Inn, find the nearest shower, and scrub Kitty's smell and our mixed secretions off me. But instead, I watched Kitty, sitting at the other end of a long table, stuffing her face. I had stayed for only one reason, one big reason, self-preservation. I needed to know what she and Andrew had drawn me into and why.

I watched her wedge another large piece of raw meat into her mouth. She didn't look nearly as pretty as when I walked through the door of the private dining room an hour or so ago. Miss 'umm-umm' Kitty had lost her 'umm-umm'. Her make-up looked like it had been hurriedly applied in the dark on a sweating face. The smeared lipstick area around her mouth gleamed with meat juices. Her shoulder-length dark hair hung limp, tangled, and dried with sweat. And her distended cheeks were gorged with food, like a nut-gathering squirrel in the fall. Her jaw muscles flexed and chomped, her teeth cutting and tearing at the raw beef.

When my tolerance of her and this terribly wrong encounter was pressed to its limit, she had the balls to ask me between chomps, "Have you ever killed anyone?"

She knew my background. She knew I was a Marine with plenty of combat experience. Killing? What the hell kind of question was that? What did she think we were doing over there? Of course I had killed. And it was a

95

subject I never discussed with anyone. Why would I want to talk about something I wanted to forget, but couldn't? Yeah, I had killed people directly and indirectly by ordering my men to do whatever was deemed required at the time. I had been responsible for the destruction or crippling of the enemy. A foe comprised of teenage boys to old men, and sometimes, by accident, women and even children, ravaged over and over again in my never-ending nightmares. Why would I want to refresh those grueling memories?

One cheek ballooned like she had a wad of Red Man Chewing Tobacco stuffed inside. She stopped chomping, and stared at me, waiting for an answer.

I leaned back, sighed, folded my arms across my chest and nodded.

She flipped her fork outward. "That's your answer, a head nod?" Her words were distorted by the lumps of meat in her mouth.

"I came here to get questions answered, not asked."

A smile further distended her jaws. "You got a lot more than that didn't you?"

"Coming here was a big mistake." The words escaped before I could stop them. I had probably slammed a door I wanted open. I stood and flung my napkin on the table.

"Whoa, whoa, whoa." She motioned me to sit with her fork-holding-hand. "It's a little late to get pompous. *We* both wanted the sex, and as I recall, *we* both enjoyed it." She paused to chew and swallow. "Personally, I've never had so many great orgasms. And if you haven't noticed, which I doubt, I've wanted you since the first time I saw you. So there, I've said it, out loud. Now sit down and relax. We're not done." The smile returned. "Your girlfriend will never know what happened here. After all, you're not married or even engaged to her, so what's the big deal? Two consenting adults enjoyed each other. It happens … and I hope it happens again, soon, like maybe later on tonight, all night." Her eyebrows rose.

I shelved my immediate reaction to inform her sex with her would never happen again, ever. I sat down. I didn't want to piss off my only information source. "Let's talk, like you promised."

She held up her forefinger and chewed.

Lord give me patience … and please hurry.

(33)

Kitty finally wiped the remnants of her feast off her face and pushed back from the table. She motioned to the couch. "Let's sit over there, where we can be more ... comfortable."

I glanced at the brown leather couch against the wall. Our body impressions lingered on the soft cushions, and I was sure our smells did as well.

"I'm fine right here."

She refreshed her coffee and stood with her brimming cup in one hand, while the other hand tugged at her scrunched up jeans. "I'm going to the couch. Suit yourself."

Kitty walked to the couch, swaying her round hips like a big city street-walker. She stopped, glanced over her shoulder with a smile, and then eased down on the divan. The rumpled Governor crossed her long legs and patted the seat next to her. "Come here, me and the couch beckon," then she pulled up her shirt exposing her large breasts, "and so do these."

I couldn't help but stare, what man wouldn't? Her breasts were the size of grapefruit, round, perfect, and yet natural with silver dollar sized nipples. A hint of heat returned to my depleted and bruised loins.

The male mind was such a diversified mechanism. My conscience overflowed with Bean-guilt and wanted to run away from this disheveled, table-manners-of-a-pig woman. But my id wanted to rush to her and climb the mountain again, slowly, until we both peaked at the oxygen-starved summit.

My base, male instinct countered my conscience's guilt with the addict's game; I had already broken my promise, so what harm was there in doing it again.

My pride and purpose for coming to this meeting stepped into the fray and forced me to gulp some much-needed air and look away from Kitty's beckoning boobs.

"Not now, Kitty." Though I was a nudge away from another 'now', I had to act like I had some control. I had come here for a much more important reason than jumping her bones, over and over. "We must talk."

She grumbled and pulled her top down. "Okay, I'll behave. But come over here." She patted the cushion next to her again.

I sucked in another lung full. I had come this far, why go backwards now? I stood, walked to the prior lust pit, and sat down.

She leaned over, her lips a breath away from my ear, her fingers lightly touching my cheek. "How 'bout a little kiss before we start."

After all the things I had seen her put into that mouth and what she had done to them, I wanted no part of it. I gently removed her hand. "Let's just talk ... for now."

Kitty sat up, uncrossed her lags, and braced her hands on her knees, her prior playful expression morphed into a look of stern seriousness, in a wink of time the governor had returned.

Thank God.

㉞

Governor Franklin and I sat on the couch of the private dining room at the Severn Gables Inn. She looked off into space, unmoving, as if using the silence to feed and organize her thoughts.

The couch, with its lingering smells of her magnolia perfume mingling with the strong odors of our prior sex, was the last place I wanted to be. The latent aromas stoked my guilt. Just what I didn't need, but deserved. I had acted impulsively, reacting to stimuli, her stimuli.

But was I totally at fault, or just normal? The woman was gorgeous with a stunning body, and she had seduced me. I had tried to stop her, though a weak, futile attempt. And Kitty was right; the sex had been a discovery, an adventure into unknown territories. Not only because of the mystique of being intimate with someone new, but because she had done erotic things to me that no one had done before, and she coached me to do wild and stimulating things to her that I had only heard of but never tried. We had gone to unexplored places together, not only physically bonding us, but mentally connecting us as well.

The sex had been great; no, it had been more than that. Although I didn't want to admit it, the physical sex, though lacking the intimacy of the loving sex I had with Bean, had been the best I'd ever experienced.

I had been seduced by a lovely, sexually skilled woman. And although I was riddled with guilt, if the scene were recreated anew, it would be an instant replay. I was sure or at least hoped I was.

Governor Kitty cleared her throat. "Dering my campaign for this office, at a crucial point when I was on the verge of losing, Senator Sparks approached me and asked for a private meeting." Her facial features scrunched together. "Just saying his name repulses me. The only thing uglier than his appearance is his personality and ... and his body odor, he reeks."

She rubbed her chin with her thumb and forefinger, obviously a thinking habit. "Trimethylamineria ... I can't believe I remembered the name ... it's the disease Senator Sparks has. After he told me what it was called, I Googled the ailment. It's a rare metabolic disorder that's currently incurable. It, ah, it makes you smell like fish." Her eyes scanned my face expecting a reaction, when there was none, she looked away. "The common name is fish odor syndrome." She glanced at me again.

"If you're waiting for me to make some lewd comment, I'm not going to," I said.

She took a sip of coffee and patted my arm. "I'm very impressed with your level of self-control."

"I'm not." The words spewed out involuntarily, a bad habit.

Her sapphire eyes fixed on mine. "Only you can fix your guilt. All I can do is redirect your focus." Her free hand touched my thigh and slid over to my crouch.

I grabbed her hand and shoved it into her lap. "You talk. I'll listen."

A brief grin rolled over her face like a glimmer of sunlight through a dense patch of moving clouds. She wrapped both hands around her coffee cup, and her eyes rolled up to the ceiling. "All my advisors told me the only way I could win the gubernatorial race was with Senator Sparks' support. I knew they were right. And I knew if I lost the race for Governor, I'd have no political future." She sighed. "I had to win. Gramps was counting on me."

She hesitated, chewing on her lower lip. "Sparks and I met, and he took me to one of his" she sat her coffee cup down on an end table and used two fingers on each hand to form quotation marks, "'hideaways.' This one was a modern-day, large log cabin deep in the woods somewhere between Langley and Washington, an admitted gift from a lobbyist."

Her words 'This one' stuck in my mind. She obviously knew about others. I wondered how many. I was prematurely conjecturing. I changed my focus. "You should've taken a small recording device," I said hoping to ease her visual tension.

She gave me a flat look. "You don't know the man or his intentions. If I had taken something to record the meeting, he would've found it. Plus at the time, I went with him because I thought I was the one collecting the favors." She emitted a sad, pathetic chuckle and shook her head. "I actually thought I was going to use him."

I thought I'd save her farther pain. "I think I get the picture."

"Do you want answers to your questions, or are you going to sit and second-guess me all night?"

"I was just … sorry. I'll shut the hell up."

She nodded. "I had dressed for a night of formal dining, thinking we would go out to eat somewhere befitting our places in society. Actually, I was hoping he would take me out to show me off so I would reap the publicity. So I had gone the extra mile, hair styled, selected borderline-sexy new designer gown, come-fuck-me heels, the works."

I could picture her, beautiful and sexy. A twinge of jealousy pecked at my chauvinism.

A smile interrupted her seriousness. "I have to say, I looked good, maybe too good."

The smile faded. "And where do I end up? At a log cabin in the woods, alone, with a fat, stinky, ugly man. Little did I know how ugly he could really be?"

Her pained expression made me want to stop her, but she had already given me a verbal wrist slap. Maybe she needed to vent, no matter how painful.

"When I asked him what we were doing in the middle of the wilderness, alone, he said he thought we'd be able to talk more freely. He valued his sponsorship and wanted to make sure he knew the person he was supporting. So many politicians had their careers upended by bolstering campaigners concealing dark secrets. Next he told me I needed to relax so he fixed me a martini and that's when things went wrong. He must have put something in the drink. The last thing I remembered was my helplessness to stop him while he struggled removing my clothing."

She took a gulp of coffee and a sigh slithered through her trembling lips.

Hearing her offensive words and seeing her lips trembling ignited my temper. I sat up on the edge of the couch.

"After what seemed like hours I awoke, naked, lying next to that nude, foul smelling fat pig. The sight of his bared rolls of blubber along with his smell and the thoughts of what he must have done to me, gagged me."

"You should've beaten him to death with a lamp," I blurted.

"I wanted to, but, ah, one of my hands was cuffed to the bed such that I couldn't reach anything off the bed. *Senator* Sparks had obviously done this before. He was asleep, snoring louder than a teen's car radio. I had to pee so I had to either wake up Prince Charming or wet myself. It was a difficult decision, kicking him to wake him swayed my choice. I kicked him as hard and as many times as I could before he stopped me."

"Kitty—" her index finger bridged my lips.

My anger was close to its boiling point. I pushed her finger aside and honored her request to be quiet.

"He cuffed me to him, tossed the key on a table, and then pulled me to the bathroom. He was smart, I'll give him that. If I could've overpowered him, I couldn't drag his unconscious four-hundred-plus pounds back to the table. He stood over me, his stinky obesity inches from me, and groped my breasts while I peed. I've never hated anyone that much before or since. Then he took me back to the bed, still manacled to him, and made me watch videos of him fucking me, along with other God-awful things he'd done to me. I was shocked that I was awake in the video, through the madness, a manipulated, but not forced, rag doll. At the time, I remembered thinking how glad I was that I couldn't remember any of it." She shook her head and looked away.

Thoughts of some of my homeless buddies came to mind. "I know some people who'd beat the shit out of him for twenty bucks."

She extended a stop-sign hand at me. "Hold on, there's more." She moved to the edge of the couch and sat upright arching and flexing her back.

I couldn't imagine how difficult telling this horrible story had to be for her, particularly now as the governor of South Carolina. No one had ever trusted me like her.

"After he forced me to watch the 'triple X' rated film, he grabbed me by my hair. And as he pulled my face toward his video-induced hard-on, he asked me what I'd do to keep our movie off the net. Unfortunately, it was a rhetorical question. Then we made another video, a silent movie without the gags recorded or the overpowering stench encapsulated. The director cunningly blocked any view of the cuffs with my body. And the star actress utilized all her skills to hasten the nightmare."

I swallowed the expletives seeking release and touched her shoulder. "I'll save you twenty bucks, I'll kick his ass."

She didn't acknowledge my touch or my words; she just stared off into space. "Unfortunately, the worst was yet to come. After I completed my second movie, he yanked me out to the dining room where one of his chefs had left a table full of food. I had to sit and watch pig-man at the trough, another disgusting memory. I'd never seen a person consume so much food in such little time."

Her words made me wonder if Senator Sparks had influenced her table manners.

"Between fork-filled gorges and chews, he told me the real price of the videos. He needed money, lots of money. He told me he had arranged for the Powerball drawings to be moved from Atlanta to Columbia. And after I became Governor, I would arrange for him to be a multiple winner, anonymously, of course."

I had to check myself from saying,"So it's true," out loud.

"I should've dropped out of the race then, but that video going public would've killed Gramps. His health wasn't good at the time." She wrung her hands together, stretching the skin and whitening her knuckles.

Mistakes were hard for anyone to voice. I thought of the day when I would have to tell Bean about tonight.

She unclenched her hands and rubbed her thighs. "After I became Governor, I turned to the one staff person I could trust, my ex-campaign manager, Andrew Hays. Somehow, and I swear I don't know, he fixed the drawings, and Camden took care of diverting the money."

"'Diverting the money?'" My voiced raised an octave. "Is that how you avoid saying Senator Sparks picked the Powerball winners, let them collect, and then killed them and took their winnings?"

She bowed her head, eyes and mouth tightly shut.

She wasn't telling me everything, there was more; I could sense it from her slumped body language. Then the obvious slammed me, head-on.

"You're still sleeping with him aren't you?"

She grimaced as she barely nodded her head.

I had to fight an urge to run to the bathroom and check to see if I had a discharge or worse, a smell.

"The money … me … again and again, it has to stop." Her voice was barely audible.

"Christ." My sympathy sparred with my revulsion. Then another thought slapped me. "Oh, and thanks one hell-of-a-bunch for making me an accomplice."

Her eyes opened, she sat up and turned to face me, her head shaking. "I … I didn't mean to … no."

My mind continued to probe into the cesspool she had opened. "But Andrew should have been the last person Camden wanted dead. So who killed Andrew and why?"

Her face lengthened as if she had been startled. "I swear I don't know."

I thought about telling her about the Powerball numbers I had found in Andrew's pocket. But I wasn't sure I could trust her. Indirectly, she was a murderer.

"What *do* you know?" I couldn't tone down the harshness in my words.

She had this lost, helpless look on her face, so like many of the homeless street people I had served. "All I know is that Andrew wanted out when he realized that Camden was having the winners killed. He told me he'd steal for me, but he wouldn't kill for me."

Her words exploded in my head, releasing slutty visions followed by logic-laden thoughts. "Were you sleeping with Andrew too?" My voice rose again.

She looked away.

Her failure to respond along with her physical reaction made me feel even cheaper. What a fool I was to have thought we had shared something special? No wonder she was so skilled. Who hadn't she slept with?

Like a lightning flash at night, in an instant, I could see everything, the whole ugly picture.

I stood and looked down at her, at her glum and yet beautiful face, her rounded breasts jutting against the sweatshirt, and her long toned lags wrapped in the tight jeans. Although she was exceptionally beautiful, she was no different than the whores I had encountered on R&R during the war.

I had to vent my stupidity or explode. I wanted her to feel my degradation, the hollowness from being used; a fool's self-loathing.

"That first night with Senator Sparks ... there weren't any drugs or cuffs were there? You seduced and fucked that fat pig in order to secure the election, to win. And he knew you would, so he taped it. And you're more pissed about him outsmarting you than you are about his tapes. He had out-manipulated the manipulator. The pig-man was the wiser politician. He owned you, and he was using you. Something you couldn't stand. You needed someone else, Andrew, to bed and use, to stop him. Now that he's dead, all you had left was me, so you fucked me."

Red-faced, she bolted to her feet.

I saw it coming, a second too late. My cheek was set on fire and my head jolted. I grabbed her hands before she slapped me again.

"What do you want from me?" I shouted.

Her moistened eyes glared at me. "I need someone, someone I can trust," she glanced down and then back into my eyes, "someone who can find out how Andrew fixed the system."

"Why?"

"So I can set up the fat pig and then blackmail him for the videos."

I squeezed her wrists to emphasize my words. "But that's not why Andrew selected me."

"Not exactly." She took a deep breath. "He said you were the only man he knew who wasn't afraid of anyone or anything. And besides being smart, you were unemployed, desperate, and ... and I," she turned her tear-streaked face away, "I could convince you to replace him, to fix the numbers."

I flipped her hands away and raised my arms in surrender. "Go find yourself another fool. I quit."

The governor of South Carolina, the conniving politician, the fraudulent, vixen loser and I stood facing each other in the private dining room of the Seven Gables Inn. The only things keeping me from leaving and never returning were the tears streaming done her cheeks and her grip on my hands.

After I had announced my job termination, Kitty had grasped both my hands and brought them together in front of us, wrapped in hers.

"Brent, you and I ... it's not what you think. Yes, I made some horrible decisions, and I did terrible things, things I—" sniff, sniff—she raised our joined hands so she could wipe her wet face on the sleeve of her sweatshirt. "You and I were different, special. The sex was the best, but only because of our feelings. I could tell you knew that." One of her hands softly caressed mine. "You've got to believe that. Yes, I need you. I ... I can't go to jail. Those tapes are my only proof of being blackmailed, and I can't get them without your help. I know I'm asking you to risk your freedom and possibly your life, but you're my only hope. If you stay and help me, you'll see that I'm not the person you think I am."

Those red-streaked blue eyes searched mine.

"You and I can have something most people never find in their lifetimes, I know it." Her expression softened. "I can feel it in your touch, and your kiss. Just give me a chance. You won't regret it. When Gramps passes, I'll inherit close to a billion dollars. We can do anything we want to, go anywhere, and live like royalty. You'll never have to work again for either money or happiness." She looked down at our hands. "I know you don't trust me. I don't blame you." Her tear-streaming eyes returned to mine. "But I swear to you, if you help me, I'll spend the rest of my life making you happy." She separated my hands and placed them around her neck. She wrapped her arms around my waist, and hugged me.

Tears continued to flow, and she pressed against me like a scared, lost child. Her vulnerability, her scent, and her curvaceous warmth extorted naked memories. I wanted to believe her, to trust her, to dream with her, and to save her. Despite everything else she was saying, she was right about one thing, I was her only hope.

I had one small problem, one tiny little thing keeping me from risking everything to save Miss 'umm-umm' Kitty, my little Tinker Bell, Bean. If I stayed not only did I risk Bean and my relationship, if we still had one after tonight, but, most importantly, I was gambling with Bean's life and mine.

I gently broke her embrace. Holding her arms, I stepped back. "You're right. I did think we shared something, ah, different. You're beautiful and successful and smart and unbelievable in bed. You're the woman every man dreams about. But I feel like a prince in a fairytale. I'm not sure if you are the beautiful princess in distress, or a self-serving witch trying to cast a spell on me. And I'm not going to risk Bean's life to find out who you really are."

She opened her mouth to speak, and I pinned her lips with a finger.

"You're either acting or you've panicked. In either case, you've overlooked one thing. You don't need me. You're a politician. Use those skills to get the tapes back. And then run to the Feds as fast as you can, before anyone else dies."

I released her arms and walked past her, through her pleading words, and out the door.

36

I drove the Taurus through the darkness, mindlessly negotiating the winding road to Charley and Annie's. I'd shower, get my stuff, check out, and drive to Walterboro and Bean. The plan made me queasy, for I'd tell her what happened, the whole body-meshing scene. That was just how I was. Besides, she always knew when I was hiding the truth. If she left me, which I deserved, I wasn't sure what I'd do. I'd probably end up on the wrong side of that soup kitchen table. No, I'd rejoin the Marines first. Afghanistan was hell-on-earth, but at least if I died, I'd have an honorable purpose.

My cell phone's cornet announced another 'Private Number.' The damned phone had taken on a personality I didn't like, one that loved to surprise me; one I feared.

I'd just left Kitty. What part of no didn't she understand? I really didn't want to talk to her again, not tonight, not ever. I cancelled the call.

As I pulled the car into the B&B, the bugle sounded again. I stopped, levered the car into park, and killed the engine. "What do you want?" My voice resounded with impatience inside the car.

"I just left there and I'm through, finished, done. I don't work for you anymore. Why can't you understand that?"

"Brent."

I almost dropped the phone. Bean's voice reminded me of a frightened little girl.

My hand squeezed the phone, the instrument that continued to fool me. I sucked some air and blew it out.

"Why are you calling me from a—" the answer jumped into my mind and was as unexpected and as painful as a sucker punch from a best friend.

(37)

All my nightmares had been combined and transformed into reality; Bean had been kidnapped. And what had I done? I'd slept with the Governor. But being regretful wasn't going to change anything. I had to save Bean, and I knew only one way to do that.

A sleepless-night and a picked-over breakfast later, I sat in Sally Kellerman's desk chair, the Lottery Drawing Manager. Waiting for her to arrive at work, sitting in the empty, early morning office, reminded me of one of the many ambushes I had led in Afghanistan. Externally, I was calm; internally my gyrating nerves were the lead performer in a rock and roll concert.

I had wanted to call the police, the FBI, the Marines, God, or anyone who could help find and rescue Bean. But that son-of-bitch who had taken Bean told me not to call anyone before disconnecting. The things he'd threatened to do to her if I did call anyone had to have cracked several of my molars. Plus my recent encounters with both the police and FBI had eroded any confidence I once had about their abilities.

So I finally called someone, I called Kitty Franklin. Thank God Kitty was as desperate to take me back as I was to rejoin the employed. If it hadn't been so late last night, I wouldn't have gotten by with just a phone call. I would have had to eat more than phone crow.

I don't know why, maybe because Kitty had divulged so much of her personal life to me, or maybe because I just needed to tell someone, so I told Kitty most of what had happened. I told her Bean had been kidnapped, and I was being blackmailed to find out how the lottery had been rigged.

Kitty promised me she wouldn't tell a soul. And she promised she'd try to help me. What a team, a sleep-around, fraudulent Governor and a dumbass.

At five minutes before eight o'clock, the starting time for government employees, the Lottery Drawing Manager, Sally Kellerman, walked into her office. I would've sworn she was wearing the same black pants suit and vest as she wore the day I met her. When her glasses-magnified green eyes locked on me, she gasped. "Wha—what are you doing here?"

"Good Monday morning, Mrs. Kellerman, my name is Brent Layne in case you forgot." I got up and motioned her to her chair.

She nodded, wrinkling her flap of neck skin, and stepped past me to her seat. "I, ah, I remember."

Her physical demeanor exuded stiff control, though her darting eyes conveyed concern.

I pulled a small note pad out of the breast pocket of my gray suit coat. "Do you have time to answer a few questions for me this morning?"

"I will make time, sir."

"Great." I was pleased her attitude-adjustment from the other day had taken root.

I took a seat opposite her and straightened my blue silk tie. "The other day, Sally, is it okay if I call you Sally?"

"That's fine, sir."

And please, call me Brent," I flipped pages on my pad. "The other day you said ... let's see, oh yeah, here it is. You said the Powerball drawings were conducted at exactly the same time, 10:59 p.m. Eastern Standard Time, on Wednesdays and Saturdays in a television studio in the basement of this building."

"That's correct."

"Each drawing is conducted in the presence of multi-state lottery draw officials, an independent auditor, and a security official."

"Yes, there are at least five witnesses." She tugged her vest down.

"The drawing equipment, including the previously auditor-sealed ball sets, is kept in a double-locked alarm vault." I raised my eyebrows seeking acknowledgement.

"Yes."

"All events are audio and video recorded when the vault is opened."

"Each and every time."

I flipped another page. "And the equipment is tested regularly; physical measurements, x-rays, as well as statistically for nonrandom behavior."

"Precisely." She leaned back in her chair, the initial shock of seeing me in her office obviously dissipated. "I'm impressed. You took very accurate notes." She braced an elbow on her desk and leaned her neck-less chin on her hand. Her big eyes fixed on mine. "So what is the purpose of your first-thing, Monday morning visit?"

"With all those controls in place, I'd like to know how you rigged the process."

"What?" She bolted upright, her eyebrows chasing her hair line.

I leaned closer to her, my elbows on her desk. "You know what I mean, how did you make the equipment pick specific numbers?"

Her jaws dropped, quadrupling her chins. "I have no idea what you're talking about. If someone is messing with the system, I would know about it," a concerned expression replaced her indignation, "or at least I think I would." Her thumb and forefinger glided up and down on the sides of her actual chin. "I think you need to talk to a 'techie.'"

"A what?" I asked.

"One of the technicians we employee who oversees the drawing process."

"And who would that be?"

"I'd suggest you start with Ms. Nancy Beltner. If there's a way to undermine our process, which I doubt, she'd know it."

"Where do I find her?" I asked, scribbling her name on my pad.

Sally snatched up her phone. "I'll have her come here. There's ah … more privacy. I don't want a breath of this being overheard by any of the busy-bees in the bullpen."

(38)

Nancy Beltner had a look, or maybe more like an aura about her. I don't know what exactly just something, like a Rolls-Royce owner with calluses. There was something out of place, something subtle: one of those things rarely sensed about a person when you first meet them. But due to the infrequent occurrence, my alarms clanged.

She was an average height redhead, late-twenties, with a disguised figure draped in baggy black slacks and a way-too-large grey pull-over. Her cropped red hair draped both sides of her face, like a certain half-closed and bridged by her wide mouth. Her mouth seemed out of place compared to her other small features. She had a cute but not memorable face, though coated with a heavy blemish-hiding foundation. Her shoulders bowed inward like an adolescent girl trying to conceal big boobs.

Sally Kellerman stood. "Nancy Beltner, meet Mr. Brent Layne, our newly appointed Vice Chairman of the Lottery Commission and head of the Audit Committee."

I stood and faced the redhead.

Nancy extended a hand and smiled, exposing wired-braced top teeth.

"Mr. Layne, nice to meet you." Her voice was high and scratchy like a teenage boy going through puberty. "Are you a ball-counter or a ball-breaker?" She chuckled.

Her greeting was rather off the wall, a strange thing to say to your never-before-met boss. I squared my shoulders and stretched to maximum height. "I can be either, depending on the situation and the people involved."

Her beady, pale brown eyes darted from me to Sally and back to me. "So I've been told." She tugged on her loose top and stood a little straighter. "So, how may I help you, sir?"

I wondered how long I could stand to listen to her chalk-on-blackboard voice. "I want you to tell me how to rig the Powerball drawing to make it select predetermined numbered balls."

Her fisted hands braced on her hips, her thin lips squeezed together and curled downward at both ends, bulging her cheeks. Those dust-colored eyes rolled up and to one side, pushing her eyebrows skyward. Her reaction questioned either my intelligence, or my sanity, or my deodorant, I wasn't sure.

"Are you asking me to do something illegal?" she asked pushing her raised red eyebrows higher.

"No, but possibly stop something illegal," I said with conviction.

Nancy scanned me from head to toe, and then, with her head shaking from side-to-side, she glared at Sally. "I thought you said *this one* had read the manuals."

"I have read the manuals," I inserted. "Now answer my question."

Continuing to shake her head, Nancy's eyes returned to mine. "The only way would be to pay everybody involved to cheat. And the probability of getting by with that … well there would be too many involved people having too much money to keep it a secret for long.

I pulled my up-the-sleeve card. "How about magic?"

She gave me a questioning look and then broke into laughter, so strong it doubled her over.

Within seconds Sally joined her, and I just stood there, biting my lower lip and wondering where Bean was and what was happening to her.

(39)

Between gasps of laughter Nancy looked up at me. The three of us, Sally Kellerman, Nancy Beltner, and I stood in Sally's office early on Monday morning. "Magic?" Nancy asked in her scratchy, squeaky voice followed by more body-quaking guffaws.

I turned to Sally for some support, but she was doubled over in laughter.

After their laughter subsided to tear wiping, I said, "I totally understand your reactions, but I'm serious. I've thought about this a great deal. The drawing process is so controlled I came to the same conclusion as you, to rig the system you'd have to pay everyone to cheat and that wouldn't work. So, that leaves only one other option, trickery. Magic is probably one of the oldest entertainment forms known to man. And almost all acts of magic, no matter how complicated or scrutinized or tested, succeed because of the simple feat of distraction. So tell me, could the process be tampered with if there were a distraction?"

"Like what?" Nancy asked, her face expressing her acceptance of my seriousness.

"I don't know, you tell me," I said.

"You're serious." Sally spoke her thoughts.

"Deadly serious," I said.

"I have a major in engineering and a minor in statistics," Nancy said. "I'm sorry. I can't help you with *magic*." She buttered the word 'magic' with disdain.

"Is there someone else in the system, someone with the skills or controls to either rig the system or create a distraction so preselected numbers can be drawn?"

Sally chewed on her lip and Nancy fidgeted with her hands, picking at a cuticle.

The silence was harder to take than the laughter.

"I can't think of anyone," Sally said. "But I don't know all the 'techies' as well as Nancy does."

Nancy wagged her head. "There are three others, and they are so specialized and geeky … none of them have the balls," she chuckled. "Excuse the pun."

My wheels were spinning, slicks on an oil patch, going nowhere fast. One of these ladies had to know something.

"Do you both agree that the system has been compromised?" I asked.

The two women eyed each other.

"I'm not sure," Nancy said. "What if these people who were robbed and murdered had legitimately won and were then selected as victims. After all, they weren't assaulted until they cashed out."

"That's exactly what the perpetrator would want you to believe. You're the one with a minor in statistics. You have to agree, the statistics are skewed. The thief made a mistake."

"Minus three sigma occurrences do happen," she said.

"What?" I asked. I was a math major and understood exactly what she said, but I wanted her to think otherwise. "Please, speak English to a layman."

"The unexpected, though improbable, can happen," she said.

I needed a different approach. "Did either of you know Andrew Hays?" I asked.

One of Sally's eyebrows flinched, her first sign of losing control. "Sure, he's the top dog, next to the governor, or, ah, was."

"Have either of you talked to him in the past few months?"

"I don't know the man," Nancy said, looking at her cuticle as if it were more interesting than the subject matter, her other hand on her hip.

"I've met him several times," Sally said. "He'd bring people through to see the process after we were awarded the drawing process." Her gaze shifted from me to the floor. "He was always nice, never full of himself like so many of the other politicians, particularly Senators."

That was Andrew, God bless his soul. "Who were these people he brought, did you know any of them?"

"No."

"Did he or any of his guests ask a lot of questions about the system?"

"No more than any other visitor," Sally said.

I rubbed my chin. I was an interrogator receiving only 'yes' and 'no' answers; no leads, no nothing except frustration.

Sally looked up at me through her magnified green eyes. "Why all the questions, was his murder connected to the lottery investigation?"

"I was hoping one of you could answer that."

They both gave me a glazed-over-eyes look and shook their heads.

I wasn't dreaming all of this. The lottery drawings had been fixed. People had been murdered. Bean's life hung in the balance, dependent on me. And I was failing. Maybe I should call that FBI agent, Nick or Jim, ah Sanders, the one who called Robin 'Bean.' My gut said no.

Maybe I should pay a visit to Senator Camden Sparks and beat the truth and the tapes out of the fat pig. That would most probably get me thrown in jail. And then who knows what would happen to Bean.

I really didn't trust anyone, including the governor. And I didn't know what to do, except to leave Sally's office.

40

I've always hated Mondays and today had to be one of my worst. Laden with fear and guilt, my meeting with the drawing controllers hadn't yielded squat. Somewhere around mid-morning I was driving back to my office, a small windowless room in one of dozens of government-owned buildings near the capitol building, when my friggin' phone blared that damn trumpet noise I'd grown to hate and fear. My heart skipped a beat. I had to summon all control to keep from throwing the phone out the window.

I fumbled the phone out of my suit's jacket pocket. "Hello."

"Brent, Kitty. I'm sitting in some unbelievably boring financial meeting with rambling accountants who don't speak my language. Come save me."

"I told you last night, Bean's the one who needs saving. Have you asked Camden if he knows anything about her, like I asked you to do?"

"Yeah, I called Mr. Obesity. He said he wouldn't talk on the phone. He always uses his paranoia as an excuse to meet me in person. Do you have any idea what you're asking me to go through just to get what we both know will be a 'No'? Why would he admit to knowing anything, even in person, and naked? Oh yeah, I forgot, that's his other game, he won't talk to me when I have clothes on."

What she had said made sense. Asking him anything was a waste of time, a costly waste for her. "Okay. Forget him."

"Did you learn anything from Sally?" she asked.

"Nothing."

"What are you going to do?"

"I don't know, maybe call Nick Sanders."

"Who?" she asked.

"Nick Sanders, maybe you know him as Jim Sanders, he goes by either name."

"I've never heard of him."

"What? He's the FBI agent Andrew recommended I use. You've got to know him."

"I met three FBI agents last week with Andrew, and the same ones this morning, and none of them have either of those names."

I had to slam on my brakes to keep from running a red light.

"I'm so fucking tired of being used and confused." I could not keep from blurting my thoughts. I would have to make a concerted effort to control my mouth. Like my WWII veteran gramps used to say, 'Loose lips sank ships.'

"Have lunch with me."

"I can't. Someway, somehow, I've got to find Bean." I pressed 'End.'

(41)

I walked into my virgin office, sparsely decorated with three chairs, a desk unmarred by reports or messages or paper of any kind, and a bare bookshelf except for those damned manuals. I plopped down in my high-back, leather chair, placed my elbows on the barren oak desk, and rested my chin in my hands.

After a minute or two, minutes that had to be excruciating for Bean, I took out my phone and stared at it. Deep Voice, Bean's kidnapper, had warned me not to call the police or FBI. He'd assigned me the free-Bean task to find out how the lottery was being rigged, more specifically how the governor was rigging it. But I had failed.

I had failed Bean, failed to keep my commitment of monogamy, and, more importantly, failed to save her. At this very moment that bastard could be raping her, and here I sat on my ass doing nothing.

I knew someone, if not all of the people I had been interfacing with, had been lying to me. So what should I do; kidnap all of them and torture them until they told me the truth?

I knew way too much about torturing people. We had administered more pain behind closed doors than I'd like to remember in both Iraq and Afghanistan. I had never been involved directly, but I was involved, I was there and knew what had happened. I didn't condone the torture, but I didn't try to stop it either. The orders came from above me, way above. Do-gooders cringed about 'water-boarding' used in Guantanamo, and we considered that to be a mild form of interrogation. The most effective method of torture was learned from the Vietnamese. Taking two prisoners up in a helicopter and pushing one out. That worked.

To save Bean, could I do that? I could take all of them up on the roof of a high building, Sally, Nancy, Camden, Nick-Jim, and Kitty, but I wouldn't know which one to push off.

Maybe I should call Kitty back and get the names of those FBI agents and call them. That was the right thing to do. But the kidnapper had warned me.

I had no other sane choice. I dug the phone out of my pocket.

At any given time, everyone seemed to know where I was and what I was doing. I needed to use another phone to call the Feds, not my own or the one on my desk. I stood and my phone trumpeted in my hand. My body stiffened. I hated the damned phone and that stupid bugle sound.

My fingers trembled as I took the call. "Hello."

"Mr. Layne, this is Sally Kellerman."

"Does everyone in the government use unlisted phones?" Again my mind spoke.

"I, ah, I don't know. But after you left, I couldn't get my mind off your reference to magic and distractions, so I did some research."

She hesitated. I hated people who made you beg. "And what did you find, Sally?" I tried to make my tone sound inquisitive, but it bled exasperation.

"Well, as you know the drawings are always made at 10:59 p.m. on Wednesdays and Saturdays. We started it, and now the public counts on that. And we must accommodate."

Another fucking hesitation. "Yes, I know that, so?"

"Well, when we took the drawing process over from Atlanta, they informed us that we'd need a back-up."

I couldn't believe she paused again. If I were there with her, I would have——my brain linked with hers. 'A back-up,' why hadn't I thought of it? "A back-up in case there was a problem with the telecast, right, Sally?"

"Yes, a video of another drawing that could be aired if we had a problem that precluded us from doing the drawing at precisely 10:59 p.m."

"'A problem that precluded,' like a distraction, right, Sally?"

"Yes, Mr. Layne."

Another heart rate-jacking pause which I was starting to love. "Sally you're giving me goose-bumps. What'd you find?"

"We have used back-up videos four times since taking over the process, two for local power failures, one for an equipment failure, and one for a cameraman becoming ill."

"Let me guess, each time you used a back-up video, the resultant winner was murdered."

"Yes, sir." Her voice dropped off exposing her shame. "We … I should have found this correlation of bizarre events in the data."

"You were distracted, Sally, trying to find a flaw in the process that wasn't there. You weren't alone. The drawing staff was distracted so another video, one with the preselected numbers, could be substituted."

"Magic," she said with a hint of respect.

"So Sally, who could switch these tapes?"

"I'm not sure."

"I want a list of names, today, as soon as possible."

"Yes, sir."

"I'll be there in twenty minutes."

㊷

On the way to Sally Kellerman's office, it struck me that this dedicated employee, my employee, trapped in a boring bureaucratic state job, had gone out of her way to help me. I needed to show my appreciation. I pulled the Taurus to the curb and checked my phone. I needed some directions.

Twenty–five minutes later, I arrived at Sally's closed office door with a bouquet of assorted flowers mixed with long-stem red roses. Though I had never met a woman who didn't like roses; I didn't. The smell of roses reminded me of funeral homes. Regardless, Sally's office could use some color and fragrance. Fabricating a smile, I knocked on her office door, and waited. Nothing. After a polite pause, I knocked again, a little harder, and the door opened. I stepped inside. No one was there. As I turned to leave, something crunched beneath my foot. Damn it, I had stepped on a pair of glasses, Sarah Palin glasses, Sally's glasses. As I bent over to retrieve the remnants, I saw a pair of feet, one bare and one wearing a black, flat shoe, on the other side of the desk.

I dropped the flowers and rushed behind the desk.

Sally was on the floor, on her side, a plastic bag covered her head. Her bulged green eyes seemed even larger than when magnified by her glasses. A swollen blood-dried gash protruded from her forehead just above her left eye. Her blue-lipped mouth was stretched open in a silent plea.

The bag was sealed around her neck with duct tape, the same duct tape that bound her hands together behind her back.

I squatted and pressed my fingers against her neck searching for a pulse. There was none.

Bent over the frail, masculine woman, a shiver rocked my body. What had I done?

Bean and I had probably gotten Andrew killed by our insistence to visit him when his killer was already there. The murder may not have happened if we hadn't called and demanded a meeting.

And poor innocent Sally wouldn't be dead if I hadn't involved her in my investigation. There were no ifs, ands, or buts to dilute the blame; she was dead because of me.

And shit, Bean might already be dead as well.

My guilt was like a covered pot of liquid heated to boiling; I was on the verge of erupting. I needed to cry, or scream, or hit something; anything to vent, to relieve the pressure. I clenched my jaws and squeezed my hands white.

Men had died following my orders, but that was different, that was war, people died. Sally was an employee, trying to help her appointed boss who had gotten in over his head.

I squatted next to her, slowly shaking my head. I wanted to rip off the plastic bag and ease her mouth and eyes closed and straightened her rumpled hair. She hadn't deserved to die, not like this, not because of me.

I should've never taken this fucking life-changing, life-ending job.

I had to shake off my emotions and think. Sally was gone. I couldn't change that.

I relaxed my hands and took a deep breath and let it out through pursed lips.

I could stay and call the police. Two murders both found and reported by me. Who would the police suspect?

I stood and looked around the office for any clues, anything that may lead me to the killer. There was nothing obvious. I eyed the desk for a list. There were papers scattered everywhere. I wanted to sort through them, but obviously the murderer had already done that. And I didn't want to leave my fingerprints. Thinking of prints, I bent down and, using my tie, wiped Sally's neck where I had checked for a pulse. I wasn't sure prints could be left on skin but I couldn't take any chances.

There was nothing more to do here. My vulnerability was testing my control. I needed to get out of here now.

I left, closed the door behind me, and paused to wipe off the knob. As I turned to walk away, I remembered the flowers, those damned horrible-smelling roses. As I turned to go back, an old black man pulling a cart carrying a plastic garbage can came around the hall corner.

The old man nodded at me and said, "Afternoon."

I could only think about leaving, getting away. I rushed by him without responding.

(43)

Death was such a one-way street, there was no return. And we all had to take the trip; I knew that. And yet when I had to physically confront death, I always got the same sickening feeling in the bottom of my stomach, synonymous with my fear of any unknown threat. I guess my biggest fear was that we all just turned to dust and life was meaningless.

The war and life in general had taught me there was a Devil. Evil existed in so many cruel and inhumane forms. Everyone had to experience evil in their lives, some more than others, so we all knew of its existence.

But God was another story, you had to blindly believe. I guess we didn't associate the good things with God as much as we should. We associated good things with the doings of people or happenstance. I wanted to feel different; I wanted to trust my beliefs. But I was a data guy, a math person, I needed logic.

So I was more mystified by death than afraid of it.

But there wasn't anything mystifying about Sally; she was dead.

I didn't know what to do or where to go. The only thing I could think of was to find somewhere to wait for Bean's kidnapper to call. I had the information he had requested. Kitty had rigged the system as he'd said, and I knew how. I didn't have any hard proof, only Kitty's verbal admittance and a hypothesis, corroborated by dates, of how Andrew had accomplished the 'magic.' I had to hope that was enough to get Bean and me out of this nightmare.

The safest place I could think of was my office. I was never there, and when I was, no one ever came there or called me on the office phone. My office was one of thousands of temporarily assigned government cubicles. And my office was new, and the location and phone number had to be sitting in some stack on some clerk's desk waiting to be entered into the annually published directory. I had to be lost in the bureaucracy.

A numb drive later, I sat in my office, door closed and lights out.

I stared at my phone trying to will it to sound the trumpet ringtone, the God-awful sound I'd grown to dread.

My mind couldn't escape the 'who' and 'why' of my predicament. Someone wanted to indict Kitty and someone else wanted to either protect her or themselves from being discovered. If I believed Kitty, Camden had to be responsible for all the murders, the lottery winners, Andrew, and Sally. My guess was that the killing of one of the four lottery winners had to have angered my caller, possibly a loved one. He had probably tried to use the authorities to seek justice, but they had failed. Somehow, he'd uncovered Kitty's involvement, but he didn't have the means to prove anything. And then along came Big Dumb; me, and my stupid 'press release.' So my caller decided to use me and Bean to gain his revenge.

If deep voice insisted on proof, Kitty would've succeeded in pulling me into her problem, both needing proof.

But what if Kitty were lying?

My head ached from the 'what if' do-loops.

My stomach growled. I checked my phone, it was past noon. Breakfast had been two cups of coffee and a stirred-more-than-eaten bowl of cereal. I needed food.

If I sat in this dark, empty office much longer, I'd admit myself to the loony-bin. Lunch would be a reprieve, a break from the madness, and a great idea according to my stomach.

I left, deciding to walk to a nearby diner. The sun was out and the low humidity, warm winds of March ruffled my government length hair. I wanted so much to be anywhere but here. I couldn't believe how I had taken for granted the walks Bean and I used to take on the beaches of Hilton Head Island. Oh, but to be there now, with her.

A gust of reality slowed my pace. I'd never be able to repeat those days, those walks with Bean. I'd never be the same person, nor would she. I had violated our relationship, and I didn't want to think about all the things that probably had happened to her. All because of greed, mine, hers, Kitty's, Andrew's, Camden's, and whoever else was involved. Hypocrites, all nothing but hypocrites, talking the words of the almighty, while totally committed to another almighty ... the almighty dollar.

I wanted out of this mess.

Ring phone, damned you, ring.

There probably was a time when Carlo's Luncheonette had been a delightful place to eat, maybe before Carlo, or before the grease had coated the ventilation system and the walls.

The actual cheeseburger and onion straws didn't resemble the succulent picture on the menu, not even close. The sandwich had some identity issues. Instead of a neat stack of two beef patties topped by fresh, water-dripping lettuce, a thick slice of fire-engine red garden-picked tomato, and an ivory white slice of onion, between two fluffy buns; the cheeseburger looked like it had been sat on by Senator Camden Sparks, all four-hundred pounds of him. And the onion straws were an overcooked glob bonded by grease. Yum-yum.

But I was hungry, so I ate. I'd had worse. Any time I thought I was having a bad meal; I only had to think of the Marines' preserved MREs in the middle of an Iraqi sandstorm.

Halfway through the mashed burger and lubricated onion straws, washed down with a watered-down diet drink, my cell phone finally came to life with the attention-commanding trumpet call. Thank God.

Afraid to guess who the "Private Number" caller was, I simply said,"Hello."

"Brent, where are you?" Kitty asked in a high nerve-jacked tone.

Fooled again.

"I'm having lunch. And I'm sorry I didn't accept your invitation before, very sorry."

"Brent, Sally … Sally Kellerman is dead, murdered. The government is buzzing with the horrible news."

My first reaction was to lie, but why do that, what difference would it make if she knew I had found Sally's body?

"I, ah, I know. She called me and told me she had found something of interest, so I want back to her office after our meeting this morning. By the time I got there someone had hit her on the head, tied her up, and suffocated her with a plastic bag."

"How awful." Her tone implied she hadn't wanted the details.

"Be glad you weren't there to see her." Sally's face frozen as if in a scream, though literally dying for air, came into high pixel-density focus in my mind.

"The police said a janitor reported her death," she said, her selected words hiding the dangling, unasked question.

The old black man with the cart came to view, the same one who probably gave the police a description of me that coupled with the flowers with the Florist's card, and the credit card record of purchase at the Florist, would have the police searching for me in a matter of hours.

"If I had called in a second killing in as many days, where do you think I'd be right now?"

She dodged my rhetorical question. "What did she find?" Her tone was void of innuendo.

Now was the time to lie. "I don't know. And if I did know something, I'm not sure I'd tell you. Anyone with knowledge about the corrupted drawing process is being murdered." A shudder rolled through me. I knew how they had rigged the game. The killer had to know that Sally had uncovered the method, so the killer probably knew Sally had talked to me. Sally had told someone other than me what she had found; the wrong someone.

I had to be on the murderer's list, probably at the top.

"What was she looking for?" Kitty asked.

Her inquisitiveness eroded what little trust I had for her. "She was helping me find out how the Powerball drawing was rigged."

"I know that, Silly, did she have someone or something she was focused on?"

"Magic," I said and disconnected.

$$\textbf{45}$$

When you have worked for an organization that provides you the tools and training for self-preservation, you never forget the training, and you retain as many of the tools as you can. Personally, I had kept my M9 Beretta Marine pistol. Like my toothbrush, I took that gun everywhere with me. The 9mm weapon with the fifteen-round clip removed, probably weighed less than the loaded clip, together about two-and-a-half pounds, a light, easy to pack, instrument of death.

I had always trusted the gun for reliability and accuracy. The weapon, several times my savior, had never let me down. But I needed some practice, and I couldn't think of a better time than now. My gut told me my skills at self-preservation were going to be tested, soon.

After making a few inquiries, I left Carlo's Luncheonette and went to a Wal-Mart where I bought one-hundred rounds of NATO standard 9mm bullets, some black thread, oxblood spray paint, some metal clang-bells, and a paperback book. Then I headed west, directed by one of Carlo's cooks, an ex-Jarhead, to a shooting range.

An hour later, wearing the residual smells from becoming intimate with a weapon, I returned to Charley and Annie's B&B. The last thing I needed was gunpowder residue on me. I washed my hands and arms thoroughly.

Although I didn't think anyone knew where I was staying, I wasn't completely sure of anything or anyone.

I spent the rest of the afternoon spray-painting the bells close to the same color as the outside walls of the B&B, oxblood. After they dried, I strung the half-dozen bells together using the thread. Then I tied the black tread about six inches high above a step halfway up the rear outside entrance to my second floor suite of rooms. The bells dangled below, blending into the background of the siding. The bells weren't obvious in the daylight, and would be invisible at night, plus they were tucked under the enclosed stairs out of the wind. I wouldn't want wind-blowing, clanging bells to cause Charley and Anne to think I was 'around the bend' or an early Christmas decorator.

I went to my room and tried to immerse myself into an Al Chaput novel, one of my favorite southern suspense fiction writers, while I waited and prayed for a phone call.

(46)

The sun was low as I sat in the B&B and tried to read a paperback. What was I thinking? With all due respect to Mr. Chaput, wherever he was, I couldn't concentrate on his book. All I could think about was Bean.

I remembered the first time Bean and I met. I'd just gotten back from Afghanistan and had come home on leave. I had met a couple of buddies, and we went out drinking. And Tinker Bell walked in and waved her magic wand and wham, my life was permanently changed. As soon as I saw her in the doorway, as crazy as it may sound, I knew I had to meet her. She could've been blind, deaf and dumb, or retarded, I didn't know. I didn't know anything about her, but I had to know everything. I wedged my way through the Friday night crowd until I stood in front of her, blocking her path. The black-eyed, tiny blonde looked up at me and smiled. And that was how it all started.

Where was she now? What had happened to her? I didn't want to think of the possibilities. I just wanted her alive and well and in my arms. We both had unhealed wounds that needed mending. Maybe we could fix them together, or at least try. I just wanted the chance.

I let my mind search through my memory, pulling out all the fun things and loving things we had done together. My mind savored each memory, like a kid eating a cupcake, slowly, first the icing then the cake, ingesting the time, the place, the clothes, the colors, the words, and the laughter.

Then I thought of her parents, George and Wanda, simple, hard working folks, who had to be worried sick. Robin was overdue. I would call them, I should call them, but what could I say, "Your daughter's been kidnapped, and I'm not doing a damned thing about it. And no I haven't called the police." A phone call would evoke too many questions I couldn't answer without sounding insane. For now, I'd have to let them worry.

I'm not sure how long I sat there lost in Bean and my memories. But when my phone trumpeted, jerking me back to reality, the sun had set.

"Hello," I said, my voice was scratchy from lack of use.

"Did I wake you?" the deep male voice asked.

"Thank God you finally called." I had to get control. I had thought about this call a great deal. And I swore I wouldn't let this man manipulate me. So what do I do first thing, I blurted out my thoughts. Control was the operative word.

"A bit anxious are you? Worried about your little cutie pie? My mother always told me the best things came in small packages."

"I want to talk to her."

"I want, I want ... and *I* don't give a shit what you want. Have you been concerned enough about this tiny, but," he cleared his throat, "sexy woman to do what I asked? Don't rush; I would love to have more time with her. I think she's startin' to like me or at least what I do to her."

Although my body trembled with rage, I kept my voice soft and flat. "I've done what you asked. I know how the governor rigged the Lottery drawings. Kit—Governor Franklin actually didn't know any of the details. Someone else thought up the scheme and managed the process."

"Great. Tell me all about it, every detail."

"I will, when Bean is in my arms, and we're both safe."

"Brent, tell him what he wants to know." Bean's voice was void of emotions, distant and strange.

My control vanished. "Bean, are you okay? Where are you? This will all be over soon, I promise. Are you—"

"Details," the male voice said.

His cold, demanding voice returned my control. "I will tell you everything, after Robin is here, with me," I said.

"It ain't gonna be that way. It's now or never."

"But you said—"

"Tell me how the governor rigged the Powerball, and I'll leave her someplace where she'll be found."

His words, his tone, everything about what he said and how he said it peaked my anxiety. "'Where she'll be found'? Why would she need finding? What are you—"

"She will be bound, gagged, and blindfolded, that's why. Now talk."

"When will you take her somewhere she'll be found?"

"As soon as we finish … if I'm satisfied with what you tell me."

"How do I know you'll do that after I tell you? Why should I trust you?"

"You have no choice."

I already knew what he'd say. I had no choice. I was powerless and hated it. I filled my lungs and let the inhaled air ease out, hoping it would take my muscle-bunching tension with it.

"The Powerball drawing is televised at the same time every Wednesday and Saturday night, a commitment to the public. In case something happens that precludes the drawing from occurring on time, like a mechanical failure or a local power outage, the drawing manager has made back-up videos of other drawings using the same controlled process that can be substituted and aired by the network on time. Andrew Hays, working for the governor, substituted videos containing preselected numbered balls for the back-up videos and then created disruptions to the scheduled drawing process on at least four occasions."

"Ahh-haa, so that's how the bitch did it. So is Andrew willing to testify?"

Bean's kidnapper obviously didn't work in the state government. Though he had a problem with Kitty, he didn't know her confidants. "He's dead, murdered."

"Was he that Pro whatever, that State Senate guy that was murdered a couple of days ago?"

"Yes."

"So how can I prove Governor Franklin did what you said?"

"You asked me to find out how, not to prove it." Despite my efforts to control my emotions, anger crept into my voice.

"I need proof. What about the drawing manager, wouldn't he know?"

"The manager is a she, Sally Kellerman."

"So ask her how he did it."

"She's dead too."

"Sounds like the governor is eliminating any witnesses."

"I don't think she's responsible."

"What? That bitch will do anything for power!"

I had pushed one of his anger buttons, one of the more sensitive ones.

It was time to eat some crow and to settle him down, if possible. "Excuse me, I spoke without thinking. She could be responsible. I don't know. And I've got some proof, albeit circumstantial. Since South Carolina has taken over the multi-state lottery drawing, every time there was a disruption to the drawing process, the resultant Powerball winner has been killed and all winnings are missing. That's all I know and probably ever will know. If I dig any deeper, I'm pretty sure someone will at least try to kill me as well, if they aren't already planning to. Now will you let Bean go?"

"I'll call you." The call ended.

47

Sleeping alone shouldn't be an issue to a veteran, a man who had slept alone, concealed behind Afghan boulders from the Arctic night wind and the searching Taliban.

I had tucked the Beretta under what had been Bean's pillow. And I had adjusted the B&B's bedroom temperature down to five degrees below cool, snuggling conditions. But I laid in the dark and stared at the blackness above me. My mind had too many unresolved problems to deal with before allowing sleep.

I sat up, fisted the pillow several blows, and rolled onto my side. This was stupid. I didn't have any answers and wouldn't find any tonight in this bed. I needed sleep. I had to be mentally sharp tomorrow. Tomorrow I had to figure out how to see Nancy Beltner, the lottery tech, without getting arrested. She had to know something.

I clamped my eyelids closed and tried to focus my mind on something soothing, relaxing, mind numbing. To my chagrin, no matter what my mind concentrated on, the logic flow would be disrupted by a three-dimensional, in vivid color, close proximity view of Kitty's yellow sweater with the neckline cut-to-barely-decent boobs exposure. Why would my mind keep taking me there? I couldn't be horny, not with Bean's life in jeopardy. Somewhere in the recesses of my brain, a neuron or two took control and redirected my focus on the rich, beautiful Governor of South Carolina and the question of why she would seduce a commoner like me. Could I believe her words, or did she have a hidden agenda like everyone else involved in the lottery seemed to have? My mind raced around that closed-loop track over and over, one body roll after another, one side to the other.

When I arrived at the point of praying for the stair-bells to ring to end my mental torment, my damned phone, the bugle blasting, nerve jamming bitch, trumpeted.

I bolted to a sitting position and groped the darkness where the nightstand should have been. After knocking over a lamp, I found my cell phone buried under an earlier tossed pillow. The illuminated face read '2:45 a.m.'

"Hello." My one-word answer oozed with irritation mixed with contempt.

"I'm so sorry, Brent. But … where are you?" Kitty's voice sounded alert; scared alert. "I've got to see you now."

Despite having not slept, three a.m. was not a good time to get a phone call.

"Hold on," I blurted into the phone to Kitty Franklin like she was just a normal person instead of the governor. Titles tend to evaporate after you've slept with the holder and particularly at three a.m.

I righted the lamp and turned it on. The shadowed bedroom of the B&B despite its warm colors seemed cold and foreign, like everything else in my current life.

"Kitty, why do you need to see me in the middle of the night?" I asked, sitting on the bed in my Jockey shorts.

"I can't talk over the phone," she said. "Neither of us can risk anyone knowing what I've got to tell you."

She certainly had a knack for getting my attention; she had done it before and now had done it again.

I released a long sigh. "Okay, I can't sleep anyway."

"You checked out of the hotel. Where are you? I'm dressed and ready to roll, just tell me where."

How could I trust anyone associated with the lottery? "I'll meet you, what's convenient?"

"We need privacy. Call me paranoid, but I don't trust my phone, my house, my office, my car, or even my clothes. I bought this throw-away phone today, along with the outfit I'm wearing. The coffee shop is open, but I would feel exposed there. Let me come to you. I'll make sure I'm not followed."

"I'm sorry, but I won't tell you. I can't afford for anyone to know where I am. I'm Bean's only hope. The FBI, the police, and probably the killer are looking for me. I need to be free to save Bean, not in jail or some ditch with a plastic bag over my head."

"Brent, I've told you my darkest secrets. You can trust me. We have no one else to trust, just each other. If I were the killer, why would I let you live this long? I could've killed you many times."

"You needed me to find out how the Lottery had been rigged. And now I have enough circumstantial evidence to convince the police to at least investigate you and Camden."

"That's true. But do you honestly think I'm capable of killing anyone?"

"I know for a fact that everyone is capable. I've lived it."

"That was the war," she said.

"Yeah, the war where killing anyone who can harm you is a necessity, a daily task. How is that any different from the situation you and I are in today?"

"Brent if I wanted to find you, all I would have to do is trace your phone, you leave it on. I'm the governor; I have access to people and tools who could find you. If I wanted to kill you, you'd be dead."

I didn't respond. My mind digested her words. She had a lot more power than I could probably fathom.

"And what I have to tell you is … I can't talk, but you've got to know this." Her voice sounded sincere. "Hold on while I go outside and then you can tell me where to go."

"Kitty … Kitty!" She was apparently on the move and not responding. She had told me things about her and Camden that if leaked could ruin her career. Her urgency and fear seemed genuine and logical. If she had wanted to find me, she could've. If she had information that could lead me to Bean, I had to take the chance and see Kitty, now. Bean couldn't afford me not to know. Every minute had to be hell for her. I had no choice but to tell Kitty where I was.

"Okay," she said a little out of breath. "What's the address?"

"There's an all-night convenient store up the road. I'll go there and borrow their phone and call you back."

(48)

Thirty minutes later, I stood in the dark dressed in black sweatpants and a black tee shirt outside the B&B. Beretta in hand, I watched a car's headlights roll into the driveway.

I waited a moment to check for a trailer, someone tracking her. Then I eased through the darkness as I had so often done in the war and positioned myself behind the car.

The headlights and engine were extinguished and the driver's door opened. In the dome light, I could see Kitty, alone in the car, as she stepped out onto the gravel drive.

I glanced over my shoulder to again make sure she hadn't been followed. Then I took several quick steps, and grabbed her, covering her mouth with my gun-free hand.

"Shhh, it's me," I whispered. "I'm just making sure you're alone." I released her and she turned to face me.

"You just took ten years off my life."

"Keep your voice down. I don't want to wake the owners. Follow me and be quiet." I took her hand and led her to a big oak tree near the road, a few hundred yards from the house.

Her dark silhouette whispered, "What are we doing here?"

"I want to be sure you weren't followed. Plus there are no distractions, no visible yellow sweater, no couch, no bed, and we can talk here."

"And I thought I was paranoid," she said.

I ignored her. "What do you need to tell me?"

"Late tonight, just before I called you, Tom Peterson called. Tom is the District Director for the FBI. We've met several times recently and he … well he sort of likes me. I can tell. Tom is old, fat and bald, and recently divorced, a lost soul, but the way he looks at me and … I can just tell. He's lonely."

"Kitty, you're a lovely woman. Even Ray Charles would like you if he could smell you or listen to your lovely voice. Now get on with it, what did he tell you?"

"He assigned a team to investigate Andrew Hay's murder. In doing so, they checked on all Andrew's phone and financial records, along with everywhere he had gone. Tom called me from Switzerland tonight, just before I called you. Either he hadn't thought about the time difference or didn't care. He was in a bank. Andrew had opened an account in that bank a week before his murder. And he had deposited a lot of money, millions."

"So Andrew was either being paid to steal the lottery funds or he was skimming," I said.

"Yes, but there's more."

"What?" Impatience ruled my tone.

"Tom asked me if Andrew was secretly married, and I told him I was sure he wasn't."

I wanted to ask her if she told this Tom guy she was certain because she had slept with Andrew, but this was not the time or place. "And?"

"Tom told me Andrew had had a "Power of Attorney" letter with him so he could stuff another account for another person with tens of millions."

It was late. We were in the dark, hiding beneath a grand oak tree in the middle of a field. I was bone tired. My patience had died long ago. I grabbed both her arms and shook her. "Who?"

"His sister, Robin Hays."

(49)

It was damned near four in the morning, and Kitty and I stood in the living room of my suite in the B&B. I no longer cared about being alone with her in a lighted room with a couch and just a few footsteps from a bed. I had guided her through the darkness up the outside steps, over the hidden string, to my three-room quarters. I needed to see her face when I asked her to repeat her story, word for word.

Kitty was dressed in a shapeless beige smock and flip-flops. Her hair was clipped up, and she wore no make-up, and I thought she was prettier without it.

I watched her blood-shot blue eyes and her blank expression as she repeated her story. If she were lying, I couldn't see or sense it.

When she finished, she folded her arms across her chest and chewed on her lower lip with one raised eyebrow, as if awaiting a response.

I glanced down and, to my surprise, still had the Beretta in my hand. I sat the gun on the two-person kitchen table, where Bean had sat and called her parents the morning after Andrew was killed. The morning she had begged me to quit my job. I should have listened to her. Sally Kellerman would be alive. Bean and I would be together. And I'd still be monogamous, and guilt-free. And I'd have no doubts about who Bean really was right now. At this point, I envied ignorance.

Could Kitty's story be true? Was it possible for me not to really know Bean? Was she consumed by greed, like everyone else around me? Had she really been kidnapped, or was all this a ruse? Had she been using me? Had she paid some man to call me and to find out how Andrew had rigged the lottery? Why, did she want more? Who was the man, a lover? Was I that big of a fool?

"You don't believe me, do you?" Kitty asked.

I stared into her ensnaring blue eyes. "I don't want to."

"Your girlfriend has a multi-million-dollar account in Switzerland. Andrew had a power-of-attorney letter from her. Someway, somehow, she's involved. Ask yourself why she would pretend to be kidnapped and use that to get you to find out how the Lottery was rigged? Why wouldn't she already know? Her brother did it. Maybe she really is kidnapped, and the kidnapper doesn't know her involvement."

"Maybe, maybe, maybe," I blurted. "This whole mess is one big maybe." I turned my back to her and squeezed my hands together.

Her hand touched my shoulder. "Brent, I wish I had the answers, but I don't. I … if you want me to, I'll go see Camden."

I spun around. "No. But I will."

"That will only get you arrested." She leaned against me, wrapped her arms around my waist, and laid the side of her head on my chest. "I'm sorry Andrew and I ever involved you."

Her body was soft, warm, and comforting; a sanctuary from the madness. She smelled like honeysuckle in bloom. I slid my arms around her and clutched her tapered back. Once again the governor had come to see me without wearing a bra, but this time, I didn't care.

We stood there for a long moment, two people clinging to each other to escape reality.

I took a deep breath and sighed it away. Then I eased her to arms' length. "I don't think you or Andrew had anything to do with my involvement."

Her eyes fixed on mine and she shook her head. "Why do you think that?"

"Because schoolteachers don't make very much money; barely enough to exist on."

"So you think—" the stair bells clanged.

(50)

It was the middle of the night, Tuesday morning, and I stood in my B&B holding Miss 'Braless' Kitty, the governor of South Carolina, at arms' length. The bells I had rigged to announce someone on the stairs to my second-floor suite were clanging.

I shoved Kitty aside, grabbed the Beretta off the table, rushed to the light switch, and flipped it off. Then, standing to one side, I jerked the door open to the outside steps. Feet hammered on the wooden steps. I jumped into the door frame and saw a bouncing, dark figure scampering down the steps.

"Stop or I'll shoot!" I shouted and sprinted down the steps.

The figure jumped down the remaining four or five steps, stumbled and rolled on the ground, and came up running.

The thought of shooting this dark invader flashed through my mind, but I focused on negotiating the invisible steps instead. I needed this person alive.

By the time my feet found the ground, the intruder had a good lead on me, in the black of night. I had run a lot in my life, in the dark, with a gun.

I could barely see the shadow streaking across the open field heading for the trees by the road, probably where a vehicle was parked, but I was gaining. When I got close enough to hear the person's panting, the figure slid to a stop and whirled. A dull ignition flashed and something burned my left thigh, the pain was so intense I thought I had been branded. I found myself tumbling, rolling on the ground. When I finally stopped flopping, my gun was gone and both my hands were clutching my singed, stinging leg.

I writhed in the darkness trying to find a way to extinguish the fire in my leg, back and forth, nothing helped. They say you don't remember pain. Bullshit. I remembered pain just like this, when I got hit in the back by shrapnel in Afghanistan, our mortars, although at the time it didn't matter, my first of two Purple Hearts, compliments of the US Army artillery. It hurt like hell then, and it was even worse now.

Somewhere in the distance a car started, an engine revved, and tires sprayed gravel.

A hand grabbed my shoulder. Were there two of them? I flailed a fisted hand in the direction of my assailant and connected.

"Aaah!" Kitty voiced her pain.

Oh shit, I'd hit Kitty. I wanted to feel bad, but I had my own problems.

"What the—why'd you hit me?" Kitty asked; her voice above me in the darkness. "I'm gonna have a hellofva knot on the side of my head." She paused. "I was just trying to help you. I saw the flash and you go down, I … I thought you were … I was scared."

"I'm sorry. It's my leg … the fucker shot me."

"Oh my God," Kitty said. "I'll call 911."

"No!" I took a breath and tried to capture some control. "Find my gun. I dropped it."

Kitty got on her hands and knees and crawled in the direction I had come. Five pain-filled minutes later she whispered, "I've got it."

"Bring it here and help me up, I think I can walk."

"Brent, someone shot you. We need to call the police and get you to a hospital."

"They'll arrest me. And what are we going to tell them, that my girlfriend is a crook?"

"That's up to the police to sort out, not you. And if Bean is guilty, that's not your fault. She's a big girl, she had choices, and she made them, not you."

"Help me up. We'll talk about this inside."

Kitty handed me the Beretta. I engaged the safety and tucked it in the waistband of my pants.

Kitty helped me stand. The burning seemed to intensify when I tried to flex the injured muscle by putting weight on that leg. I stood on my good leg.

I put an arm over Kitty's small shoulder and hopped to the B&B's outside stairs. Surprisingly, there were no lights on; either the proprietors were sound sleepers, or they weren't home. But why would Charlie and Anne leave overnight when they had guests? Unless my intruder had visited them first. Enough conjecture, I'd check on the owners later, I had stairs to climb, a whole bunch of them.

(51)

Out of breath and tolerance for any additional stair-climbing, Kitty eased me onto a kitchen chair. She retreated and flipped on the light switch. The left leg of my black sweatpants was gashed open thigh-high on the side and was soaked with blood.

I pushed up off the chair to a standing position, removed the gun from my pants, and put it on the table.

"What are you doing?" Kitty asked.

I inserted my thumbs into the waistband of my sweatpants and pushed them down. "I'm taking my pants off. We've been here before, so don't act embarrassed, help me. I need to see how bad this is."

I got the pants off my butt and flopped back down on the chair.

Kitty finished removing my pants, taking care not to add to my pain.

I looked at my leg. A pinky-wide, two-three inch long gash oozed blood on the side of my thigh.

"Thank God, it's just a graze," I said.

"A pretty ugly graze," Kitty said.

"I'll need some antiseptic cream, some gauze pads, and some tape."

Kitty leaned down and then squatted by my side. She lightly touched the skin around the wound. "Bullshit. You need stitches, Brent. The wound is too deep."

Her fingers felt cool and momentarily took my mind off the burning. "Stitches will require a doctor and too many questions," I said.

"This wound could have been caused by a lot of things other than a bullet. Tell them you were taking an early morning jog and a broken tree branch gouged you. Something, but you need stitches if you want to be able to walk today or tomorrow."

She was right about that. The opened wound screamed every time I flexed the muscle.

She looked up from her squatted position. "Let me clean it up and take you to a hospital." Her magnetic blue eyes studied my face for an answer.

I leaned to my side and looked at the wound. "A tree branch, huh?"

She stood, hands on hips. "Yeah, that'd work," she said.

I glanced at her smock. I had smeared the side of her dress with blood when she helped me walk and climb the stairs.

"I'm sorry I hit you and … and I've ruined your dress." I pointed.

She looked down and flared the skirt of her loose smock outward with her hands. "No biggy. This was just something I bought to wear that was safe; something I knew wouldn't be bugged. I didn't wear anything from my closet, not even shoes."

"I know, including underwear."

Her face spread into a smile, adding sparkle to her already sparkling eyes. "A girl can hope, can't she?"

I loved her smile, and my ego couldn't help loving her flirts. I reached out and took her hand in mine.

"The press will have a field day with the no-underwear Governor carting a wounded man into a hospital in the middle of the night."

"Let me worry about that." She squeezed my hand.

"Then what?"

"Then I'll take you to breakfast, Brent Layne. My treat."

I dropped her hand, stood up balancing on my good leg, and grimaced from the on-going burn. "Someone's trying to kill one of us or both of us, and you want to go to breakfast?" I shook my head and returned her smile. "How can I refuse that?"

$$\left(52\right)$$

Kitty and I checked on Charlie and Annie before leaving the B&B for the hospital. They weren't home; thank God.

Kitty dropped me off at the Emergency entrance to the hospital. She waited for me in the parking lot. Surprisingly, the reception personnel, nurses, and even the doctors bought my story about snagging my leg on a cut-metal post while running.

After spending four hours in the hospital, of which over three-and-a-half were spent sitting on my ass waiting, Kitty and I sat at a local, family-owned restaurant that served breakfast twenty-four-seven.

My stitched-leg was sore and the combination of the bandages and the pain made me walk stiff-legged.

Kitty took a sip of coffee, and then she covered her mouth with a hand and tried to hide a giggle.

"What's funny?" I asked and scowled, enunciating my reaction to humor.

A little grin wrinkled her cheeks. "Your leg, the way you walk, and my name, I think I'll start calling you Chester."

"What?" I shook my head.

"'Gun Smoke', the TV western with Miss Kitty, Matt Dillon, and his stiff-legged sidekick, Chester, don't you remember? The re-runs are still aired." She leaned forward, excited. "Wouldn't it have been wild if the doctor who stitched your leg would have been Doc Adams, the character

Millburn Stone played on 'Gun Smoke'? If only you needed a blacksmith? Did you know Bert Reynolds played—"

My open hand smacked the table, bouncing the plates and cups. "Kitty, forget that trivia bullshit. We need to talk about what we're going to do, before anyone else gets killed, specifically Bean, you, or me."

"What a grouch." She sat back. "You can't believe that Bean is in jeopardy, you and me, yeah, but Bean?"

I flipped my hand at her. "Fine, whatever, but you and I need to do something, like talk to Nancy Beltner. She's got to know something, like who Sally may have talked to about her discovery. Nancy could be the killer, although she doesn't look capable. But looks don't matter. She worked for Sally. Maybe Sally told her what she'd discovered, and Nancy killed her."

"So why would we want to meet with a possible killer?" Kitty asked with a touch of frantic in her tone.

"She might slip up, give herself away."

"And she might kill us."

"I'll have my gun with me, and there's safety in numbers. And if she's not the killer, she may be able to lead us to the killer. We got to do something, at least call her."

"I've got a better idea," she said, as she toyed with her fork. "Let's call Tom Peterson, my FBI buddy, and tell him everything. Let him talk to Nancy and Camden and whoever else he can think of, while you and I take a little trip somewhere." She reached across the table and touched my hand.

I wasn't sure if it was her cool fingers on my skin or me swimming in her blue-lagoon eyes that eased the tension in my shoulders. There was something, more than looks and intellect, to this woman; something special. At the possible expense of her political career, which she had paid so dearly to obtain, and maybe her freedom, she was offering me an out. Her concern for me was eroding my doubts and mistrust. Taking a get-away trip with her sounded wonderful.

"You're wound up tighter than an eight-day-clock as my mom used to say." She patted my hand. "We both could use a break."

Reality and chivalry stomped on my yearnings. I couldn't let her lose everything for me. "That'd be great, except the FBI would insist we meet them. And we have no proof to support anything we tell them. You'd be locked up for at least fraud, and I'd be a prime suspect in two murders. And if Bean is kidnapped, who knows what would happen to her. If we call Peterson and then run; you'd have my problem, with both the killer and the FBI after you. And no matter where I've gone so far, one or both of them seemed to always find me."

"You're leaving your cell phone on. They can track you if they know your number."

"I have to, if I'm going to stay in touch with Bean's kidnapper." I shook off my frustration. "And the last FBI agent I met was more than suspicious."

"I doubt that man, the one Andrew recommended to you, whatever his name was, was with the FBI," she said, her fingers fondling mine.

"About Andrew, did you sleep with him? You never answered me."

She withdrew her hand. "Why do you care who I've slept with?" Her head canted to one side.

I didn't have an answer other than I wanted to be someone she wanted to sleep with not just another person she needed to use. "Did you?"

"No." She folded her arms over her unsupported breasts, tucking her hands under her arms. "Andrew was a friend. He was my campaign manager when I ran for Governor. I wouldn't have won without him. So I helped him get elected to the State Senate and appointed to Pro Tempore. And he helped me when Camden blackmailed me. That's how politics work, collecting or performing favors."

"Andrew may have initially rigged the lottery for you, but afterwards he either did it because someone was paying him, or because he was skimming," I said.

"Or because his sister found out what he was doing and saw an opportunity to get rich."

I wasn't going to pursue her conjecture. "You said Andrew told you he wanted out after the killing started."

"Yes, we both did."

"I can understand why Andrew would want me involved. It gave him an out, and maybe he thought I'd stand up to Camden." I shook my head. "But if Bean knew about this, which she must have since she gave Andrew a power-of-attorney letter, why would she drag me into it?"

"That's simple. Who else could she manipulate in order to keep the money flowing?"

"She's no different than her brother. Bean wouldn't condone murder no matter how much money was involved. She begged me to quit."

"When?"

"After a phony masseur visited her at the hotel."

"Someone visited her at your hotel? Can you prove that?"

"No."

"What else haven't you told me?"

I looked away and then back into her angry blue eyes. What the hell else could go wrong by telling her everything? "My mystery caller, the one who allegedly kidnapped Bean, is after you. From the first call on, he has wanted me to find out how you rigged the lottery. He wants me to get proof against you. Do you have any idea who or why anyone would hate you so much?"

She shrugged and sighed. "Does anyone like politicians? The only person I can think of would be Camden. He needs someone to take the fall."

"Camden Sparks, the man with all the proof. It's time he and I had a talk."

"He won't meet with you."

"No, but he'll meet you. And I'll be there. I'll have your back, or maybe I should say your naked back." I chuckled.

She reached out and smacked my hand, "That's not funny."

(53)

I sat in the passenger's seat as Kitty maneuvered her new Jaguar XJ through the morning traffic on the outskirts of Columbia. I didn't have a clue where we were. I checked the glove box to make sure my Beretta was still there, where I had left it before entering the hospital. It was present and accounted for, with a full fifteen-round clip.

Kitty plugged her throw-away phone into the dash and pushed several icons on the display window. Then she tapped a button on the steering wheel and a phone rang in the car speakers.

"Governor Franklin's office, Ms. Cummins speaking."

"Jeanette, this is Katherine. Please cancel all my appointments today. I will not be in the office until tomorrow."

"Yes, Governor. You've had several phone calls this morning. Your grandfather, Senator Camden twice, and a FBI Director, a Mr. Peterson also called, would you like me to text you those messages?"

"Yes, send them to my private number."

"Would you like me to forward all your calls to your country home for the rest of the day?"

The mention of 'your country home' got my attention and made me glance at Kitty.

"No. Just text me if there's anything you deem important."

"Yes, Governor."

"Thanks, Jeanette, have a good day." Kitty touched another button ending the call.

"You have a country home?" I asked.

Focusing on the curvy road, she nodded.

"Is that where we're going?"

Her eyes swept over me. "You look so uncomfortable. That seat has all kinds of buttons for your comfort." She touched my shoulder. "Please, relax."

I adjusted the lumbar section of my soft, new-smelling leather seat. "Nice car. No wonder people are greedy."

"People are people, most good; some bad. Me, I just like the car. Gramps always owned Jags. It's a sweet car. Handles, rides, and maneuvers like a dream with power to spare. Plus it has a paddle shifter and displayed icons and buttons for everything. Want to drive it?"

"Why be tempted by something I could never afford." The thought made me think of Bean and her Swiss bank account. Maybe she had the right idea. You only live once, so why live poor. I pushed the conjecture aside. Plus my ego didn't want to dwell on Bean's finances.

I scanned Kitty in her frumpy, blood-smeared beige smock. She had no make-up on, though she didn't need any, and her hair was a mess. She looked like a woman who had been up all night, except in this case, a very pretty woman.

"I've only known you a few days, and it seems like a lifetime," I said. "Over and above our roll-in-the-hay, I think we've formed a bond, a special relationship. This probably sounds crazy, but you're like a war buddy. People are dying all around us, and others are trying to kill us, and we're helping each other through the hell. We barely know each other, and yet we'd each risk our life to save the other."

She glanced at me with a furrowed brow. "'Roll-in-the-hay'? Please don't degrade what we did. I thought our love-making was wonderful." Her eyes returned to the road. "But you know what? You're right. I've never been in combat, but there is something special about how I feel about you, something I've never experienced before, but I wouldn't call it a bond. I'm not sure what to call it."

"You know a lot about me, and I really don't know anything about you. Tell me about yourself."

"Well, I went to Brown in undergrad and—"

"No, not that stuff, tell me about you, your likes and dislikes, your friends, your lovers … about you."

She shrugged. "There's nothing unique about my likes and dislikes. And regarding friends and lovers, they come and go. The only two people I care about right now are gramps and … and you."

Although I had some doubts about Bean, I had a commitment to find both her and her side of the story. I needed to change the subject.

"Your Gramps raised you. Was he a stern parent or did he spoil you?"

"He was stern and yet so loving. He taught me to never lie or cheat," her blue eyes flashed my way, "and that trust is earned."

"But you're a politician."

Eyes fixed on the highway, she sighed and nodded.

I had painted myself into a corner. It was time for another subject change. "Where are we going? Don't you need to call Camden to arrange a meeting?" I glanced at my cell phone. "It's after nine a.m. Isn't Congress in session by now? He'll be on the hill in DC at work. Can you reach him when he's in session?"

Her sapphire eyes, reflecting the morning sun, glinted my way. "Listen to you." Her long nails drummed on the leather-wrapped steering wheel. "You sound like an old woman." She patted my good leg. "There, there, Dearie, relax, everything is going to be alright. Mama will take care of you."

I brushed her hand away. "Cute. Now, where are we going?"

"We're not going to DC to see Camden. You'd never get near him with me. He's too cautious."

Why did I have to constantly pry information out of everyone? Was there something wrong with my approach or the way I talked? I leaned my head back against the headrest and tried to relax. I had been able to maintain control of my emotions in much worse situations, far worse. I sighed. "Then where are we going?"

"I have a place … a private place. All spot-lighted politicians have a 'place.'"

"Kitty, I don't—"

Her fingers covered my lips. "You need time to heal. And we need time to decide what we're going to do … a plan versus a reaction."

I took her hand off my mouth and held it. I wasn't sure why I intertwined my fingers with hers. I owed her for helping me after I was shot. Maybe I was needy due to my doubts about Bean's sincerity. I didn't know. I just wanted to touch her. "Will you have security there? Other than your office and your chauffeur, I haven't seen you with any bodyguards. Why?"

"My security manager is a personal friend. He bends the rules for me. And no, there won't be any guards there. No one knows about this place. The house is off the beaten track on ninety acres in the country and sits back from the road, hidden by a hill and woods. It's listed under my ex-husband name, including the title. He inherited it. I paid him cash for it. We have … an arrangement." Her fingers played with mine and maneuvered onto my bloodied sweat pants. "And there are probably even some of his clothes there that may fit you."

Either politics paid better than I thought, or her gramps, or the lottery was bolstering her income. Like my thoughts about Bean's bank account, I didn't want to dwell on any guesses about Kitty either.

The personal contact relaxed me. Toying with her hand was like finding a middle ground for us, somewhere between wild sex and her position as my boss, the governor. "I know I'm repeating myself, but I can't help it. 'No one', not even your friends know about this place?"

"Only my ex and he wouldn't tell anyone about it. I couldn't trust him around other women, but I do trust his word now that we're divorced."

"Ms. Cummins knew about your 'place'." I leaned toward her.

"All she knows is that I have a place in the country, and now she has my throwaway cell number. That's it. I don't own a phone with a hard line."

It was time to change the subject, before I started to repeat myself. "Okay as long as we're going to make a plan and nothing else. I've got to find Bean. I have to know she's safe, even if she hasn't been kidnapped."

She squeezed my hand, nodded, and smiled.

I studied her while she drove. She was a beautiful, smart lady, and a politician. Though she repeatedly flirted with me and insinuated she liked me, I had to keep in mind who she was, a politician and maybe a killer.

Kitty's 'place' was definitely secluded. The five-bedroom ranch sat at least a half-mile off the two-lane country road. A wooded hill concealed the house from the road just as she had said. The eighties home had been modernized with the latest appliances, new furniture, and such amenities as towel warmers, large walk-in showers, satellite televisions, five of them, and a recently stocked refrigerator.

After being given the grand limp-along tour, I removed the gun from my waistband and eased down onto a white leather sectional in the great room. This combined kitchen, dining room, living room was larger than any house I had ever lived in. I shook my head as I put the weapon on an end table.

"Tired?" Kitty asked. "Is your leg bothering you?"

"Not really, I'm ..." I raised my hands skyward, "I'm overwhelmed with how you live. Obviously you must have a maid service, a landscaper, and who knows who else takes care of this place. It wouldn't surprise me if there's a cabana next to an Olympic-size pool somewhere on the property, and maybe even a golf course. Oh, I almost forgot the stable with thoroughbred horses."

She stepped closer, her blue eyes widened over a smile. "Do you ride? Oh please tell me you ride. I don't have a golf course, but I've got a polo field and polo ponies."

I couldn't hold back a chuckle.

"What's so funny?" She sat down next to me and pinched my arm.

"Ouch!" I rubbed my skin.

"Well do you—" her expression morphed to a threat as she held up her pinchers—"ride?"

"Currently no, and previously not well." I sat upright and turned to face her. "You've got to pay all these maintenance people. So they have to know you stay here."

She dropped her pinchers. "You're paranoid. She sighed. "My ex pays all the bills. It's part of the arrangement."

My eyebrows climbed skyward. "Is casual sex part of your 'arrangement'?" Another thought that should have remained a thought and not spoken.

Her chin sucked inward as she leaned away from me. "Do I detect a jealous tone? Or do you just think I spread my legs for everyone?"

I glanced away. "I'm sorry. I really don't know anything about you." I looked at her. She had folded her arms over her chest, and her facial expression conveyed hurt. "But if a single 'spot-lighted politician' like you wanted to have a fling, they'd need a place like this." I waved an arm at the surroundings.

"True. But just to set the record straight, with the exception of," a scowl invaded her features, "Camden and you, I've been a virgin Governor."

"Okay." I wasn't sure I believed her, but it was past time to talk about something else. "Now, can we talk about a plan?"

She slapped her thighs with her hands. "We just got here. We need to relax a little first. And since you brought it up—" she unbuttoned one of the shoulder straps on her smock. The material fell away exposing her tanned upper chest. She smiled.

When her hand moved to the remaining button, I grabbed it. "Is sex all you think about?" I dropped her hand and buttoned her drooping strap. "Don't you realize if Bean really has been kidnapped, every minute must be hell for her? I wished you'd heard what that son-of-a-bitch threatened to do to her. I need to do something to find her. Maybe we should call Peterson." I shrugged. "I don't know what else to do."

"You are absolutely right. Why would I want a man who is hung up on a girl who has lied to him and used him? One fool in our little party of two is enough."

I rubbed my neck. "Okay, you're probably right. It's just … what if she is kidnapped?"

She spread her hands, palms out. "What if? What If?" She shook her head. "I'm sorry." Her hands clamped the sides of her head. "Sex is the only way I can take my mind off all this shit. And," she dropped her hands into her lap, and then reached out and took one of my hands in hers, "and sex is so wonderful with you." She bowed her head and massaged her temples with her free hand. "And I don't have any ideas about a plan; none. Truthfully, I don't think there's anything you, or me, or Peterson can do to find your … your girlfriend."

I thought for a moment, as our fingers played tag. Maybe I was a fool. This gorgeous woman was trying to help me evade reality, the reality and ego-stomping pain that Bean was a crook. But I had to know the truth. I needed data. "Would you ask Peterson to send you a copy of Bean's Swiss bank statement and the power of attorney letter?"

Her head snapped up, and she dropped my hand and fisted her hips. "You don't believe me do you?"

Women just loved to throw men into minefields. I glanced away from her piercing eyes. "I want to see if it's Bean's signature on the letter, and I'm curious about how much money it would take to … to change her."

"Two accounts, twenty-five million dollars each, one for Andrew and one for her." Her tone was tainted with resentment.

"Ask him to send you a copy."

"Why would he do that?"

"Cause he 'sort of likes' you."

"Most men do." Her hand took mine again, fingers toying. "Do you like me, Brent? Am I more than a war buddy?"

(55)

Kitty and I sat on her couch at her country home. Morning broached mid-day.

My leg ached, and I hadn't been this tired since my last five-day op in the 'Ghan.' Then as now, it was hard to sleep when people were stalking you, trying to kill you.

Kitty had to be exhausted as well. Neither of us had slept last night.

Kitty's fingers flitted over the face of her phone. She stood. "Brent, get out of those bloodied clothes and get in my bed. You need to rest. When you awake, take a shower. I'll lay out some of my ex's clothes for you. I'd guess they'll fit. He's a big man like you." She smiled. "But not nearly as handsome."

Though flattered, I had no response.

She touched my arm. "Come on, you need sleep. I have calls to make, including Peterson, and then I'll join you," she canted her head, "for sleep. God forbid I wouldn't want you laying there worried about being sexually molested." She offered a hand to me.

I pushed her hand away. "I'm not worried. It's just that ... I'm okay." I stood. "But I do need rest, and so do you."

"I'll just be a minute." She touched my shoulder. "I know you're okay, but do you need help getting undressed?"

My head involuntarily rocked back, liked someone had punched me.

Kitty slapped my arm. "I didn't mean it like that. I'm serious."

"Sorry." My eyes locked on hers. "Thanks. Thanks for helping me."

"You shouldn't thank me. I'm the one who dragged you into this. In retrospect, that press conference I made you give wasn't such a good idea. But I have this feeling that you and I will survive this mess and be better people because of it. At least that's what Gramps always told me about adversity."

"I hope both you and your gramps are right."

"He's a wise man. I hope you get to meet him someday."

"I think I'd like that."

"Now get to bed. You're cutting into our time to sleep together." She winked.

"You are something else. Whatever happens, don't change. I like your spunk."

"Is that all you like about me, Brent Layne?" She giggled like a mischievous lover.

I picked up the Beretta. "I'll take this just in case."

"In case of what?" Her tone climbed to indignant. "I told you no one knows about this place."

"In case you try to molest me." I chuckled and limped toward the long hallway, leading to the bedrooms. "Make your calls. And while you're at it, call Nancy Beltner and ask her if she knows who Sally Kellerman talked to after I left her office. Maybe if the governor asks her, she'll talk, or if she's guilty she might make a mistake. Wake me if you find out anything important, particularly about Bean."

When I awoke, a warm body was pressed against my back and the sunlight was no longer fighting to get passed the red floor-length drapes. A light from the adjacent bathroom dimly lit the bedroom.

I jerked upright. I was sleeping away Bean's life.

Kitty stirred, and her squinted eyes opened. "Wha—what?" Her hand patted the bed next to her. "Lie down." Her eyes closed for a second and then popped open. "Come ... snuggle with me. I—" yawn "—promise I'll be good." Her lids closed.

"Kitty, wake up. What did you find out? What did Peterson say? What did Camden want? Did you call Nancy?" I shook her. "Wake up."

One eye opened, and she pushed my hand off her shoulder. "Leave me alone. I'm tired and … and—" her eye closed.

I got up, gimped to the bedroom door, and flipped on the overhead lights. I was naked. I scanned the room for my clothes. They were gone, but a stack of men's clothes lay on a chair fronting her dresser.

"Turn those damned lights off." She pulled the covers over her head.

I grabbed the covers and pulled them off the bed. Kitty, naked, curled into a fetal position and pulled a pillow over her face.

Without taking my eyes off her; I couldn't if I'd tried; I limped to the chair and stepped into a pair of men's boxer underwear. A groan escaped when I bent my wounded leg. She was beautiful and climbing back into bed and cuddling with her was tempting. But I had more pressing priorities. "Get up, Kitty. We're wasting precious time."

"No." She wiggled like a little girl wanting her way.

I limped to her side of the bed. I yanked the pillow, but she clutched it, causing me to lose my one-legged-balance and fall on top of her.

As I rolled off her, trying not to hurt her or my leg, she climbed on top of me.

Before I could protest, she covered my mouth with hers, squirming her naked body against me.

I pushed her off and sat up. "Damn it, Kitty. This isn't the time for sex. I need some answers. What did you find out?"

She rose on an elbow and scowled at me. Then she stacked pillows behind her and scooted back against the black walnut headboard, unabashed about her nakedness. She sighed away the frown, rubbed her eyes, and leaned over to the nightstand and retrieved her cell phone. "I got Camden's and Nancy's voice-mail." She yawned. "But there was something." She shielded her eyes. "Could you just turn on one lamp and douse those overheads, they're blinding me."

I eased off the bed and complied with her request. "'There was something' what?" I asked standing at the foot of the bed.

Her index finger scrolled over the phone's face. "Oh yeah here it is, a message from Director Peterson. This is why I didn't wake you." She stretched and yawned.

"What, for Bean's sake?"

"He says he can't send me the documents, Bureau policy, but he verified Robin Hays' signature. And she admitted to signing the letter although—"

"She admitted to signing the letter?" Without regard for my screaming leg, I climbed onto the bed and crawled next to her. "He talked to her, to Robin? Let me see that message."

She shook away her drowsiness and pulled her phone out of my reach. "Brent, maybe you—"

I yanked her hand back so I could see the screen and read Ms. Cummins' text summarizing Mr. Peterson's message.

"'When Peterson couldn't reach Bean on her cell phone, he called her parents, and'"—my eyelids compressed the tops of my cheeks and then fluttered open—"'son-of-a-bitch, 'she was there.'" Two pounds of broken glass entered my stomach and started tumbling.

(56)

Wearing only another man's underwear, I sat on the edge of Kitty's bed in her country home. Kitty was asleep in the bed where I had covered her nakedness minutes earlier. She softly snored.

I wasn't sure where her home was located, somewhere in the boonies near Columbia. It was dark outside. I didn't know what time it was, I had left my watch with my other personal items including my gun when I had showered before sleeping. I really didn't care where I was or the hour. Time and place no longer meant anything to me.

My back and shoulders were in a sag contest. Elbows on my knees, I covered my face with my hands. How could I be such a fool? I should've wondered why Bean's parents hadn't called me. Now I knew.

Duped, used, lied to, passed over for money by Bean, I was an idiot. How could I ever be sure I knew anyone ever again? I thought I loved her, and all the while she was laughing at me, using me like a throw-away toy. How could anyone put another person through the anguish of a pretend kidnapping? There is no way she could care for me. And how long was she planning to continue the ruse?

I pushed my anger aside, I needed to think.

Bean was waiting for something. I sat upright and snapped my fingers, the Wednesday's drawing, the numbers in Andrew's shirt pocket. Somehow, probably Andrew had told her, she knew the numbers and had bought a ticket. Bean was going to screw Andrew's killer out of half the winnings. She had to be pretending to be kidnapped so she could hide from the killer and me. No one would ever expect to find her at her parents' home. After the drawing, she'd anonymously claim the money and disappear as if the kidnapper had murdered her and buried her body in some woods or the ocean never to be found. People disappeared every day in this country and were quickly forgotten.

I found my pants in a laundry bag in the bathroom. I retrieved my phone, the gun, my wallet, and the sealed note. I returned my pants to the laundry bag and put everything else in a sink drawer except my phone. I used my phone to 'Google' the Powerball. The Powerball was currently worth two-hundred-ninety-five million dollars. It'd be over three-hundred million by tomorrow night when the drawing took place.

I wondered what kind of 'magic' or distraction the killer would use to force the playing of a taped show? And who would substitute the tape? The killer either had to be one of the drawing attendees or had bribed one of them.

Maybe I should go out and buy a ticket, why not? I'd cut Bean's cheating money in half and the killer's bloody money to a fourth. I could always return the money.

Maybe I should call Bean's parents and demand to talk to her. They'd just tell me she wasn't there.

Returning to the bedroom, I scratched my head. Something didn't work. There was a hole in my logic. Why would Bean go home, to her parents' house, if she were trying to hide from the killer? I stopped a step from the bed. She could go anywhere if the killer thought Bean had been kidnapped. I sat on the edge of the bed. The only person Bean would think I had told was—Kitty's warm hand touched my shoulder, and then she leaned her bare chest against my rigid back.

Kitty had rigged the lottery. But I didn't want to believe she had anything to do with the murders. But I would've never thought Bean was a liar and thief either.

I had to have faith in someone in this deceitful mess. I needed an ally. Plus Kitty had helped me. No, Kitty wasn't a killer. For all the wrong reasons, I trusted Kitty. Regardless, it was time to get out of this death trap.

"Let's call Peterson," I said and patted her wrist.

She slid her hand from under mine and pulled her warm breasts from my back. "Why? What's he going to tell us that he hasn't already said?"

I looked at her over my shoulder. Naked, she sat on her folded legs and chewed on her lower lip until she caught me looking at her.

"I don't know, but I'm gonna find out," I said.

Her expression changed to sultry, and she arched her back pushing her breasts up and out.

"You don't have to feel guilty anymore about Bean, so why don't we mess around before you call Peterson. It'll save us the time of undressing later." She leaned forward and kissed me, one of her oh-so-soft-and-tender sister kisses, like the one she seduced me with at the Seven Gables.

One thing for sure, the woman knew how to kiss, and, as her hands roamed over my skin, how to pleasure as well.

And she was right, I didn't feel guilty anymore. Robin Hayes was a memory, a bad memory I didn't want to recall. And time was no longer a concern. No one was holding or torturing poor Robin. I was free, free from all prior commitments, free to do as I pleased, or, better yet, free to let others do to me as they pleased, especially a beautiful, sensual woman.

But there was this little part of my brain that wouldn't be quiet. I still had some trust issues. I broke the kiss and eased Kitty away.

She tilted her head and pouted her lips. "Don't say it. I know. You want to call Peterson. I'll get me phone."

She started to crawl by me and that was all the trust I needed for the moment. I grabbed her and pulled her into me.

Her eyes met mine. Her questioning look faded into a silent, sensual conveyance.

Our mouths collided.

Kitty's lips were so soft and her fingers—Peterson could wait.

Kitty eased me down on the bed and rolled on top of me without losing lip contact. The warmth of her body, her pillow-soft lips, her curious, exploring tongue, and those skilled wandering hands … the world would have to wait.

(57)

The dim light of dawn defined the gaps between the bedroom drapes and the window frames. Either the thin, dull gray lines awoke me, or the soft snoring inches from my ear of the resurrected Miss 'Umm-umm' Kitty. Regardless, I was awake. I lay naked in Kitty's bed, next to the defrocked Governor of South Carolina. Together, skin against skin, we snuggled under a sheet and comforter. The chilled bedroom of Kitty's country home enticed me to stay in our nest of warmth.

The first time Kitty and I had sex was an extemporaneous experience, a happening, two people trapped in a moment. The sex had been wild, new, and wonderful. I had been the student guided and instructed by a highly trained teacher.

This time, I wasn't burdened by guilt. I had consented before she took me beyond refusal. I wanted her. I took the reins and spent a long time pleasuring her, over and over, until she begged me to take her. Though our first time was indelibly printed in my memory, the second time, being guilt-free, was even more memorable.

I realized our stress-packed situation, surrounded by murdered people, stalked by a killer, wounded by betrayal, and facing possible career-ending decisions including possibly imprisonment or death, played a major role in our physical relationship. We were bonded by common threats and our need for an emotional escape and empathy. But I sensed there was more to us than just common problems and physical sex. Although, trust was still my major concern with her, I was starting to fall for Katharine Franklin, like I had never fallen before, dangerous ground.

What did I know? A day ago, I would've sworn Bean wasn't a liar, and never a thief. Kitty could be a killer. I was a fool being lead by his penis, or was I? My guts said no, but my batting average would've benched an all-star.

Now wasn't the time for dealing with unsupported feelings.

I eased my arm from under Kitty's neck, stacked pillows, and pushed up to a sitting position.

I smelled and tasted like Kitty, and she smelled and tasted like more. And I knew it would only take a touch, a brush of her lips with mine, and I'd have Miss 'Umm-umm' all over again. The thought attempted to morph into a stimulus, but was blocked by a mental alarm; today was Wednesday, and the Powerball drawing was tonight at 10:59 EST.

Schemes flashed through my brain, like finding the nearest seller of Powerball tickets and buying ten … no, one hundred … no, one thousand tickets, all with the same number that Andrew had in his pocket. The Lottery computers would go crazy. The state commissioners would be notified and they'd realize the system had been compromised. No money would be awarded. I couldn't imagine the look on Bean's and the killer's faces when they found out they were getting nothing, not a penny. That would kick their greed in the groin.

But one person wouldn't buy a thousand tickets all with the same number. That made no sense and would raise a red flag.

I'd probably only need to buy three or four hundred tickets with the same number to create a lottery computer alert.

Kitty stirred, springing a thought to life in my searching mind. I knew who could buy several hundred identical tickets, my soup kitchen street people. But did I have enough time to make that happen? I'd need to find my buddy, Charlie. I could do this. And if three or four hundred tickets of the same number didn't alert the system, so be it. There'd be some rich street people, and some disappointed crooks.

"Good morning, Governor." I leaned down and gave her a smooch on the cheek.

"Coffee." She rolled away onto her other side, her bare, tapered back to me.

"Ah-ha, I've finally found someone else who is allergic to mornings. Thank God."

Her top arm flipped in the air as if swatting at a menacing mosquito. "Coffee."

I eased out of bed and limped to the chair where Kitty had placed her ex's clothes. "And while I'm rummaging through all the kitchen drawers trying to find the stuff for the coffeemaker, I want you to dream about how much cash you can get your hands on today."

$$58$$

While the coffee brewed, I showered, and then I dressed. Though another man's clothes felt strange, they were clean and fit, almost. The belt she'd left compensated for the pant's large waistband.

I woke Kitty with a steaming mug. She grumbled for me to leave. I returned to the kitchen. I sipped coffee and used my phone's GPS to locate Kitty's home and then searched for lottery ticket sellers in the general area near the soup kitchen.

A half pot of coffee and three ticket locations later, Miss Kitty made her grand entrance, trailed by a wispy scent of vanilla. Her hair was combed, make-up light but noticeable, and her demeanor seemed close to human. But there was a problem. She wore nothing but a short, pink, transparent teddy.

She held her arms out to her sides and pirouetted. "What do you think?"

No woman had ever made me want her as much as I wanted Kitty. The thought gave me a twinge of guilt about Bean. But the reaction was quickly erased by Bean's lies. It was sad to think the Bean I had known and loved no longer existed.

I consumed Kitty with my eyes. "I can't." My words sounded subservient.

She smiled. "Good, the teddy is doing its job." She swayed her way to me, wrapped her arms around my neck, and pressed her curves into mine.

She looked up at me, her head slightly tilted. "I called in sick and so did you." She pecked my lips.

Thank God she hadn't given me one of her soft kisses, I'd been totally subjugated.

"Pour me another mug of coffee, grab some snacks, and let's spend the day in bed," she half-whispered, her lips inches from mine.

I wanted her, but not as much as I wanted revenge. I pulled her arms off my neck and eased her to arms' length. "Get dressed. We've got things to do."

Her eyes played tag with mine, going from one to the other and then back. "No one knows about this place. You turned off your phone yesterday. We're safe here. Your girlfriend is a memory, or at least she should be after last night." An eyebrow rose, and a smile flashed across her otherwise pleading expression. "I want you and you want me, and we have a whole undisturbed day to enjoy each other and get to know each other. Now what 'things' could be more important than that?" Her blue eyes sparkled as she thumbed one of her spaghetti straps off her shoulder and let it slid down her arm.

I gulped some restraint. "Did you think about what I asked you to dream about?"

Her features scrunched as her eyes looked up and away. "You mean about how much cash could I get today?"

"Yeah." Sandbagging my flooding testosterone, I pushed the strap up, onto her shoulder.

She sighed and placed her hands on her covered though visible hips. "Gramps taught me a long time ago to keep a stash of 'walk-away' money. Will twenty-grand take care of your needs?"

"A thousand would do nicely."

She pushed my arms aside, stepped closer, and undid my belt. "We can talk about for what later."

I stopped her skilled hands and re-hooked my belt. "You and I need to go see some people about buying some Powerball tickets; three or four hundred would be a good number."

She stepped back, brows arched. "Why?"

"Get dressed and I'll tell you. Please."

Head down, she slumped off into her bedroom.

Five minutes later, to my surprise, she returned, still wearing the teddy. My id wished she would've changed because she did more for the sexy garment than it did for her. I had to fight the stirrings from my conscience-less organ.

I flipped my arms out to my sides. "What now?"

"Why do you want to buy Powerball tickets? What's going on?"

"Like I said, 'get dressed, and I'll tell you.'"

"I don't like this game," she said.

"It's not a game."

"Then tell me now." Her sapphire eyes pleaded.

I wanted to think about how to answer her, but there wasn't any time. Plus, I didn't like games either. "When, ah, when I found Andrew, dead in his home, he," my gaze slid away from her captivating body, seeing nothing but the hand-scrawled figures, "he had a note in his shirt pocket. Numbers ... all that was written on the paper were numbers, five coma-separated numbers followed by a dashed sixth and three slashed-numbers, today's date. The six other numbers had to be Powerball numbers. Andrew, or someone, had rigged the drawing one last time, tonight's drawing."

My eyes returned to her seeking a response. She stood slump-shouldered with her head bowed. One of her arms folded over her visible breasts and her other hand covered her groin.

"What's wrong?" I asked, stepping closer and clutching one of her arms.

"I've been such a fool." She shook her bowed head. "You don't trust me. After everything we've been through together, you still keep things from me." Her sad, imploring eyes found mine. "Why? What else are you hiding?"

I squeezed her arm. "Nothing." I hadn't meant to hurt her. I paused collecting my thoughts. "Listen to me for a second. People are dying all around me, people I know, and the woman I thought I knew and ... and loved was using me, how could I trust anyone?"

She pulled away from my grasp. "I trusted you."

"Why not, you researched me before you hired me, plus people were dying before I got here."

"So, do you trust me now, this very minute?" Her eyes searched mine.

"I do." And I did, though blindly and unearned. Was I like a shipwrecked sailor floundering in the ocean for something to cling to? If so, I didn't care, she was keeping me afloat.

"Do you? Did you keep the note you found on Andrew?"

"Yes."

With lips pursed, she nodded her head. "Then tell me where it is, or show it to me?"

My hand patted my pants pocket, her ex's pants. "Ah, it's in your bathroom, in a sink drawer, with my watch, wallet, and gun."

"Really?"

I took her arm. "I'll show you."

She pulled free. "That's okay. I don't need to see it. I *trust* you."

My gaze shifted away. "I deserved that."

"Do you *really* think I'm involved in these killings?"

I just stood there. I didn't have a good answer.

"You can't answer me." She exhaled a disgusted sigh. "And what makes you think either of us could buy lottery tickets? Oh, I guess we could buy them, but we could never cash them in, we're both affiliated with the lottery. We can't legally play."

"I've got that covered."

"Oh, another secret?"

Before I could respond, she snatched my phone off the kitchen table. "I need to borrow this," she said, holding the phone toward me. "I'm getting dressed." She darted into her bedroom, and closed the door, leaving an angry sob in her wake.

(59)

Kitty had been in her bedroom longer than my guilt would allow. She was right, and I had been wrong; wrong to have kept secrets.

I took a step toward the closed door to her room. A thought blocked my path. Kitty said Andrew wanted out of the lottery fraud. But what if Andrew and Bean wanted one last big pay-off and Camden found out about it? What if the Andrew's killer had visited him that night because he knew Andrew had made another substitute video? Rattled by the surprise visitor, Andrew hid the numbers in his pocket. And Bean and I arrived before the killer could search everywhere. The police hadn't found the numbers and exposed the lottery fraud, so the killer suspected I found them and purposely let me live, a shot to the leg versus the head.

Bean had to know the numbers. Kitty was right, Andrew couldn't buy or cash-in lottery tickets, but Bean could. A truth-enlightening shudder jolted my limbs. Bean had seen me studying the note I had found on Andrew. She had asked me about it. Maybe Bean had shot me. She wouldn't or would she?

What if Kitty and Camden were partners, and she knew about the note? I rubbed my temples.

Kitty was a governor striving to climb the political chain. She didn't need money, I looked around, she had tons of bucks, and her gramps had even more, mega-more. Kitty had recruited me because she was scared, not greedy, like Andrew or Bean. And unlike Bean, Kitty wanted me, both an exhilarating and refreshing thought.

I had 'what-ifed' myself into a mental corner. I blew out a long breath. It was time to call Peterson and tell him everything and let him sort it out. Kitty was right, we should just stay here. We were safe here. Forget about buying tickets and the drawing, forget about everything in the past, including Bean.

I knocked softly on her door. "Kitty, I'm sorry. You're right. I have no reason not to trust you. And I feel we—" I took a deep breath—"there's more to us than just the sex. Although I've never wanted another woman as much as I want you. I … I both care about you and trust you. And when all this is over, I want to spend some normal time with you, away from here on some quiet beach. Let's call Peterson, I'll tell him all I know, and let him handle this. Then we can spend the rest of the day, in bed, getting to know each other. I'd love to do nothing else but talk and mountain-climb all day and all night."

Nothing but silence responded.

I knocked again, harder, louder.

"Kitty? Answer me. Are you okay?" I tried the door; it was locked. Strange. She had nothing to hide.

I pounded on the door. "Kitty, open the door."

Nothing. Why? Had the killer come back? Was he in the bedroom muffling Kitty's attempts to scream for help? Had he hurt her? I slammed my shoulder into the door and bounced off. The ten-foot high door was solid wood, not a fabricated, hollow door. My aching shoulder informed me I couldn't force it open.

I checked the handle and headed for the kitchen. I rummaged through drawers until I found a box of toothpicks.

Back at the bedroom door, I inserted a toothpick into the small, round aperture in the handle. The lock released. I opened the door and rushed inside. The teddy was on the bed, and Kitty wasn't in it. I searched the bedroom and bathroom. Kitty was gone and so were Andrew's note, my Beretta, my phone, and my wallet. I checked the French doors leading to the outside patio and hot tub. They were unlocked. I ran outside around the house to the driveway. Her Jaguar was gone.

She'd taken the lottery numbers, my gun, and my phone and left me here, defenseless.

I shook my head. I must have 'easy' scrolled on my forehead, everyone used me. How could two women fool me so badly? My hands clenched into white-knuckled fists. "Son-of-a-bitch!" I screamed into the emptiness.

A thought, a survival instinct, pushed my anger away.

Worse than being used, I was afraid I was no longer needed by Miss Kitty. I had become expendable.

$$\textcircled{60}$$

The rim of the late morning sun kissed vertical as I approached the detached garage, a leg and mind wounded man in another man's clothes. Though I didn't think it was possible, my ego physically ached.

I needed wheels. Peering through a side window, the garage was empty. I had scurried around Kitty's country estate on a gimpy leg like a starving man chasing a rabbit, from outbuilding to outbuilding. The maintenance shed was just that, a shelter for landscaping tools and equipment. I didn't think I'd get very far on a Cub Cadet riding lawnmower. I could see a barn roof over a distant hill; so I limped toward it.

The barn was locked with an armed, flashing red light, security system. With my leg bitching about the hike, I peered through a dust-covered window. The barn contained two John Deere Tractors and two Polaris four-wheelers. If any of those transporters had an ignition key and gas, I had wheels-ish. I had driven both types of equipment in my life, tractors for my grandfather during the summers when I was a teenager and four-wheelers with a high-school buddy on his daddy's farm.

Now all I needed was a barn key. If I broke into the barn and set off the alarm a four-wheeler or a tractor would probably not speed me away from the police unless I went cross-country. And how far could I get before I ran into a fence or a stream? I could head east on the highways. But even if I were lucky enough to find Columbia without getting pulled over for riding a stolen four-wheeler on the road, what would I do then? I had no clue where Kitty went. And I didn't know where Bean was. So what would I do?

A thought slammed me. I could go to the drawing tonight, after all I was the State Lottery Commissioner in charge of auditing. There would have to be a diversion and a substitute video. And the person who substituted the video would be there. Maybe I could tell who replaced the tape. I picked up a rock.

A side window to the barn gleamed vulnerable in the noonday sun. I stood in front of the window tossing the rock from one hand to the other. I hated people who damaged the property of others, and I hated thieves. Plus I had a better chance with no alarms. The drawing wasn't until almost eleven o'clock tonight. I had time or did I? I understood why Kitty had taken the lottery numbers, but why my gun and my phone? Maybe the intruder at the B&B hadn't followed her; maybe she'd brought him there. Had anything she told me about Peterson or Bean been true?

I shattered the window with the rock. The alarm pulsed a high pitched ear-hurting screech. I climbed inside and smashed the alarm box with the shovel, silencing the noise, although I was sure it was still sounding in the house as well as at the alarm company.

The four-wheelers both had keys and full gas tanks. I mounted a blue one and keyed its engine to life. I eased out the clutch and rolled out of the barn. I bounced over the dirt trail that ran past the house and up the wooded hill blocking the house from the road. When I reached the dense-tree summit a flash of light from the driveway near the road focused my attention. I stopped the four-wheeler. A black Chevrolet slowly rolled on the drive toward the curve around the hill. I shut off the putt-putting motor.

The car stopped in the curve hidden from the house by the hill. Nick or Jim Sanders got out, gun in hand.

I had watched enough television and read enough to know the FBI never went alone after a suspect. Mr. Sanders had just confirmed my suspicions, he wasn't with the FBI. But he had come looking for either me or Kitty with a gun. Or Kitty had sent him here for me. No matter, the man was a liar with a gun at 'a place no one knew about.' I was in deep shit.

My hand instinctively reached behind me to my waistline and found nothing. Kitty had taken my gun, maybe now I knew why.

(61)

Sanders trotted to the base of the hill and peered around at the house. I had no doubts, he was looking for me; no he was hunting me. He maneuvered from one bush to another until he reached the house and then eased his way to the front door.

It was my turn to make some moves. I skidded from tree to tree down the steep slope of the hill toward Sanders' car. A man who possibly may have to make a quick getaway would surely leave the keys in the ignition.

I fell and slid on my butt for twenty or thirty feet and grabbed a tree to stop my slide. I got up and limp-hopped to the flat ground. I ran as fast as my leg could go to the car. The keys were in the ignition. *Thank you, Lord.*

I eased the car door open, slid in, and started the car. The engine roared to life, way too loud. I jerked it into gear, spun the wheel, and swung the car around over the grass and back onto the driveway heading toward the road. I floored the gas. As I turned onto the road going back in the direction Kitty had come from, a gunshot caused me to duck while something plinked into the body of the car. I pressed the jammed accelerator even harder against the floor. Mr. Sanders definitely wasn't here to sell encyclopedias.

A curvy mile or so later, I eased up and began driving normally. The road was one small knob after another with too many curves. I could almost relax at thirty-miles-per-hour. My search for lottery ticket-sellers had verified where Kitty's home was located. Although I hadn't memorized the directions, I knew I had to head east.

Tonight was the Powerball drawing, and Kitty had the numbers. She no longer needed me, so she had sent Sanders to kill me. How else would he have known how to find me?

I checked the glove box and the console hoping to find a weapon. They were empty except for a tire gauge in the glove box.

No manuals, no maps, just a tire gauge, strange.

As I straightened up behind the wheel from my search, movement in the mirror caught my eye. The blue four-wheeler had rounded a curve about a half mile behind me and was gaining ground.

(62)

I had taken the car versus the off-road vehicle because I needed a car to enter the city. If I had been familiar with this road, I would have taken the four wheeler's keys.

I had enough experience on a four-wheeler to know the man with the gun chasing me had the advantage. The unfamiliar road had too many blind curves hidden by small humps in the pavement for me to out run a four-wheeler. When Sanders got close enough, he'd start shooting and both the chase and I would be finished. There was only one solution. I cinched my seat belt as tight as it would go.

As I negotiated the car over a knob, a county sheriff's car passed me going the opposite direction. I checked my rearview and watched the 'county-mountie' disappear over a hill. Either his presence on this road was a coincidence, or he was responding to the alarm I had set off by breaking into the barn.

Maybe he'd stop Sanders for driving an off-road vehicle on a county highway. I doubted it, my luck wasn't that good.

A moment later, I saw Sanders top a hill. I accelerated as fast as I dare and repeatedly checked my mirrors to see if the cop had turned around to pursue him. A mile later the only thing I could see was that damned four-wheeler gaining ground.

My time was limited by the closing rate of Sanders, too limited for the time it would take for the cop to check out Kitty's estate and head back this way. I had to act now.

Traversing a knob, I saw a driveway and braked hard. I sideslipped the sedan into the gravel path, reversed onto the road, and headed in the direction of the oncoming four-wheeler. I may not have a gun, but I had mass on my side.

Just as I popped over the small hill, Mr. Sanders in his off-road vehicle was just rounding a curve at the base of the hill. I floored the gas, yanked the steering wheel left into his path, braced with gritted teeth, and slammed into the driver's side of his front bumper. I don't know how I did it, but I kept my eyes open and the gas-peddle floored through impact. There was a horrendous jolt accompanied by the sound of metal crunching metal. And as if in slow motion, I watched the four-wheeler rise off the ground and flip over top of my car just before my vision became blocked by an airbag. Something burned my face. I locked the brakes and listened to the tires scream as the car spun around and around. When my car finally stopped, the airbag collapsed. I was staring through burning eyes at the spinning tires of the up-side-down four-wheeler in a ditch on the opposite side of the road. Smoke wafted from the front of the inverted vehicle.

I checked my hands and arms and couldn't feel or see any damage. I wiped my eyes and face on my shirt sleeve, relieving the burning. My legs and feet moved without any additional pain. I unhooked the seat belt, forced open the jammed door, and eased my way to my feet. Except for chemical burns from the airbag and my prior leg wound, I was fine.

I looked around for a weapon, a stick, a rock, anything, but there wasn't anything usable in sight.

I ran to the overturned four-wheeler. It was in a deep ditch. I slid down the driver's side of the ditch, dropped to my hands and knees, and peered under the vehicle. The roll bar had dropped into the crevice slamming the strapped in Sanders head-first into the opposite embankment. His head was at an odd angle to his body. His contorted face and fixed eyes were turned toward me. He was dead.

I had no remorse, none.

I looked under and all around the wreck for the gun but didn't find it.

All the kneeling and clamoring in and out of the deep ditch had made my leg wound sing.

I gimped back to the Chevrolet. The left front head light and fender were destroyed. But the car started and rolled, although things scrapped and ground if I turned too hard to the left.

I headed toward Columbia. I had a meeting to attend.

(63)

An hour after leaving the 'scene of the crime', I sat on a park bench, three blocks from Sally Kellerman's office. The Lottery drawings were performed in the basement of that building.

I had left Sander's wrecked Chevrolet parked on the street a few blocks in the other direction from the park.

I was hungry but had no money, no credit cards, no wallet; nothing but a set of car keys. The last time I'd eaten was last night when Kitty and I had eaten sandwiches and snacks after our sexual escapades. My stomach growled. What I wouldn't give for a cup of that soup I used to hand out. Now I understood the look on most of the faces across the table at the soup kitchen.

I would've had no clue about the time except there was a clock mounted on a post in the park, how convenient. It was half-past three in the afternoon. I had more than seven hours to kill. I couldn't sit here that long, no way.

A thought pulled me to my feet. I hadn't really searched Sander's car. He had to have clothes and stuff somewhere like the trunk. Maybe he'd left a hotel room key in the trunk or under the seat. I had nothing better to do, so I limped back to the car.

The trunk was spotless and empty. As I rummaged under the driver's seat, my hand found something, an envelope. I pulled it out and it bulged. I opened it. I was jammed with one-hundred dollar bills, thousands of dollars. I sat in the seat, closed and locked the doors, and counted; there were a couple dozen hundred-dollar-bills shy of ten thousand dollars. Maybe I was in the wrong business. Nah, I had done more than my share of killing in the service. Money wasn't an incentive for taking a life.

It was time to eat.

$$\textbf{64}$$

Even though my clothes didn't fit, and they weren't dress clothes; I didn't care. I walked into what looked to be a nice restaurant between the Chevrolet and the park. The eatery was called the Full Fishnet Restaurant. It was a little after four, too late for lunch and too early for supper. Except for three people sitting at the bar, the place was empty.

After having to almost lasso and hog-tie a waiter, I ordered surf and turf and all the trimmings, including escargot for an appetizer. I would've order the best wine, but I couldn't afford to dull my senses. The surprised waiter explained that my order would take a while since the staff wasn't quite prepared for dinner service yet. I nodded. I had lots of time.

Three cups of coffee and a tossed salad with too much buttered German bread later, my meal was served. The filet was cooked perfectly, medium-well, and the lobster was steamed and ready for dipping in the drawn butter. My mouth salivated as I cut into the steak.

After I had consumed half the filet and lobster, I was dipping a forkful of Maine lobster tail into the cup of drawn butter when something stopped me. When things happen like that, they're hard to explain; I had this strange feeling someone was staring at me. It's the closest I'll ever come to telepathy or extrasensory perception. Regardless of whatever was occurring, I knew it to be real. The hairs on my arms bristled, I was vulnerable, exposed. My short-term-memory-hand quickly dove behind me and vainly searched the waistline of my pants for my gun. I glanced around and there standing at the entrance to the restaurant was Kitty, not Governor Franklin, or Katharine Franklin, or Miss 'Umm-umm' Kitty, just Kitty, standing there staring at me with those bluer than blue eyes.

God she was beautiful.

(65)

The previous impressive ambiance of the Full Fishnet Restaurant faded into a dull backdrop after Kitty Franklin appeared.

Kitty had changed clothes since I'd last seen her. The loose fitting smock had been exchanged for a form-fitting high-necked, knee-length, satin green dress with matching green heels. Her hair looked like it had been styled, and her make-up was perfect.

What was she doing here? How'd she know I was here? And why was she dressed like that? She looked ready for work. If she knew I was here, who else did?

I wondered if she enjoyed toying with my feelings, first the trust, than the lust, and now the disgust. Who was she?

I watched her glide across the room, her dark hair flowing in her wake, her hips swaying to a slow, captivating song.

I needed to fear her, to protect myself with the steak knife, but there was this serge of warmth throughout my being. I wanted her. I was a penis-controlled fool and didn't care.

She stopped at my table, her magnolia scent catching and passing her, and bathing me.

"Hello, Brent," she said in a normal tone.

"Hello, Governor," I responded as calm as my struggling self-control could muster.

"May I join you?"

I motioned at the chair across from me.

She sat in the chair next to me.

I opened my mouth to speak and her fingers touched my lips.

She shook her head. "You eat, and I'll talk." Her hand dropped from my mouth to my hand. "Surprised that I found you? I'll bet." Her head nodded at me. "The clothes, my so-called ex's clothes, they're bugged." She patted my hand. "But I'm sure you're glad to see me." She guided my hand between her breasts and pressed it against something hard, foreign. "I picked this dress out just for you and," her forefinger of her other hand bridged her lips, "and the meeting I have to go to with the DOT later." She slid a hand behind her head as if to message her neck, lifting her hair off an ear exposing an ear-piece. "Think those highway boys will like it?" She was wired. Someone was feeding her words and listening. We were being monitored.

"You'll have them eating out of your hand," I said. "So what's going on?"

She wagged a finger at me. "You're 'spose to be eating while I talk."

For some unexplained reason, like a Pavlov dog, I put the forkful of butter-dripping lobster in my mouth.

She sighed. "You're more resourceful than we thought."

The 'we' had me baffled. And I'm sure my expression telegraphed my reaction.

"Mr. Smith, er, Sanders, was supposed to, ah, take care of you. But since you're still here," she pressed her hands together as if her prayer had been answered, "and the police know you found Andrew, you have become the last missing piece to the puzzle. We assumed you came here to go to the drawing tonight. That's perfect. We want you to go." A tear streaked her cheek. "Someone had to take Andrew's place to rig the drawing. Who better than his sister's newly appointed Lottery Commissioner live-in boyfriend. The man who has decided to eliminate all his ties, Andrew, Sanders, and … and Robin—"

I swallowed the half-chewed meat.

"And keep the last big lottery pot all to yourself and run." Kitty continued after my choking swallow. "After you found out Andrew and Robin were hiding money from you in a Swiss account, cheating you, why not? Perfect."

I stared at Kitty. Her lips quivered, and her eyes brimmed with tears.

Bean was dead. Rage boiled inside me. I wanted to turn the table over and throw the chairs and break—it didn't matter. I gulped some air and flexed my fisted hands. Kitty was just a messenger. Or was she?

Bean *had* been kidnapped, but not by some vindictive Kitty hater. The lottery thieves had taken her and fed me a story so I'd find out how Andrew had rigged the lottery and not go to the authorities. They wanted one more, big score. So then they convinced me Bean hadn't been kidnapped, but was involved in the lottery fraud. They turned my trust to Kitty, playing me, until I revealed everything I knew, including the drawing numbers.

We had all been used, Andrew, Bean, and me. And when Andrew and Bean's usefulness had been spent, they had been killed. I'd probably soon be just as dead.

My tiny little Bean, murdered, gone, and to think I had thought she was involved, thought her to be a liar, a cheat, a—such a fool, I was such a fool. Someone had to pay.

"Hear my words." My voice failed to squelch my rage. "I'm not going to do anything you ask. All I'm going to do is find you, all of you, and kill each and every one of you."

She shook her head. "You'll do as we say. Robin is still alive and well, and she'll be released if you cooperate." Kitty reached into her purse and removed an envelope and handed it to me.

I tore the envelope open and found a time-dated picture of Bean, naked, gagged, and tied spread-eagled to a bed. Her almost black eyes were wide open as if voicing a plea. The time stamp was an hour ago.

"After all, we need someone to cash in the winning ticket, and it can't be you or me," Kitty said, parroting the words spoken to her.

Kitty fidgeted in her purse and removed a little cardboard box. "You need to put these on before I leave. There's an ear-plug receiver and a clip-on miniature microphone. Put them on, and leave them on, if you want to see Bean again."

I opened the box and clipped the mic to my collar and inserted the plug into my ear.

Kitty dabbed her mascara-smudged eyes with a napkin and stood.

"Good luck, Brent. I—I hope ... good luck."

"Where are you going? What's going to happen to—"

"Be quiet!" a deep male voice boomed in my ear.

I wasn't sure it was the same voice as before. They both had been enhanced by a modulator of some kind.

"From now on you only speak when told to speak and what to say." The voice ordered. "Do you understand?"

This male voice seemed different; raspier. Could they be different people?

My focus was diverted by Kitty. I watched her walk away as I sucked in a gulp of air to smother my frustration. "Yes, I understand."

I wondered if I would ever see Kitty again.

(66)

I sat at a table in the almost empty Full Fishnet Restaurant with a half-eaten plate of 'serf & turf', losing both its warmth and its appeal, in front of me.

Kitty's magnolia scent lingered. Though Bean was still alive, I wanted Kitty to return.

The attention-focusing deep voice spoke into my ear piece, "In retrospect, it was probably a bad idea to order Smith to kill you … particularly for Smith. Plus we couldn't get Kitty to leave you at her country home. We had to gag and drag her out of her home. Not a pretty scene. Besides, you've been very helpful. Not only did you provide us with the winning Lottery numbers for tonight's drawing, but with you alive, it's much easier to get Robin, er, ah Bean to buy the winning lottery ticket for us. Which, by the way, she's doing as we speak. She isn't alone, mind you, but she is also wired up and listening right now. Would you like to say hello? Just be wise about your words, as I said she isn't alone. And neither are you."

"Bean?" My eyes scanned the restaurant until I found a man with a NFL lineman's width and breadth seated at the bar with his glass raised toward me.

"She can only hear you," the deep voice said. "She can't talk to you."

"Bean, I'm so sorry about all of this. I should've quit when you wanted me to. Bean—run, run now!"

"That was real bright, Layne. Do you want her manhandled or worse?

193

We can oblige. We've all had her; so smacking her around a little is no big thing. We've all done that too. It made her much more willing and even aggressive the second and third times, or was it the fifth and sixth?"

My internal pressure rose to eye-bulging. Bastards, spine-less hiding-behind-microphones bastards.

"I will kill you."

The man chuckled. "Oh yeah, I almost forgot … the special ops guy, the killer. Which reminds me," he coughed and cleared his throat, "now it's your turn to be of service."

Brent nodded as if there were another person present. "I knew there was another reason I was still around."

"Aren't you astute?" The man coughed again. "Kitty is waiting for you outside. She's in her limo."

As if on cue, the big man at the bar stood and walked toward me. He had a folded newspaper under his arm. He stopped at my table, towering above me, and put the paper on my table and slid it next to my place setting.

"There's a loaded snub-nose .38 inside the paper," deep voice said. "If you try to take it out of the paper before you get into the limo, both you and Bean will die."

I watched the big man's broad back as he walked back to his bar stool.

"Take the folded paper and join the governor in her limo," deep voice ordered. "And then kill her and her driver. If you don't, Bean will die."

(67)

I sat in the Full Fishnet Restaurant staring at a folded newspaper on my table. The deep voice in the microphone in my ear had said there was a gun wrapped in the paper.

This was crazy. I was being told to kill Kitty and her driver, or Bean would die. Hell, Bean would probably die anyway. And how could I kill Kitty? I couldn't even kill her driver, a man I didn't know.

Yeah, I had killed before, but that was war, an enemy I didn't know who was trying to kill me and my men. And even then the killing wasn't easy. Taking another person's life robbed you of your innocence, scrambled your scruples, and left an indelible mark, a scar, on your soul, a never forgotten night-visiting memory.

I was exhausted, my mind numb, and I had no time to gather my thoughts. I picked up the paper with hands that trembled from fear mixed with rage.

A thought slapped me, what if Bean was dirty? What if she was an accomplice to deep voice? What's a naked photo amongst lovers? And Kitty, who must be innocent or they wouldn't want me to kill her, had said her FBI friend had talked to Bean at her parents' house.

Who should I believe?

Throughout this nightmare, I had been kept stupid and used. I was sick of it. Could I dare risk Bean's life?

Bean hadn't been blindfolded in the picture. Was that a mistake? Or had her kidnappers worn masks? If she wasn't an accomplice, they couldn't let her live. She had to have seen and heard things, body markings, sizes, voices, too many things to be left alive.

I couldn't kill Kitty, but could I be responsible for Bean's death?

A rambling idea caused me to stuff my napkin into the newspaper when the monster man wasn't looking. I couldn't kill Kitty, but I couldn't let her talk either. She talked too much anyway.

I got up and walked to the door.

They'd had given the wrong man a gun.

68

Toting the newspaper-wrapped gun was like carrying the execution order for a friend, or maybe more than a friend, a lover. The door to the restaurant was too close, I needed time to think, but I was already there, my shaking hand on the knob.

I glanced over my shoulder and the big man sitting at the bar, perched like an elephant on a milking stool, watched me. He whispered into the lapel of his suit coat.

I had no choice, I couldn't hesitate; the big man would get suspicious. I opened the door and went out into the warm, sun-setting air.

I slid my hand into the paper and clutched the pistol and napkin. I was oblivious to the rush-hour people and cars flowing by me, heading home. All I could see was the large limo with its opaque windows idling at the curb. Unbeknownst to Kitty, the extended black limousine was, per deep voice's orders, soon to become her hearse.

(69)

The twenty feet or so from the restaurant's front door to the curb-side limo seemed like a mile of anxiety and a foot for planning.

Kitty's driver had to be a bodyguard, which meant he was packing. I'd have to deal with him first.

When the limo was between me and the restaurant, I eased the napkin out of the paper, unclipped the microphone from my collar, wrapped it in the napkin and shoved it into my pants.

I let the newspaper fall to the ground and flipped open the gun's cylinder. All six chambers were loaded. I snapped the cylinder back into place.

I tapped on the driver's window. And I-think-his-name-was-George opened the window.

As always when the governor was on board, the blackened window was raised between the front seat and the rear compartment. Kitty couldn't see or hear what I was doing.

Cocking the gun, I jammed the barrel through the opening against the driver's cheek.

"George, right?"

"Ya—yes, Mr. La—layne." The man's eyes were wide with fright.

"Carefully remove your weapon and place it on the dash. Then unlock the door and slide over and face the side window and don't say a word."

George obeyed. His weapon, lying on the dash, was a 9mm Glock.

Keeping my gun aimed at George, I got in, closed the door, and placed his gun between me and my door.

I reached into my pocket and removed the napkin and unfolded it revealing the microphone.

I scanned the dash and found the button for the glass divider and lowered it.

Kitty leaned forward and her brilliant blue eyes enlarged. "Brent what are you—"

I crossed the gun barrel over my lips and opened the sunroof.

Then I extended my napkin-holding hand into the rear compartment and motioned at her to remove her microphone and put it into the napkin.

She did.

When her clipped transmitter hit the napkin, I fired a shot through the roof opening. It sounded like a cannon had discharged in the close quarters.

The driver spun around to find my gun in his face.

I motioned for him to turn around and waited for Kitty to stop screaming. Then I fired two more rounds through the gapped sunroof. I squeezed the napkin closed around the microphones and stuffed the wadded cloth into my pants pocket.

I levered the car into gear and sped away. A glance in the rearview mirror confirmed my expectations; the thug from the restaurant was at curbside with his back to me waving. He must have more associates in the area. But he was too late, as I maneuvered the long limo around a corner.

(70)

I turned on the limo's radio and jacked up the volume as I mirror monitored; no followers. After putting six staggered city blocks between me and the restaurant, I leaned over to the driver.

"Relax, George, I'm not going to hurt anyone, just be quiet and everything will be fine," I whispered.

George looked over his shoulder to see if the governor was okay.

I glanced in the mirror and saw Kitty give George the thumbs up.

"Layne, what the hell happened?" deep voice asked. "Where do you think you're going?"

I drove with my gun hand and fidgeted in my pocket with the other. If George were half the man I thought he was, he could've subdued me then.

He just sat there and watched me.

Frantically I pulled out the wadded up napkin out of my pocket and placed in on the bench seat.

George helped me straightened the cloth exposing the two microphones, exact replicas.

Which one was mine? I couldn't hear Kitty talking when I was in the restaurant, and I'm sure she was, so the two mics had to be set on different frequencies. If I used the wrong one, deep voice would know I was messing with him.

I picked one of the microphones up and smelled it, nothing. Then I smelled the other one, magnolia, Kitty's mic.

I clipped on the non-Kitty's mic. "They're dead; both of them. At least I guess they are. They're both still and gushing blood."

"What took you so long to respond?"

"The governor tried to get to the gun, and she knocked my mic off. I had to pull over and retrieve it from the floor."

"I want to see the bodies."

"And I don't want to die in prison. A whole bunch of people had to have heard those shots. You can see the bodies on the six o'clock news after I dump them somewhere."

"Don't fuck with me, Layne, or I'll—"

"Shut up! I did what you asked. Now tell me where I can find Bean. And she'd better be alive and well."

"She'll be at the governor's country house, in the cabana by the pool."

"No. You leave her somewhere in the city where it's crowded." My mind ached in search of a good spot. "I know; the underground parking lot below the Capital Building."

The mic was silent for a moment, and then a deep chuckle focused my attention.

"You're arrogance astounds me. I give the orders here. You are powerless. The slightly used but still kicking Bean will be at the cabana, ah, or maybe somewhere else, maybe the garage. She'll be there after the drawing—" he coughed—"a week after, or maybe a month." His laughter interspersed with hacks.

"What? You said—" the receiver became lifeless, nothing, he was gone.

Fucker. I tore off the mic and pulled out the ear plug.

71

I rolled the limo to the curb five or six blocks from The Full Fishnet Restaurant. My hands were shaking from the prior adrenaline rush.

"George, take over, I need to talk to the governor."

"Hold up," Kitty said from the rear compartment. "Before you do anything, you need to ditch your clothing and that gun. There's at least one bug, maybe more, somewhere in those clothes and I'm sure they are planning someway to use that gun with your prints on it. I know, they gave the clothes to me and insisted I make you wear them."

I glanced at her beautiful, squinted blue eyes in the rearview mirror. "What do you suggest? Oh, wait, I know, you want me to come back there and strip naked and throw the clothing out the window."

A smile creased her lovely features. I needed her smile. Hell, we both needed some form of relief. Maybe I would get in the back, and we'd both get naked.

Her smile faded as she chewed on her lower lip and rubbed her chin with her thumb and forefinger. Then she snapped her fingers. "I've got it. Both of you get back here and I'll drive. You're about the same size. You two exchange clothes, while I drive to a rental car company. Then George you need to take the limo on a long drive somewhere."

I nodded as I climbed out of the car. I trusted Kitty. I really didn't have much choice, but I did.

Kitty and I traded places, and George and I traded clothes down to my

202

underwear which I discarded; a strange experience, but necessary.

A wiped cleaned, trashed gun and a rental car later, George was on his way in my clothes and alone in Kitty's limo, minus a pair of binoculars, his gun, and a Tazor. He was headed to Bean's parents' home to see if by chance she was there. Plus, it was a trip deep voice may think logical.

Wearing George's gray slacks and white starched shirt, black socks and black too-large shoes, I drove with no destination and Kitty sat next to me, in her pretty dress, playing with my fingers. And despite the shithole I had fallen into, she again was able to distract my thoughts.

There was something about this woman that went beyond her beauty and her curvaceous sex appeal, something I wanted to know more about.

(72)

I drove Kitty in George's rented gray Ford Escape out of the rental company's parking lot. This was the first time we'd been alone since we were at her country home, an eternity ago.

"Any ideas where we can go for a while ... until the drawing?" I asked.

She grabbed my arm. "You're not really planning to go to the drawing, are you?"

"You know a better way for me to find out who's behind all this?"

She blew out a long breath. "We need to talk."

I nodded. "Where?"

Her thumb and forefinger jumped to her chin; thinking mode. "I've got it, the perfect place where no one would ever look for us."

⑦③

Kitty and I sat side-by-side on a leather couch in Andrew's study, away from the great room with its blood-stained carpet. The glow of the fading sun was losing its battle with the darkness.

I never liked going back to places where I'd lost men, people I knew, in either Iraq or Afghanistan. I don't know how others felt, but to me, death seemed to leave an invisible but irremovable residue. The places were forever tainted by images, smells, horrors, and ghastly sadness, things that needed to be buried in mental recesses, but couldn't, not if you were there again.

Kitty was right; no one would ever look for us here. It was the last place I wanted to be.

"I'd ask you how you knew where Andrew's back-up key was hidden, but I don't want to know," I said as my eyes scanned the room.

"You need to know. My only response is the truth." She wiggled her torso more upright on the couch and her snug, green satin dress rode up her smooth thighs. "Andrew was my confidant, never my lover."

"Okay, I believe you." I dreaded the next subject more than the hidden key. I sighed and turned to face her. "You said earlier that 'they insisted' you make me wear the bugged clothes. Who and how?"

She reached over and took my hand and played with my fingers. She had to know that was one of my weaknesses.

She lightly touched my face with her free hand. Her fingers conveyed soft, warm, wonderful feelings.

I prayed her gestures were sincere. Although my first priority was still to find Bean and the truth, I cared for this woman. I had no clue what I'd do after I found Bean. I just wanted to find her ... alive.

Kitty dropped her hand to mine and squeezed my hand with both hers. "There's something I need to tell you. It'll probably sound weak and ... I don't know, unbelievable." Her blue eyes looked away and then returned to mine, moistened with brimming tears. "I, ah, I think ... no, I don't think, I know." Her tears streamed. "I know that I love you, Brent Layne."

(74)

Kitty Franklin, the governor of South Carolina, had just told me she loved me; me, Brent Layne, a nobody.

I sat in Andrew's dim-lighted study next to Kitty and shook my head, not in disgust but in disbelief. I didn't know if my ego or my soul wanted Kitty to love me, regardless, I wanted it. It was wrong, Bean wrong. But I didn't care, I liked hearing her say it, and how she said it. What had happened to me? Who had I become? How many times had I told Bean I loved her, and how many times had she told me? But my reaction, the feelings stirring inside me, hadn't been the same when Bean had told me she loved me. My reaction to Kitty's words had to be ego, or male-chauvinist stupidity. But I liked the stirrings.

Kitty refocused my attention by squeezing my hand again. "That first day when you walked into my office with Andrew, I knew then there was something special about you. I had this feeling, I can't describe it, it was like a desire, a need, an impulse; I had to get to know you better."

Kitty lifted my hand to her lips and softly kissed it.

Her wet, soft mouth and her words sent a warming electric current up my arms and down to my loins.

"And the more time we spent together, the more time I wanted to spend with you. It was like you had me under a spell. And then when we made love that first time, the shared feelings, your unselfish tenderness, and the never-before-reached highs, were all unbelievable. I had never experienced anything like that. I think that's when I fell in love with you."

She cleared her throat. "Since then, my feelings have gotten stronger. You're all I think about. I know you must think I'm either crazy or lying; we barely know each other. This isn't infatuation. I've been there before. I can't help how I feel. I know what love feels like, though it was a long time ago. I do love you."

She released my hand and covered her face with both her hands. She stayed that way, face buried in her hands, for what seemed like a minute.

I wanted to reach out to her, but thought better of it. There were unexplained matters on the table, a whole bunch of them.

She dropped her hands and gave me a blank stare. "With that said, it's time to get back to your 'who and how' question." She tugged on the hem of her dress. "The morning after Andrew's murder, early in the morning, around four or four-thirty, my cell phone rang and woke me. A handful of people have my cell phone number, and Andrew was one of them, his cell I.D was displayed. A man, the same man who was on the microphone today, spoke." She diverted her eyes as more tears flowed. "He told me Andrew was dead. And when I quit sobbing, he told me he knew I had Andrew rig the lottery and that there was another fixed drawing planned. He wanted the numbers and the date." She shook her head. "I told him I didn't know. He told me I'd better find out before the drawing because he had irrefutable evidence that would indict my grandfather for insider-trading as well as me for fraud and murder. He said," she looked down, "he said he owned me," her flooded eyes met mine, "and he has, ever since that call."

"And right after that, you called me using the news of Andrew's death as an excuse, a means to invite me back to Seven Gables," I said, fighting to suppress my disappointment and confusion.

She closed her eyes and nodded.

(75)

The shadows invaded and grew inside Andrew's study, as if the darkness was feeding off the dwindling light, consuming it. I finally risked turning a small desk lamp on and then returned to the couch. I pulled Kitty into my arms.

She rested her head on my chest.

I rubbed her back through the cool satin material of her green dress.

She had just admitted loving me and using me.

My head involuntarily shook from side to side. I was her stay-out-of-jail fool. Could I really believe she loved me? I wasn't sure what or who to believe anymore.

She turned, her hair brushed my chin, and her magnolia scent caressed my nose. Her smell was an aphrodisiac, a stimulus for warm, vivid memories.

I wanted to believe her. What choice did she have but to use me? I was her only means for saving both her gramps and herself.

The look on her face and the emotions in her words when she had voiced her love for me more than implied sincerity.

I was so easy, just a head turn and a sniff put my trust issues on a back burner.

Did I love her? I was confused about love because of my relationships with Bean and her. And yet I had this yearning to tell Kitty I loved her, to scream it from the top step of the State Capital Building.

Even if our love was real, where would Kitty and I go from here? What would I do about Bean? And what would we do about the caller?

Deep Voice had what he wanted; the winning Powerball ticket for tonight's drawing. Did he still want us dead? Why take the risk? Although we were the only links to him, we couldn't identify him. If he didn't try to kill us, he'd at least provide the authorities enough data to indict us. He needed someone to absorb the legal heat. We were his pawns.

I blinked away all my unanswered questions and conjectures. All those issues would have to wait until tomorrow. Today, I had only one purpose and that was to find Bean. And I had only one way to do that. I had to go to the drawing tonight.

Going to the drawing was insane. They'd expect me, and I had no means to protect myself. But what choice did I have?

I reached down, hooked Kitty's chin with a finger, and raised her face until we made eye contact.

"Where is my gun?" I asked.

Kitty's eyes darted from side to side. "Ah, they took it, the two hooded men who kidnapped me from my bedroom. They took everything, the drawing numbers, your phone, your wallet, everything."

I sighed, looked away, and bit my lower lip. I wondered who they might kill with my fingerprinted gun.

Her warm fingers brought my face back in alignment with hers. "Brent, do you love me?"

Her purse, on the floor by her feet, blasted 'The Yellow Rose of Texas".

76

The windows in Andrew's study were blackened by the darkness outside. Kitty pulled away from our embrace and reached for her music-playing purse. "Hold your response. I've got to get this. That's my new ring tone for Jeanette," she glanced at me, "ah, Ms. Cummins, my dad's ... my assistant."

She retrieved her phone. "Yes, Jeanette."

She listened and then shaking her head said, "No ... oh my God, no." Her lids-pinched eyes fixed on me. Her head shook as if trying to rid herself of what had been said. "Hold on a second, I want to put you on my speaker phone and have you repeat what you just said." She paused. "Brent, Brent Layne, the Lottery Commissioner."

Kitty pushed a button on her phone and sat it on the coffee table fronting the couch.

"Okay, Jeanette, I've got you on the speaker."

"Where are you, Governor?"

"We're safe."

"Ah, just a moment ago Casey, from down the hall, bolted in here. She was blabbing so fast I barely understood her. Anyway, she said there's a news bulletin and ... Senator Sparks was found dead this afternoon; shot, an apparent suicide. There was a note. He admitted to lottery fraud. Then a friend of mine at the precinct called and said there was a detective with a squad of policemen heading to your office with a search warrant. What's going on? Do you want me to leave and lock the place up or what?"

"Just go home," Kitty answered and disconnected.

Senator Camden Sparks was dead.

Kitty and I stared at each other in disbelief. My prior focus on getting out of this place, this dead man's home, were pushed aside. The silence was menacing.

My mind flittered like a moth at an outdoor lamp sale. And I wondered if the gun Camden had used was mine.

The good news was there was a whole bunch of less stinky fat in the world. The bad news was men with humongous egos like Camden's didn't normally commit suicide. My money was on someone killed him and left a note. Camden was a scapegoat. All this time, could Camden have been a marionette to another puppeteer? Who?

Who had the most to lose? I looked at Kitty as she sat next to me, gazing off into the shadows of the room while she wrung her hands.

I grabbed one of her hands and held it gently between mine. "Before I go to the lottery drawing, maybe we should call your gramps."

Her dull blue eyes searched mine. "What on earth for?"

"Who would want to protect you more than anyone else in this world, even me?"

Her eyes fell away. "Gramps." Then her eyes leapt back to mine. "But Gramps didn't even know Camden, let alone what he'd ... he'd done to me, or how he'd blackmailed me. And why would Gramps leave a suicide note that involved me? And obviously the note mentioned me. Why else would the police want to search my office?"

I nodded. "You've got a good point. So someone else is involved. Someone who's either desperate for money or has a motive they'd kill for. And your gramps definitely doesn't need the money."

Her eyes questioned mine. "But what about the man on the phone, he threatened to expose my grandfather. And he's proven he'd do anything to get the money from tonight's drawing. Why couldn't he be the one who killed Camden?"

"He could be. I just don't think so. I don't think the mystery man who called me, threatening Bean, is the same person who called you. I think the person who called me really hates you or your grandfather. Somehow, I think Bean's involved with that person."

I clutched her shoulders and turned her to face me.

"The man who manipulated you probably worked for Camden, or at least Camden thought he did. He was either under orders to kill Camden or got greedy. And maybe he killed Camden because he got greedy or feared Camden would give him up if he got caught. But my gut says no. I think this is more complicated than that. There's something we're missing. I think we need to look for motives other than money."

She tugged on the hem of her dress. "If I were the caller, I'd let the FBI know you were planning to attend the drawing tonight."

"Yeah, I would too."

"So what are you going to do?"

"I don't know."

The sun had set and the security of darkness made it easier for me and Kitty to drive the streets of Columbia in George's rented Ford.

"Have you ever been to a lottery drawing?" I asked as I slowed for a red light.

"I guess so, if you call the commemorative drawing a real drawing," Kitty said as an overhead streetlight slid up her face erasing the shadows masking her beauty.

I had gazed at her often, and yet I couldn't pass up another opportunity. Looking at her face had to be like a junky looking at a needle full of dope, she was my means for pleasures that got better with each dose. I had trouble assimilating that this lovely creature actually loved me. Unsure why, barring ego, I hoped her love was real.

I had to force my mind back to my mission. "What happened?"

"As I recall, it was boring as hell. They went through an in-depth explanation of each step, and its additive value to the security of the process." She yawned as if the memory invoked boredom." She crossed her legs exposing half her thighs and the streetlight caressed her muscled, shapely limbs.

"Who was there?" I refocused my eyes on the road as the light changed.

"Over and above the bevy of reporters, three or four TV people, the announcer, a make-up artist, and four or five appointed process monitors … I'd say close to ten people."

"How'd you get into the building at that late hour?" I risked another glance.

Her thumb and forefinger went to her chin, her thinking mode.

"We entered through the front door. I remember that because a guard met us at the main door and checked our I.D.'s. I thought that was rather odd with me being the governor. But he did it anyway."

"So everyone entered the building through the front door?"

"Well we did that night, I assume that's standard."

"Were there security people outside the building?"

"I don't know. I got out of the car by the front door and went inside. The front door was the check point. Both Andrew and Camden were there. And I think we had to go through a metal detector … yes, we did because Camden made a joke about the metal staves in his corset. And he winked at me and stared at my chest. The only staves he was thinking about were in my bra." She shook her head. "Is it sinful to celebrate someone's death?"

"You're asking the wrong person about sins. The war blurred my right-versus-wrong vision."

"Is that why you haven't answered my question about whether you love me or not? Because of what I … Camden and I—God the memories makes me sick. I can't even say the words. They seem so ugly when his name is included."

"I must say the thought is repulsive, but"—I took her hand—"the thought of making new memories with you overwhelms whatever happened in your past."

She squeezed my hand. "How sweet." She kissed the back of my hand resurrecting the arousing warm flow through my system. "So what is your answer?"

"I can't answer you until I have closure with Bean. You've got to understand that, don't you?"

"I'm not a person who likes being second."

"And I'm not a person who deliberately hurts someone close to me."

"That's a good trait." She patted my hand. "I'll accept that answer for the time being." She pointed ahead. "The building where the lottery drawing is held is three blocks up and two over." She glanced at her watch. "It's quarter 'til ten. The attendees will be arriving soon. What's the plan?"

Kitty and I sat in the parked car two blocks away and across the street from the government-rented building where the lottery drawing was held. A single streetlight per block dimly lit the area. There were a few other cars parked on the street, so our car didn't raise unwanted attention.

I focused George's binoculars on the lighted entrance. A State Trooper guard was moving about just inside the glass door. And the metal frame of a magnetic detector was visible just inside the door.

Kitty sneezed inches from my ear causing me to jerk.

"Bless you," I said out of habit.

"Thanks. I've been coughing and sneezing most of the day. I hope I'm not catching something. You and I would make a fine pair, sneezy and gimpy."

"Maybe you got too close to Deep Voice. He was hacking a lot when we talked to him."

"I never saw him. All his orders came via the earphones. Plus my problems are allergies, I inherited them. When I was a kid, my—"

"Whoa, some people are coming up the walk." I focused the glasses. "Two men and a woman I think." I waited for them to step under a streetlight near the building's entrance. "Wait a minute, son-of-a-bitch, I don't believe this. Did you know your secretary, Ms. Cummins, was one of the process monitors?"

"What?" Kitty snatched the binoculars.

Kitty leaned forward and propped her elbows on the dash of the rented Ford. Her shaking fingers eased the knurled focus spindle on the binoculars she had pressed to her eyes. The light from a distant streetlight glinted off her gold diamond-tipped pinky ring. She had worn a ring to a stake-out that probably cost more than all the money I had ever made.

Two blocks away and across the street, two men and a woman stopped at the entrance to the building where the lottery drawing was held.

"Son-of-a-bitch!" The words popped from Kitty's mouth. "It *is* Jeanette. What is she doing here?" She released a long sigh. "I don't recognize the two men, they could be process monitors, I wouldn't know. I didn't pay much attention to them at the commemorative drawing."

"What do you know about her?" I asked as I watched one of the men's face glow when he lit a cigarette.

"She's divorced and used to work for my father. He suggested her to me after the election. And," she lowered the binoculars, "and she's always been very reliable."

"Why the hesitation?" I asked.

"Well, ah, sometimes she seems a little nosy."

"How so?"

"Well like before, when she called to tell me about Camden, she asked where I was. She asked questions she shouldn't, like she's prying." She lifted the glasses to her face and scanned the group of people again. "Her questioning always seemed a little out of place, but I never thought much of it until now."

"The lottery scam has always been based on deception", I spoke my thoughts.

She eased forward pressing the glasses to her eyes. "That man, the one smoking, he's waving at us."

Deception—my eyes swung to the rearview mirror. A dark figure rose up behind our car and then slid out of view.

"Get out of the car. Now! And run. Run!"

I jerked open my door, leaped out and ran down the sidewalk as fast as I could. I glanced to my right and Kitty, dress hiked up and heels in hand, was keeping up with me on the street.

An explosion followed by a wave-force of heat lifted me into the air, into nothingness.

Someone was patting my cheek, over and over again. I wasn't sure I wanted to open my eyes. Then I heard Kitty calling my name. I eased my eyes open. It was dark, and I was lying on my back in wet grass. And Kitty stared at me with concern, her blue eyes, close to mine, reflected a bright flickering light.

"Brent. Are you okay?" Her hands slid over my chest and legs.

I pushed up on my elbows. I was stiff and sore. I rotated my head from one side to the other. The situation, Ms. Cummins and the two men, the shadow behind our car, all came roaring back. I glanced over my shoulder. The remnants of our car with George's gun and Tazor were engulfed in flames, and I coughed as the acrid smell of plastic and rubber burning engulfed us in a cloud of black smoke. "Help me up. We've got to get out of here."

Kitty hooked one of my arms in hers and tugged me to my feet.

My back felt like I had been stretched to a new height and was unsure if all the parts were still connected. But I could walk.

A half block away, arm over Kitty's shoulder, we rushed-walked into an alley and headed for the lights of the next street.

Kitty squeezed my arm. "You saved my life back there."

I patted her arm and glanced into her lovely, but scared eyes. "Ms. Cummins worked for your dad, and he recommended her to you?"

We entered the next street and turned right to add distance between us and the burning car.

I hesitated and glanced over my shoulder to make sure no one was following us in the alley.

Arm-in-arm, she walked and I limped.

A few paces down the block, brow furrowed, Kitty glanced up at me. "Yes to both questions. What's your point?"

"What's your dad do? Is he rich like your gramps? You never talk much about him."

She stopped, tugging me to a stop. "Whoa, whoa." Her head swiveled. "I don't like what you're implying, not one bit."

I flipped my free hand out to my side. "I'm not implying anything. I'm just asking some questions. But I think you must agree, your secretary just tried to kill us. And she used to work for your dad. We need to know who all is involved in this if we want to stay alive. So my questions are not out of line."

She started walking again, tugging me along.

I pulled her into what looked like a local neighborhood bar. We needed to get off the street. There would be people looking for us. The saloon was dark and its occupants couldn't be seen from the streets.

Scattered, lighted beer signs on the walls and a turned-on TV were the only light sources in the small, tavern.

Most of the dozen or so stools were filled with hunched-over silhouettes and a basketball game played on the over-the-bar TV.

We wound our way past the bar through scattered, mostly unoccupied, tables and chairs to a table in the back. The darkness in the rear of the bar was our friend. I pulled a chair out for Kitty, and she plopped down. I sat next to her, my back to the wall.

A bulky bartender approached and I could feel the floor move with each of his steps. The big man, oblivious to the nervous tension of his two new customers, took our order for two draft beers.

After the bartender brought the beers, two of those thick, heavy frosted mugs, and was paid, he returned to the bar.

Kitty took my hand. "What're we going to do?"

It was my turn to kiss her hand, a soft slow kiss. "Tell me about your dad, Kitty."

She took a swig of the beer. And then, so unlike a woman, let alone a governor, she wiped the foam off her mouth with the back of her hand.

(81)

Kitty pulled her hand from mine and wrapped her long fingers from both hands around the frosty mug of beer. The bar was dark so I couldn't see her features, but I assumed she was grimacing. I'd had asked her to tell me about her dad, the man she never talked about, and she was taking her time to answer. The story had to be a bad one.

"I don't talk much about my dad 'cause there's not much to say." She took a large swallow of beer.

"My mom, ah … she left my dad and me when I was little. She was always a forbidden subject around our house." Her fingers sought her chin.

"Dad didn't think he could raise a child let alone a girl by himself, so we moved in with Gramps and my grandmother. And Gramps hired a nanny to watch me, even though she wasn't necessary. Gramps did most of the watching and entertaining of yours truly." She brushed loose hair from her forehead.

"My dad was one of those kids who had been given everything during his childhood. So he had zero aspirations. He didn't have to study or learn a trade, that was work, and he didn't need to work … for anything. When he got to college age, he—" I raised my hand stopping her.

A man in a dark suit had entered the bar; his silhouetted-bulk filled the opened doorframe. He looked more out of place in this neighborhood bar than the governor of South Carolina did. He scanned the interior until his eyes found us, we had to be two shadows in the back of the bar; either

222

lovers or hiders.

The hairs on my neck braced to attention. Kitty and I were trapped.

Kitty turned to see what had captured my attention. "What'll we—"

My lips silenced her words, and I wrapped her in my arms.

As if by habit, or to run from her thoughts, her tongue sought mine.

Heavy steps approached our table and then a bright phone light spotlighted Kitty and me. For the moment, our meshed faces concealed our identities.

"Hey you two, I need to see some I.D.," the man ordered.

In one motion, I jumped out of the embrace and the chair, lunged, and slammed the thick heavy mug of beer into the big man's jaw.

His limp body thudded on the floor. I knelt next to him and used his phone light to find and take his revolver. I shoved both the gun and the phone into my pants pocket, grabbed Kitty's hand, and limp-trotted to the front door.

I stuck my head out the door and glanced both ways. A black sedan with tinted windows, resembling government-issue, sat idling by the curb. The car was at the most twenty-feet down the street; a problem, a big problem.

I turned to Kitty. "I want you to run out there to that car parked outside and scream for help. When he or they get out of the car, point at the bar and yell 'In there.'"

Kitty, eyes wide, nodded and slid past me.

She ran out of the bar and stopped in front of the car. "Help! Help!"

Another suit climbed out of the passenger's door, and faced Kitty, his back to me.

Three large steps and I was behind him with the gun stuck into his back. Unlike his partner he was shorter than me and thin.

"Don't move. Don't say anything." I leaned down and checked the car, it was empty. I reached around him, found, and took his gun and his phone. "Now walk away, quickly and don't look back. Someone tried to kill us tonight, maybe you." I prodded him with the gun. "We're not in a good mood. Don't look back."

For whatever reason, the man didn't argue.

As he walked away, I grabbed Kitty. We got in the car, and I drove away.

(82)

I had trouble driving within the speed limit. I so wanted to floor the accelerator. I caught a green light at the next intersection and eased into the late-hour sparse traffic.

"I'm the freakin' Governor of the State of South Carolina, and I'm running for my life. This shouldn't be." Kitty slammed her fist into the padded dash. "Damned Camden, I hope he rots in Hell."

"No time for damning anyone." I glanced in the rearview mirror and saw nothing suspicious. "We've got to find a place to hide and think."

"Where … what? My mind is blank." Her tone reflected her battle between fear and anger.

"I was hoping you'd tell me." I turned left at the next light, going nowhere in particular except as far from the bar as possible.

"Who were those men?" she asked.

"I'm not sure. See if these tell you something." I pulled the phones from my pocket and handed them to her. "If they're FBI, both this car and those phones are probably traceable. We can't stay in this car very long, and we need to dump the phones." I pulled one of the guns from the waistband of my pants. "Oh, and take one of these." I sat one of the guns on the console. "The way things are going, you'll probably need it."

"That's just what I needed to hear."

Kitty placed the phones in her lap and carefully picked up the gun like it was a deadly snake.

"My gramps taught me how to shoot, but it's been a long time."

"Sounds like your gramps taught you things my dad taught me. Make sure the safety is on."

She gave me one of those 'I don't like what you just said' looks. Then she turned the gun over in her hands until she found the safety. Kitty put the gun in the glove box and picked up one of the phones.

"Okay, let's see who's on the contact list," Kitty said as she tapped phone icons.

Two quiet blocks later, Kitty put the phone down. "Congratulations, Mr. Layne. You just cold-cocked an FBI Agent."

"Turn those phones off and throw them out the window." I grabbed her arm. "No wait. Call your driver first and see if he can meet us somewhere. We need to get rid of this car."

She finger-poked the phone. Seconds passed. "I got George's voice-mail. He must not be receptive to calls from the FBI. I'll leave him a message." She paused and then voiced her request for her chauffeur to call her back at this strange number.

The traffic was very light, and yet I had lights behind me, strange lights, one headlight a little higher than the other. I made another left turn at the next block and shortly after the skewed lights followed again. A block later, gun in hand, I pulled into a gas station. And the lights behind me never appeared. The vehicle had stopped somewhere close by.

"Why do you have your gun out, and why are we stopping?" Kitty asked.

"We've got company." I leaned over and took the other gun out of the glove box and handed it to her. "Take the safety off and make sure a round is chambered."

We both prepped the 40-caliber Glocks. I couldn't help but notice Kitty's hands shaking as she readied the weapon.

I had parked next to the pumps as if I were going to fill up but didn't get out of the car or shut off the engine. I wanted to give whoever was following us time to relax, to drop their guard.

"Get down," I said.

And questioning-eyes Kitty laid her head into my lap.

I eased the car out of the gas station onto the street in the direction I had come. A half-block away a solitary, dark car sat by the curb in a 'No

Parking' zone. As I passed it, I floored the accelerator.

I glanced in my mirror and watched uneven car lights fish-tail into position behind us.

I tightened my grip on the steering wheel, game on.

(83)

I ran a red light and glanced in the mirror. The offset headlights behind me not only ran the light, but were gaining ground. My mind bounced like a tennis ball in an extended exchange between surrendering to the FBI and running. The FBI would probably incarcerate us, and if we ran, we'd only add to the charges when they finally caught us. What to do?

I made up my mind in an instant, when the rear window exploded.

"What the hell!" Kitty pushed her body lowered in the seat. "Get us out of here."

I tapped the brakes and skidded around a corner to the right and then floored the v-eight. The FBI wouldn't be shooting at us, not without a warning. Or would they? I had assaulted one of their agents. It didn't matter; I'd take my chances running.

At the next intersection, the light changed to red and traffic started to pull out from the intersecting street. I blew the horn and sped into the intersection. Cars screeched to a stop, sliding and spinning on both sides of us. There was a jolting thud and the rear of our car went sideways for an instant until the accelerating tires caught hold, and we were in the clear. I glanced in the mirror and no lights came through the tangle of cars.

Three turns later, no one was following us.

One of the cell phones in Kitty's lap rang. She sat up. "What should I do?"

"Answer it. If it's not George, it's got to be the Feds. Ask them why they're shooting at us in the middle of town."

She hesitated and then tapped the phone on and said a weak "Hello."

After a pause, Kitty said, "I'm the Governor and you're shooting at me! Are you insane? Your agent didn't identify—" she chewed on her lip listening. "Yes shooting. You just shot out our back window in the middle of the city!" Her eyes fixed on mine. "What? Oh my God!" She shook her head from side-to-side.

I grabbed the phone out of her hand and disconnected the call.

Her enlarged blue eyes gleamed in a passing streetlight as it flowed over them.

"The FBI isn't following us." Her voice stumbled over each word.

(84)

The lighted city streets of Columbia, South Carolina flowed by Kitty and me, one after another. It was like we were watching a movie filmed from the front seat of a car driving through Columbia at night versus actually being there.

I glanced at Kitty as the streetlights washed over her, the green satin dress shining along with the gun in her lap. I'm not sure why, maybe a tension release, I smiled.

My smiled vanished with a glance in my rearview mirror; those familiar skewed headlights were back.

I jammed the gas pedal to the floor.

"What now?" Kitty screamed as she braced against the seat.

"The shooters are back. Get down."

She glanced over her shoulder before she lowered her head into my lap. "Shit."

I skidded the car around a corner, sped through the block, and slid around the next intersection.

I glanced back and the goofy headlights were there, as if they were attached by a long chain.

I removed one of my white-knuckled hands from the steering wheel long enough to pat Kitty's shoulder. I hoped the gesture made her feel better. It didn't help me at all.

Both hands back on the wheel, I skidded into an alley.

Halfway down the alley, two gunshots boomed, jerking my already tense body with each report. The second shot seem to drop my seat. The rear end of the car swerved sending debris lining the alley flying into the air. Kitty's fingers dug into my thigh.

The bastards had shot out one of my rear tires.

I jerked the bouncing car into a main thoroughfare as the tire disintegrated yielding a high pitched screech of metal carving concrete.

"What'll we do now?" Kitty's high pitched voice rose over the nerve piercing wheel-rim-on-street noise.

"We can't outrun them anymore," I said through clenched teeth.

"Shit." She pushed up and swiveled on the seat.

Before I could protest, she fired three shots thought the missing back window. The booming gun next to my ear both jolted me and shocked me with pain. For a second I thought I'd been shot. I glanced back and the now very close funny-headlights-car swerved and slowed.

"I, ah—oh my God—I think … shit." Kitty flopped down on the seat and leaned into me, smoking gun in hand. She rubbed her shaking chin with the thumb and index finger of her free hand.

I patted her leg. "You did good. I don't think they'll follow us anymore."

"But what if I—"

"Shhh. You can't change what's already done."

Three turns and two sparks-flying, shrieking blocks later, I pulled into an alley to change the tire.

Kitty sobbed the whole time I worked. This wasn't a façade; this was real. She was in pain. The woman had a conscience, and it was berating her for her actions.

I knew; I'd been there.

I wanted to hold her, soothe her, and caress her pain away.

At that moment, I knew I loved her.

85

Kitty got out of the car when I started to jack it up. The alley was dimly lit, and as she walked around the back of the car, her foot kicked something. I prayed it wasn't any the lug nuts I had removed.

She wiped the tears from her eyes, though she'd never wipe away the memory of shooting someone for the first time. I knew. She eased past me and stood behind me.

I welcomed her magnolia scent over the smell of cat urine mixed with other vile odors in the alley.

"Anything I can do?" she asked over the noise of a passing car at the end of the alley.

I looked up at her over my shoulder, her back was to me.

One of the phones I'd taken off the FBI guys rang. Kitty's bloodshot eyes met mine.

"You can answer that phone," I said.

She retrieved the ringing phone from the car and returned. Her long index finger tapped the phone.

"Hello," Kitty said, sounding like she had congestion.

Her eyes locked on mine. "George, can you meet us and exchange cars?" She paused. "Well it belongs to the FBI and probably has a transmitter attached somewhere."

She looked at me and raised her eyebrows for concurrence, and I nodded.

"If you keep it long, you'll be picked up. Just take it somewhere and dump it."

I finished raising the tireless rim off the ground while she listened.

"Where are we?" she asked.

"We're in an alley across from a theatre on Taylor." I stood and stretched my cramped legs.

She repeated my words into the phone, and then listened.

"No, make it ten minutes," she said. "I don't want to stay here one second longer than necessary. There are people hunting us; trying to kill us." She chewed on her lip. "Yeah, we're okay. Hurry." She disconnected.

"He knows where we are and is on his way," she said as she eyed the phone. "What do you want to do with these?" She held the phone up.

"Turn them off, and we'll leave them here. Why don't you take your gun and those phones and go stand watch at the end of the alley. Leave the phones there and stay out of sight until you see George."

"Do you mind if I leave the gun here, I … it makes me sick to … I—"

"Leave it, Kitty." I knew what she felt. That God-awful, soul-scaring moment when you shoot someone for the first time, maybe kill them, remains forever.

I leaned into the trunk and lifted the donut spare out of the trunk well. "I'll join you in a couple of minutes."

She wiped the gun off with the hem of her dress and put it in the trunk. Then she walked through the dark alley toward the lit street.

Though her posture was bowed from stress and worry, and she was only a silhouette, to me she was gorgeous.

Ten minutes later, I had the spare tire installed, the car on all fours, and the jack and distressed rim stowed in the trunk. I had a gun wedged in both pants pockets. On the run stuffed with guns. One or two more weapons and I could be another Clyde Barrow, and Kitty could be Bonnie.

I found some old newspaper to wipe my hands on and turned to join Kitty at the entry to the alley. I couldn't see her in the shadows of the alley.

It was dark but unless she was crouched behind something, I should be able to see her. Was she hiding? If so, why, had she seen something? Had something happened to her? The closer I got to the alley entrance, the faster I walked. I increased my pace and pulled one of the guns from my pocket.

At the street, I looked both ways, Kitty was gone. All the excuses to stave off my real concern flew through my mind. She saw George go by and ran after him. She had to go to the bathroom. She took a walk. Why on earth would she do any of those things?

I moved back into the alley and my foot kicked something. I moved toward the sound and found one of the cell phones. I kicked the wall. And without thinking, I threw the phone against a building wall, shattering it into pieces.

I took a deep breath, pocketed the gun, and pushed aside my anger. I looked around for any other clues. The other phone was also shattered against the corner of a building wall forming one side of the mouth of the alley.

I clenched my hands into fists. Though I wanted to scream out her name or hit something; I sulked back into the darkness.

Kitty was gone. Someone had taken her.

(86)

The alley and the night air were almost as dark as my mood.

Before I could completely vent over Kitty's apparent abduction, a car pulled up, a light-colored sedan, and blocked the entrance to the alley.

I raised my gun and aimed at the side window.

The window lowered and George yelled, "Mr. Layne, is that you?"

"Yeah," I replied, lowering the gun.

"Where's the Governor?"

I limped-ran to the car and leaned in the window. "Someone just took her."

"And I think I know who. Get in."

I hopped into the car. Before I got the door closed, George made a 'U' turn, and accelerated down the street.

"Who?" My voice was louder than I expected.

"Senator's Sparks' limo just passed me a block from here going the other way. I'd recognize that car in a blizzard. I've followed it enough."

"Who would be in Camden Sparks' limo that wanted Kitty, ah I mean the governor? Sparks is dead."

"Since when? Who told you that?"

"Kitty got a call earlier from her secretary, Ms Cummins. She said Camden killed himself."

"I've listened to several news broadcasts today, and none of them mentioned it. I'd think that would be prime news."

"Fuck." I shook my head. The truth had to be on an extended vacation.

Something George had said tickled my mind. "You said you had followed Sparks' limo a lot. Why'd you do that?"

"Every time Governor Franklin went with the Senator, she asked me to follow her and wait for her, and follow her back without being seen."

"Those had to have been some long nights," I said, speaking my unwanted thoughts.

George flipped a hand.

"Can you catch them?" I asked.

"Maybe. But if I don't, I think I know where they're going. I've been to all of his little hideaways, several more than once."

Although he gave me hope for finding Kitty, I didn't need or want that much information.

"This is going to be more than a follow, sit, and wait trip. These people are dangerous." I reached into my pocket and pulled out one of the guns. "You may need this."

George patted his coat under his left arm. "No thanks, I prefer my own."

I sat back and watched George weave through the light, late-evening traffic, like a snake through a stand of trees.

George's words echoed in my head, "I've been to all his hideaways, several more than once." I shook his words and the accompanying scenes away. I loved this woman, and her past was behind her and didn't matter. What mattered was finding her alive.

$$\widehat{87}$$

In ten or fifteen minutes, George and I were out of Columbia and the city lights on an unlit country road. He pushed the car and me to our limits on the winding, rolling, two-lane highway.

Suddenly he slowed.

"What's wrong?" I asked, trying not to show too much of my anxiety.

"There are lights ahead of us. See the faint glow."

I leaned forward as if that would help. "Barely."

"Now the fun starts." He switched off the car's lights.

Though there was a sliver of moon, I couldn't see anything. We were rolling along at forty or fifty miles-per-hour into blackness on a tree-lined snake of a road. I pressed back into the seat and grabbed the armrest.

"Can—can you see anything?" I asked. "'Cause I can't see shit."

"I'm fine. My eyes adjust quickly, plus I know this road. When I was a kid, me and my buddies used to go moon-runnin' on these roads with our dates all the time. You know, to scare the girls and to impress them. It normally worked. That was a hoot; this—well this is a whole bunch different."

"I'd say so."

My body swayed and lurched out of control as George maneuvered the car through bends and over hills I couldn't see. It was hard for me to believe that anyone could ever think of this as fun. The indentations my fingers were leaving in the console and the door's armrest would be permanent.

As my eyes adjusted, I tried to relax, but George was driving too fast. I had to concentrate on Kitty to keep from verbalizing my fear each time we were on the verge of sliding out of control in a curve or popping over a hill not knowing what was on the other side. My mind flashed all the wrong scenarios, like another sharp bend or a vehicle of some kind pulling out of a barnyard. So I tried to think about the woman I thought I loved and how all this was necessary to find her and save her. It almost worked.

"I know you're uncomfortable, but Senator Sparks' driver has always had a heavy foot. I don't want them to get too far ahead of us."

He reminded me of the Humvee driver I had in Afghanistan. The corporal who drove those mountains roads like he was in a race. I wasn't sure who was worse. Nah, those 'Ghan' roads in the daytime, let alone at night, were much worse. There were three-thousand-foot drop-offs and people out there waiting for us with guns and RPG's; plus the road-side bombs. This was a child's ride in an amusement park in comparison.

I pushed out similar words I used to say back then, through clenched teeth, "You're doing great. Don't worry about me."

The better my vision became, the harder I squeezed the console and armrest. George was driving way faster than I would like in the middle of a sunny day.

I closed my eyes and let my body react to the car as it swayed through curves and bucked over pop-up hills. I redirected my thoughts to Kitty. I could see her magnetic blue eyes, I could taste her soft lips, and I could feel her—the car decelerated in time with the screaming tires. My eyelids flipped open; we were skidding sideways.

A slice of moon on a roller-coaster-like country road, and I was in a car going way too fast with no headlights on, fun. Even more fun when the driver, George, lost control of the car, and we were skidding sideways.

I opened my eyes and saw why he'd slammed on the brakes and cut the wheel. In the faint glow of what little moon existed, I could see the outline of a car blocking the road ahead; not very far ahead. Our car, my side, was sliding at the road-blocking vehicle, eating up the pavement separating us. I stiffened, bracing for impact.

"Hang on!" George's words seemed more of an apology than a warning.

"Shit!" The word burst from my lips.

George pulled the wheel and hit the gas. The car straightened and then skidded in the opposite direction.

At least now George's side was in jeopardy. But I remained braced for a collision.

Our car finally came to a stop, almost sideways in the road, ten or fifteen yards from the car blocking the highway.

Two bright flashes spurted over the hood of the other car. Glass shattered. George's body bounced in time with the flashes, and I was splattered by warm globs of something.

As George's body slumped onto the steering wheel, reality smacked me. George had been shot.

I ducked below the windows, pulled my gun, and cocked it. I shoved my door open. The dome light came on. More glass shattered. I wedged out onto the road in a squatted position leaving the door open hoping the light would be a distraction.

I heard feet softly slapping pavement, like gym-shoes running on carpet. Someone was coming to finish the job.

Cocked gun gripped in both hands, I bolted to a stand-up position. Just feet away, a man with a raised gun rushed into the sphere of the dome light. I put three rounds into his chest.

He went down, and so did I. Puffed bullets whizzed past. The man had at least one accomplice.

I shoved the car door closed, returning the burnt-gun-powder air to blackness. I had learned the hard way to adjust to the darkness as well as the adrenaline coursing through my system. Those lessons had seemed so long ago, until now. At this moment, it was as if I had never left those far-away lands; as if my nightmares had come to life.

I had killed before, too many times. Though I didn't like it, when pressed, I was a killer, guns, knives, hands; whatever. Then as now, I had no choice, either me or them. This was war.

At least now I had an edge. After taking down one of them, those remaining had to be at least as scared as me.

I took a deep breath and eased it out, hoping to calm my shaking limbs. I needed to move. Unmoving targets got holes in them. Plus, I needed surprise on my side.

I checked both sides of the road. One side was full of dark clumps, bushes of some kind; the other was a field dotted with sparse trees. The bushes would be noisy and if they were palmettos, they'd cut me to ribbons.

I slid into the ditch and crouched-ran away from the car several yards before I crossed the ditch and crawled into the field.

I snaked my way as fast as I could to the nearest tree. I couldn't tell how much noise I was making because my heart was thumping in my ears. I put the mature tree between me and the car and pushed up to my feet.

I peered around in the direction of the car. All I could see was a blob of darker mass than the surroundings.

What would I be doing if I were them? I'd be flanking the car. And the bushes weren't the way to go. He or she or they would be coming this way.

I held my breath and listened; nothing, not even a cicada or a cricket. My training and experience had taught me the dead quiet meant humans were near.

I was debating whether to move again when a woman screamed, near the car. It sounded like Bean. No way, my mind was fucked up. Could it be Kitty? It didn't sound like Kitty. If it were Bean, what would she be doing out here with the people who kidnapped Kitty?

I shook my head trying to clear my mind. Maybe they were trying to distract me, trying to get me to lose control and do something stupid. I needed to focus. A woman had screamed. I needed to log the data and go from there. At least one killer would be coming for me soon.

"Brent!" Bean called. "Is that you? "Help, I'm—umm-ummm."

Not a doubt in my mind; that was Bean. She *was* alive, alive. My rock-hard shoulders drooped. Her voice brought back all the wonderful memories, memories she had buried with money. No matter what she had done, she was alive and needed my help.

The bait had been cast. It took all my willpower to stand still. My breathing had doubled along with my heart rate. I took a long deep breath to quiet my anxieties.

Like the caves of Afghanistan, there was a time to move, and a time to be a stalagmite. I eased the gun up to my chest, and then froze.

Again I held my breath and listened. Dried leaves crunched close by in the woods, maybe twenty or thirty feet. Then glass crunched near the car. There were at least two more. If I exposed my position now, they'd pinch me in a cross-fire.

I gripped the Glock tighter as my palms perspired.

I had to become part of the tree, unmoving.

A beam of light burst from near the cars and darted from tree to tree. Fuck.

I had to risk moving, I had to put the tree between me and the light. I inched my way to my left and there was a flash from the woods and a chunk of the tree splintered away. I dropped and fired at the flash. Then I rotated and fired three rounds at the light, one to each side and one just below it. The light fell, clattered, and rolled on the road. It stopped with a man's face frozen in the beam, mouth and eyes gapped open.

He resembled one of the men accompanying Ms. Cummins to the

drawing. But I wasn't sure.

I angled my body putting the tree between me and the tree splintering shot.

Running feet headed for the cars through the woods. I bolted to my feet and pursued. I couldn't let them escape and take Bean again and maybe Kitty. No way.

A car started, the engine roared, and tires screeched.

I ran to George's car totally disregarding my throbbing leg, opened the driver's door, and pulled George's body out of the car. I slid in, keyed the engine, cut the wheel and floored the gas. The steering wheel was slippery with George's blood. I used my shirt to wipe it off.

Lights came on in front of me. They were all I needed. I left my lights out. A passing thought had me wishing George was driving, poor George. He'd given his life to try to save the governor, like Andrew. Would I be next?

The chase was on. One if not both of the women in my life were in that car. I couldn't let them get away.

(89)

When George was driving this country road with no lights, I was scared. Now that I was driving blind, I was terrified. The one consistent thing about both events was the road; it was a winding, mini-rollercoaster.

My concentration on following the lights three or four car-lengths in front of me kept me from dabbing sweat dripping from my forehead and nose.

Right in the middle of a curve, the leading car's lights would disappear over another hump in the road. I would blindly trust my aim of where I thought the car had been; over and over, turn after turn, hill after hill.

I wondered if they knew I was behind them. I refused to use my brakes. I had to be a dark blob in the blackness beyond the wake of their tail lights.

There had to be a tree or a drop off ahead waiting for me. But I didn't have time to dwell on it. I was going too fast.

Just as I was negotiating what seemed like the zillionth blind hump, when I popped over the hill, there were no lights in front of me. I jammed on the brakes and pulled on the lights. Then I saw the side road defined by their car lights as I slid by it.

Now they had to know I was following. I left my lights on, backed up, and turned onto the road.

What I thought was a road turned out to be two gravel wheel tracks. Either this was a driveway or a farmer's access to his fields. Either way it wasn't made for speed, at least not for the speed I was going. I wasn't sure which would fail first, my body or the car, as I bounced and skidded along closing the distance with the lead car.

When I got within a hundred yards of the car, it veered off the path and disappeared into a barn-like structure. There was nothing else around; this had to be a storage shed sitting out here on a wooded hillside.

Seconds later, the car's lights went out. I skidded to a sideways stop fifty or so yards from the barn and doused my lights. I had kept the car between the barn and the driver's side.

With the second fully loaded gun in hand, I hopped out of the car, and closed the door. Expecting to be shot, I hopped-ran from the car to a nearby tree. The barn was black and quiet.

I moved low and as quick as my leg would allow to another tree, closer to the wooden dark structure hopefully housing Kitty and Bean.

I had one of those moments when I knew something was going to happen just before it happened.

"Brent, is that you out there?" Bean called from the barn. Her voice was high- pitched; her fearful voice. "Answer me. They said they won't hurt us if you put your gun down and come in here."

Between Kitty and me, we had probably wounded if not killed at least three of the kidnappers. If I went into the barn unarmed, they would kill me. At least, that's what I'd do if I were them.

I maneuvered to another tree, ten or fifteen yards from the barn.

Several slapping noises followed by a woman moaning came from inside. Then seconds of silence ticked by until another slap and a gagged mumble.

I stood there imagining horrors taking place inside the dark space.

"Brent?" This time it was Kitty calling my name.

She was there and alive. My skin tingled. The bastards were slapping her to make her call my name. My grip tightened around the Glock.

"Hit me again and I'll—" smack, smack, smack and a thud.

The fuckers were beating Kitty, whose hands had to be tied. Cowards. I took several steps toward the barn before I got control of my anger.

I'd seen anger kill young men before, too many times. I limped back to the tree.

"Brent, please Brent, she's ... she's bleeding. Don't hit her anymore!"

Bean pleaded.

Another smack and Bean wailed.

Someway, somehow, I had to get in there and make the beaters pay. I couldn't stand here and listen to Kitty and Bean being beaten. And the bastards knew that.

I moved to another tree and then another.

"No! Don't, please don't!" Bean screamed.

I took three running steps and slid to a stop. When I got there, what was I going to do, jump through the door and start shooting in the dark? I'd probably shoot Kitty or Bean and get killed for my stupidity.

I needed a new plan, one conceived without emotional bias. I reversed my direction and headed back to the car.

Only shades of gray mingled with black existed in the night-time woods. The barn or storage shed housing Kitty, Bean, and their captors was a gray blob in the blackness.

I hobbled from tree to tree, refining my plan as I got closer to George's car. Planning help me control the fear and anger that had my sweating hand squeezing the Glock's grip. I'd get in the car, flip the lights on high beam, drive it into the shed's opening, and jump out. The car would block their escape, and the lights would reveal who the bad guys were. Then I'd lean into the door and start shooting. The bastards would pay for killing George and Andrew, and for smacking women, my women.

Two trees from the car, a beam of light from the shed found George's car and dropped to a wheel. Two gun flashes later, the tire whooshed and sagged flat.

Were the bastards reading my mine?

I put a tree between me and the shed and took aim at the dark opening.

A few heartbeats passed before a car engine started and lights came on illuminating the interior of the shed. The engine revved; the car bolted out backwards like it had been catapulted and slid around to a stop, bathing the woods in light.

I tried to get all my parts behind the tree. I thought about shooting at the tires or the lights, but I didn't want to risk hitting one of the women.

Before I could think of any other options, the car sped off down the gravel lane.

Useless gun in hand, I stood in the dark watching the tail lights disappear.

Sagging back against a tree, I released a muffled expletive. Two women had depended on me to save them, and I had failed. The woman I loved and the woman I used to love may both lose their lives because of my incompetence.

⑨1

I had started George's car and used the headlights to search the empty barn.

Changing a tire in semi-darkness was a real knuckle buster. My only solace was the brain-dead labor gave me time to think. I was a wanted man with nowhere to go. Who would take me in or better yet help me? There had to be someone. Then, as I was putting the flat tire in the trunk, it hit me, like a gun flash in the dark. Someone who valued Kitty's life as much as I did; her gramps.

I folded into the driver's seat, started George's car and explored. Yes, he had a GPS, why wouldn't he, he was a chauffeur.

I input 'Joshua Franklin' and an address popped up on the screen. As expected, George had Kitty's gramps in his system.

An hour later I parked the car on a street in a posh residential section on the outskirts of Columbia. The address was a city block of property surrounded by a twelve-foot-high brick wall. An ornate iron gate blocked the entrance. Gramps either liked his privacy or required protection from his enemies.

Joshua Franklin didn't know me unless maybe he'd seen my face on the news, or he was current on the FBI's wanted lists.

I thought about ringing the bell by the lighted gate, but what would I say when asked who I was and what I wanted. And breaking in could get me shot.

I had to do something. I had driven here; I couldn't just sit here. Kitty needed me and so did Bean.

I walked over to the gate and rang the bell.

"How may I help you?" a cracking, high-pitched male voice asked.

"Is this Joshua Franklin?" I asked.

"No. How may I help you?"

"I need to talk to Mr. Franklin about his granddaughter, Governor Franklin, now."

"State your name and your purpose," demanded another male voice, deeper and more assertive.

I looked up and saw a camera scanning me. I looked at myself. I was wearing another man's ill-fitting clothes, gray slacks and a white shirt smeared with blood.

I stared into the camera as if it were a person whose attention I must gain or kill.

"Kitty has been kidnapped, and I need your help to save her." My tone was flat, seriously flat.

(92)

The mansion was larger than the Seven Gables Inn, and I was seated in what my grandmother would have called a parlor. A fire crackled in a marble-faced fireplace to ward off the night chill.

I had no idea what time it was; maybe midnight. Too late to be calling on someone, that's for sure.

The furniture was old and stiff and made me wonder if the owner was the same way. The room had indirect lighting from scattered table lamps. Circles of light and darkness interplayed on the high ceilings painted with cherubs shooting arrows. A baby grand piano angled across one corner.

Why would anyone with endless money live like this, in the past?

I wasn't sure why I was here, except I had nowhere else to go. Kitty's 'Gramps' loved her like a daughter and had money and connections. And all I had were two guns, a car with a 'donut' tire, every cop in the city looking for me, and no idea of where to look for Kitty and Bean.

The door opened, and the same two large men who had brought me to this room walked in and took positions on each side of the door. I almost expected "Hail to the Chief" to start playing somewhere in the background.

A tall athletic-looking man rushed into the room with uncombed long dark brown hair graying at the temples and a full gray beard trimmed short. He wore jeans and a red 'Gamecocks' sweatshirt.

He moved like a twenty-year-old and fronted me before I could stand

and square my shoulders.

His brown eyes darted to his watch and then to my eyes. "It's after midnight, Mr. Brent Layne, and you've got a lot of explaining to do. Let's hear it."

The man was almost as big as me and in great shape. His face was chiseled with concern and few lines. I had expected someone pushing eighty or more.

"Are you Joshua Franklin?" I asked.

His eyes glanced up and right like I was boring him. "Yes, yes. Now get on with it."

With the exception of the sex, I told him everything, including how I felt about his granddaughter. When I finished we were both seated with empty cups and an empty carafe of coffee in front of us.

Joshua's head was down, his chin rested on his turned under fists, his elbows braced on his knees.

He remained still for what seemed like a minute. I wasn't sure if he was dead or had fallen asleep.

"Mr. Franklin," I said.

He raised an index finger and then his head. His thick brown eyebrows arched as he sucked in air and released it.

"The only related news I've heard is that Jeanette Cummins, Kitty's secretary was found shot to death in a car earlier."

I flinched. Ms. Cummins must have been driving the car chasing us. Kitty had shot her secretary. Thank God she didn't know that.

"Did you know Ms. Cummins? Is she involved in this?"

"I've met her, but I didn't know her. And yes, she's involved. She tried to kill Kitty and I earlier."

"Son-of-a-bitch." He nodded his head. "Did you kill her?"

I clamped my teeth on my lower lip and shook my head.

He seemed to deduce from my reaction who had shot Ms. Cummins, and changed the subject. "Camden Sparks isn't dead. I'd know it if he were. It's a shame he isn't. I may have to—" he stood—"I think I know where Kitty is."

The hair on the back of my neck erected. I grabbed his surprisingly muscled arms. "Where? Have you talked with her? Is she alright?"

He peeled off my clutching hands and turned. "Charles, get the helicopter warmed-up." He swiveled to face me. "If I'm right, Kitty is fine. And as for you, Mr. Layne, you'll need to stay here."

I shook my head. "That's not going to happen without me and your boys making a mess of your home."

He glanced away with his lips pressed together as if he were considering the options. "Okay. I'll take you, but if she's there, I want your word that you'll not pursue this … this conundrum any further."

"What? Kitty and I are both wanted by the FBI and the police. And my—ah, Bean, Robin Hayes is also missing. Will she be with Kitty?"

"I can't answer that. I don't know anything about Miss Hayes. But I will be able to take care of any issues you and Kitty have with the authorities."

I straightened and stared into his eyes. He was serious, and he had connections. He could do what he said. A sigh escaped my lips as some of my burden fell off my back.

"That … that'd be great, but I can't give you my word. Not until I find out if Robin is okay. And I *am* going with you." I glanced at the remaining big man by the door. I couldn't remember the last time I had fought and didn't want to remember it. I hated fighting, but I could kick some ass when forced to. I clenched my fists.

He put his hands on his hips and stared at me. "Okay, but if you continue to probe into this matter, you'll have to deal with the FBI and the police. You'll be on your own."

I nodded. I had learned to be on my own, not dependent on anyone, long ago. My parents were wise. I had listened and profited. No one had ever given me anything. I had to earn whatever I wanted. If I had to go to jail trying to find and save Bean, so be it.

⑨③

Feeling the seat cushion push up against my spine, the vibration under my feet, and watching the mansion's night lights drop out of sight, brought back too many memories of too many helicopter rides.

The night missions were always the worst. The Hindu Kush mountain range was somewhere in the blackness waiting to eat another chopper. And what the mountains didn't bring down, the Taliban tried to shoot down.

Joshua's voice in my ear phones erased the images. "So you think you love my granddaughter?"

I adjusted my headset. "Yes, I do." I looked at Joshua. He sat next to me in the back seat, a silhouette in the dim instrument lights. I couldn't believe I had openly divulged my feelings about Kitty. My feelings for Kitty made me wonder if I had ever really loved Bean.

"Not as much as I do." Joshua's voice pulled me out of my guilt pit. He cleared his throat. "Have you met Preston?"

"Preston?"

"Kitty's father."

"No." Kitty hadn't gotten to finish telling me about her dad. To her it was a sensitive subject, maybe one I should avoid with her grandfather. But Joshua had brought it up. "She talks a lot about you and never mentions him."

"I'm not surprised."

"I asked her about him, and she didn't get a chance to reply. We, ah, got interrupted."

I thought he'd inquire about the interruption, but apparently he had target fixation.

"Preston is different. I, ah, I made some mistakes with Preston, costly mistakes. Throughout his youth, I was consumed with making money. When I wasn't working and my wife wasn't going to one of her club meetings, we were socializing. Preston was raised by several nannies, the nanny turn-over rate should have been a wake-up call to us, but our greed got in the way."

He paused as if he were looking for sympathy. I didn't know what to say, so I said nothing.

"There are no excuses. I … we, my wife and I failed miserably as parents. I guess that's why I spent so much time with Kitty. I needed to prove to myself that I could be a loving, giving parent. And Kitty was so easy to love."

"I can attest to that," I said, meaning every word, but only speaking to make the conversation two-sided.

"Preston never had to work for anything, and he didn't. He either got kicked out or flunked out of the many private grade schools and high schools we sent him to. But we kept pushing him away, hoping one of the boarding schools could fix what we hadn't taken the time to even try to fix."

He paused as if the cutting edge of his own words had opened old wounds.

"We had to buy him acceptance into a third-rate college. And that turned into four years of partying without a degree. The only good thing that came out of his college era was Kitty, the lovely result of a one-night drunken interlude." Joshua shifted in his seat.

"Ever since then, Preston has been a leech, a money sponge. And we've supported him financially through his drug and alcohol battles and his many marriages. All of our mutual mistakes have killed any respect or love between us. And the relationship Kitty and I developed over the years has made things worse with Preston. I truly believe the intensity of hate is enhanced by the need for love."

Joshua's words reminded me of my mother's words. 'To really hate someone, you need to love them first.' But, based on his story, I didn't think love had ever existed between Joshua and his son, only the need. And I wondered if there was any love between Kitty and her father.

The question was hanging there, so I asked it. "So why are you telling *me* this?"

Although I couldn't see his eyes, I knew he was staring at me.

"Because I think Preston is involved in the lottery fraud, up to his eyebrows."

(94)

My inner ear and gut told me we were descending. And the contrasting shock of the bright circles of the landing lights to the surrounding darkness verified we were nearing the ground. Our descent slowed until the ground gently greeted us. As I suspected, we were at Kitty's hideaway. I could see the outline of the barn I had broken into what seemed like days ago although it had only been a few hours. I glanced at the instrument panel, it was two a.m. And then the instrument panel lighting was extinguished.

As I straightened after clearing the slowing prop, I could see lights on in Kitty's house. I reached into my pocket for one of my guns and found nothing but the memory of Joshua's two big men taking them. I glanced at the weight-lifters as they hustled by me, guns drawn, sprinting toward the house.

Joshua grabbed my arm and pulled me to a stop. "Let them check out the house. We'll wait here."

"But Kitty's—"

"Everybody within a mile knows we've landed. Let my men do what they're trained and highly-paid to do, secure the place before I enter."

"But Kitty—"

"Don't worry." He patted my arm. "They know she's in there. They won't shoot anyone. These guys are good."

"I hope you're right. What about us? We're out here alone, defenseless."

Joshua reached into his jacket and handed me one of my guns. "Based upon what you told me, you're pretty good with one of these. So defend me."

I breeched a round and wished my eyes would adjust to the darkness quicker.

I lead Joshua out of the open area to the side of the barn. We leaned against the barn, and I tried to be patient.

Glass broke, the lights in the house went out, and a woman screamed.

And I left my patience and Joshua in the shadow of the barn.

(95)

Joshua Franklin's two rent-a-thugs had entered Kitty's country hide-away in the middle of the night. And I was on their heels after glass broke, the lights went out, and a woman screamed.

I wasn't sure who had screamed.

I should've been use to getting left in the dark by now. But I wasn't. I did my stiff-leg run to the darkened house.

A man yelled, "We work for Joshua Franklin, the governor's father, and we're not here to harm anyone. We just want to talk. We're comin' in."

Because I was certain Kitty and Bean were in the house, my first instinct was to rush inside. But in the dark, no one would know who was who. Joshua's men could shoot me or I them. Or worse, the kidnappers could kill all of us including the women. But what if Joshua's men shot Kitty or Bean?

I stopped by the rear door. Even in this fast-paced, fluid situation, I needed to think versus react. This was no different than going into one of those damned Afghanistan caves at night after my men had entered and shooting started. It was no different and just as hard.

I couldn't remain outside. I had to do something.

"Joshua Franklin's men, I'm coming in behind you," I yelled into the opened door.

"Brent?" Bean called.

At least I knew Bean was alive.

Crouched low, I entered the rear door to Kitty's dark home into the mud room. I held the gun in front of me with both hands.

I eased through the small room to the kitchen entrance. I stood by the door frame and scanned the black, quiet room for movement. There was nothing. And then light filled the gap at the bottom of the door to the great room.

I jerked as gunshots, one after another, three, no four, and then five and six in offbeat succession. I had no choice; I had to go in and prayed I wasn't too late.

A man moaned in the great room followed by footsteps, fading and coming back and fading again. I limped to the door and listened. More heavy-walking, a pause, and then a man said, "Hold on, I'm goin' for help."

I stepped to one side of the door. It swung open, and one of Joshua's men walked past me.

"Hold it," I said as I flipped on the light.

He tensed and froze.

"Relax, it's me, Brent. What happened? Can I go in there?"

The big man raised his arms and swiveled to face me.

He lowered his arms. "Phil's in there. He's been hit at least once. We went in there and didn't even have our guns drawn. We just wanted to talk. And some fuckin' woman shot him."

"A woman?" My mind sped into warp mode. Kitty, Bean, which woman? And why would any of them start shooting? I was pretty sure Bean had never shot a gun, or at least that's what she had told me. And Kitty had been so upset about possibly shooting the person chasing us; I couldn't believe she'd shoot someone without at least being threatened.

"Yeah, the bitch shot him in the back from a bedroom, and then everything went wrong. Phil must've shot her after he went down. The ol' man's gonna be pissed." He turned and headed for the rear door. "I've got to call an ambulance for Phil, and there's no reception in this house. I checked the other rooms. You can go in. All the others are dead, or at least I think they are."

My stomach rolled with his words 'all the others are dead'. I pushed through the door just as a car started outside and roared past the house.

Someone had gotten away. I hoped Kitty and Bean were in that car.

There were two bloodied bodies on the floor of the great room, both men. Phil lay on his side, moaning, to my right near Kitty's bedroom door. The other man was face down behind the couch.

I walked over, stooped, and checked the man behind the couch. He was dead, but he had a gun and it smelled like it had been just shot. I stood and kicked his gun away out of habit.

Phil groaned. I went to him and then saw that Kitty's bedroom door was opened. And even though the lights were out, a pair of a prone woman's feet filled the gap of light in the doorway. My need to know overwhelmed my fear, and I ran to the bedroom.

I stopped at the doorway to the unlit room and eased the door fully open. The light from the great room illuminated the shoeless woman's feet, small feet. Although to me, all women had small feet.

My nights were already plagued by nightmares from too many bad memories. I took a deep breath to steel myself for the worst case scenario, Kitty, or Bean. I flipped on the light switch and stepped into the room.

96

My worst memories of the war were the ones where I had seen things that both took my breath and imprinted the image in my brain. These images were never voluntarily recalled; they had an ability to capture your mind whenever, but mostly in the still of the night. And when they did return, they were in vivid color accompanied by all the sounds and smells that took your breath again and again.

This was one of those moments.

Robin "Bean' Hayes, my little Tinker Bell, lay on her back on Kitty's bedroom floor. Her once beautiful black eyes and her mouth were wide open as if she had been shocked, or scared, like she was trying to say, "No, not me."

I stood there unmoving, not breathing. Sadness filled me, weighted me, sagged my shoulders, and bowed my back.

Breath came back and exited with a moan and tear-blurred vision.

"Oh God, why Robin, my little Bean, why?" I whispered.

I dropped to my knees to check her pulse though I knew she couldn't have survived the massive bloody exit wound on her chest. She had no pulse.

I held her, rocked her, and wept.

What had changed the woman I was once sure I knew? Had the lure of riches altered her? Could she have been warped to the extent to try to kill a man who wasn't even threatening her? Was she that guilty and that desperate to keep her millions? Had my knowledge about her been built on lies? Had she used me? God, I hoped not.

Did I really know anyone?

All the death I'd seen, and now Robin; there couldn't be a God.

I closed her eyes but couldn't close her mouth. Death was so cold, so final.

Bean was gone.

"Oh my God, no." Joshua said behind me, startling me from my tear-dried mourning funk.

I turned and Joshua knelt by the dead man behind the couch. He had rolled the man onto his back and was cradling his head.

"I'm so sorry, Preston. For so long I've feared this day would come. I ... I failed you so badly." He sobbed.

I eased Bean from my arms and stood. For the first time, I took in the room.

A gun lay on the floor by Bean's right hand. Bean was left-handed. My curiosity took over. The wall next to the bedroom door was smeared in an arc with Bean's blood going away from the door. One of the three windows in the room was open and the curtains fluttered in the night breeze.

Bean had been shot in the back. The impact had slammed her into the wall and she had slid down to the floor and rolled onto her back. Phil hadn't shot her. The person who shot Phil, had murdered Bean. Then they tossed the gun next to Bean, went out the window, and escaped in the car I had heard.

I bent and checked Bean's wrists for ligature marks, there weren't any.

Had she trusted someone, like I had trusted her?

I took one last look at Bean and walked out of the room.

I stepped outside. I needed to find a phone. Unraveling this mess and possibly saving Kitty, if she needed saving, was now up to Agent Peterson. I didn't want to be the one to find Kitty, not like this. I couldn't take any more horrible images plastered in my brain. Plus I now had no clue where to look.

Kitty and I should've called Peterson long ago, too many dead bodies ago.

I wasn't sure what would happen to me, but I wasn't concerned any more. I just wanted this to be over. I was broken and tired beyond being useful to anyone.

"Hello, Federal Bureau of Investigation, how may I help you?" a woman asked.

"I'd like to speak to Agent Peterson. I believe his first name is Tom, and he's the regional director," I said.

"Ah, I'm sorry, sir, we do not have an Agent Tom Peterson in this district or … let's see … or anyone by that name in the Bureau."

97

Two Weeks Later,
Beaufort, SC

"Why if it ain't Mr. Layne, arisin' from the dead. Semper fi."

I looked up from stirring the new pot of steaming hash, another helper and I had minutes ago sat on the serving table.

The dirty, unshaven face was sort of familiar, but I knew the coat. And then the short man smiled, exposing the void where his front teeth used to be, and I remembered him. "Semper fi, Charlie. And my name is Brent." I gestured at his coat. "It's a little warm for that coat, isn't it?"

"Ya'll don't sleep outside much do ya."

His words brought back the death-threatening cold of Afghanistan winters. "I've done my share."

The gray-haired man's red-streaked brown eyes looked into mine. "I thought you got a job. Shore didn't last long. What happened, you get caught chasin' the boss' secretary?" He grinned.

I evaded his probing stare and dished up a bowl of hash, remembering to add an extra ladle full. If I told him, or anyone the truth, they wouldn't believe me. "Somethin' like that."

Instead of taking the offered bowl from me, he grabbed one of my arms. "There was a time when I led men like you." His words were clear and enunciated, unlike earlier. "I took them into Hell and brought most of them back. And after Nam, I formed and ran my own company for thirty years until … anyway, I know many influential people. If you need help finding work and are willing to tell me your skills, I may be able to link you to the right people. As you probably already know, networking is the best way to find work."

I shook my head and sat the hot bowl down. "What are you doing here, on the street?"

"I'm not asking for help; I'm offering it, from one Marine to another."

"What was your discharge rank?"

"Colonel. Eight years, three tours, Third Marines. How 'bout you?"

"Captain. Four years, two tours, First Marines."

"So would you like my help?" he asked, taking the bowl.

"I, ah, I don't really need a job right now."

Another man stepped up for soup.

Charlie eyebrows arched. "Fooled me." He walked away and sat at a table by himself.

Charlie had to think I was an ingrate or worse; a spoiled rich guy or a sponge. Regardless, I didn't like how our conversation had ended. Three bowls of hash served later; no one else was in line. I took a break and walked over and sat down next to him.

"I want you to know, I appreciate your offer. It's just that … well I got a sort of severance from my last job." The State had given me my three-year salary as a reward, and I had kept what was left of the cash I'd found in Nick's car. But Charlie didn't need to know any of that. "And right now, I don't want to be tied to a commitment. I, ah, I need some time, some free time."

He nodded. "I can relate to that." He grinned. "And there's no need to apologize." He scraped the last remnants of hash from the bowl with his spoon and ate it. "Out of curiosity, what were you doing?"

Paranoia made me glance around. "Ah, I was a South Carolina lottery commissioner," I said in a half-whisper.

He jerked erect. "What? You were involved in—"

"Shhhh!" I raised both palm-out hands to stop him. "Keep your voice down," I said in a hushed voice. "I don't need everyone knowing my business."

He wagged his head. "Whoa. I would've thought you would've gotten jail time versus a severance."

"I told them how the lottery was fixed and who did it."

"So you got a reward and a pink slip."

"Yeah, that about sums it up." I said flatly. I wished I could forget the whole damned thing.

He crossed his legs and arms and leaned back. "Did you know these people you put in jail?"

I didn't know why I was talking to a stranger about my dark past, but I needed to vent, at least a little. "I knew them, but I didn't put them in jail. They escaped."

"Aren't you worried they'll come after you?"

I sighed. "No. I think they're too busy enjoying all that money they stole."

"And how much was it?"

I shrugged. "Oh, I'm not sure exactly, close to a half-billion."

He tried to whistle but couldn't without front teeth. "That's a whole bunch of 'enjoying' there."

He studied me for a moment. "You more than knew these people didn't you?"

I looked away. "One of them." I sighed.

"A woman, right?"

I nodded.

"We have a lot in common, you and me." He pointed a dirty finger at me. "We're both here because of the same reason."

"Do you also read palms?" I started to get up, and he grabbed my arm.

"Sit for a moment." He looked around. "The food line is done. Talk to me. I don't get much opportunity to talk to intelligent people."

"The last thing I am is intelligent."

"Believe me I know how you feel. So a woman played you, welcome to the club," he extended his hand, "Charles Forrester Townsen, President and Chief Executive Officer."

For some silly reason, I shook his hand. "Forrester?"

"It's a long story. My great grandfather made a fortune buying and selling land for the railroads. Plus he started paper mills and used the lumber he cleared for the roadbeds; smart ol' man. So I come from old money and old names. But this is about you, not me.

Don't feel bad; women have been manipulatin' men since Eve."

"She more than played me, and I'm not sure why." The acid faucet in my gut started dripping. "I'll probably never know why. She's missing."

The little man's eyes enlarged. "Wait a minute. The missing governor and her secretary, so I was right, you were chasin' the boss' secretary. You and the missing governor's secretary had a ... a thing?"

"Somethin' like that," I said with my voice trailing off.

His squinted brown eyes fixed on me as he cocked his head. "I remember their pictures in the paper, hell I slept with that paper for three or four nights. The governor's administrative assistant wasn't much to look at, but the ... you were havin' an affair with the governor! Hot damn, I'm hangin' with royalty."

"You're hangin' with a fool."

"Oh I know what it's like to have a woman lead you around by your pecker and then use you and abuse you." He looked away and blew a long breath out through puffed lips. "I probably could've recovered from losing all my wealth and material things. But when you're hollow inside you don't care anymore ... for nothin'." He wiped a blue-veined hand over his mouth. His focus returned to me. "So the luscious governor was up to her pretty nose in the lottery fraud and used you?"

The big invisible weight I knew too well compressed my frame. "I wish I knew the answer to that." My stomach burned as it did every time I thought about Kitty. Was she alive? Was she living the good life? I hoped so. Otherwise, she was probably dead. I had made so many mistakes; the biggest was letting her out of my sight in that damned alley. Maybe she would've eventually told me the truth.

No, that wasn't my biggest mistake. I should've listened to Bean when she asked me to quit. She was trying to save us. Bean hadn't used me. All the things Kitty or her secretary had said that Peterson had found were lies. Peterson didn't exist. Andrew hadn't taken any money or set up a Swiss bank account for him and Bean. And Bean had never returned to live with her parents. She must have been kidnapped by whoever had called me before she could get home.

Either Miss Cummins was using Kitty or they both were using me.

I should've listened to Bean. None of this would have happened. Bean would still be alive, and maybe she and I would have made it.

My fists clenched as they always did each time I thought about my stupidity. The guilt and grief brought to life all the painful memories, like the way Bean's parents looked at me at her funeral. Bean's funeral and all the other funerals I had caused jammed my mind. I wanted to scream and hit something, me.

My stomach gurgled. Kitty, if she were alive, owed me some answers.

Charlie plopped an elbow on the table and rested his chin in his hand. Those beady brown eyes of his played tag with mine; from one to the other. "You're lettin' the guilt eat your insides. You need answers, closure. You need to find her, don't you?"

I bowed my head and didn't answer him. I didn't want to talk about my stupidity any more.

He sat back and folded his arms. "I know how to fix your problem."

I'd had enough lecturing from a vagabond. "Bullshit! It's been weeks, and the FBI can't find her or any of them; not a trace. How are *you* gonna do what a large, trained and equipped, government agency can't?"

"Alive or dead, if you want me to, I can find her for you."

(98)

Charles Forrester Townsen and I sat at a back table of Lou's Libations, a local bar around the block from the soup kitchen. The daylight revealed cracks and chips in the dirty blue linoleum floor, yellowed white walls, and marred furniture. The smell of stale cigarette smoke and beer made me crave the spring-like outdoors.

Curiosity had brought me here. Could Charlie find Kitty, and did I really want to find her? What would I do if I did find her?

Charlie washed down the last bite of his cheeseburger with a large gulp of his second beer.

Charlie had been eating slow, too slow for me.

He wiped his mouth on his frayed blue dress-shirt sleeve. His grungy pea coat, my old coat, hung on the back of his chair.

This street-person, this bum, this ex-Marine needed saving. Marines never left another Marine behind, particularly a wounded Marine. And Charlie had been injured badly on the battlefield of life. I couldn't leave Charlie in his current state, but I wasn't sure I had the tools to save him. But those issues would have to be resolved another day. Today, Charlie was going to save me, or at least that is what he'd said.

Charlie pinched the last five or six french fries in his dirty fingers and stuffed them into his mouth.

Unlike my self-appointed savior, I didn't have the courage to eat any food in this place. Drinking their draft beer was risky enough.

268

"Okay, the food's gone," I said, my patience depleted. "You're halfway through your second beer. It's time to talk."

He arched an eyebrow as he chewed and swallowed. "You think I'm using you too, don't you?"

"Well let me just say that I'm having a hard time believing you can do something the FBI with all of its resources couldn't do." I took a sip of my draft beer.

"I owned and managed several companies in my time; one of which was a loan company."

His spot-on diction coupled with his words stiffened my back, pushing me to a sitting- attention mode, and I had trouble swallowing the beer. Charlie had been a business owner, living proof of the old 'never judge a book by its cover' adage.

"Made a lot of money—" a belch escaped Charlie's attempt to block it with his hand. "In the loan business, it wasn't uncommon for people to take the money and their collateral and run. But I employed a man who could find anyone, and he always did, always. Not only did I pay him well, we became good friends." He pointed a finger at me. "I'll guarantee you, he'll find whoever you want him to find in less than a week, and it won't cost you very much, three or four hundred dollars a day plus expenses."

I leaned toward him. "You're going to guarantee me? How are you going to do that?"

"Ah, well that was a figure of speech. But if I could, I'd financially back my words. This guy is better than good and the FBI. As a matter of fact, the Feds frequently hire him to find people for them. If they'd asked him, he would've found Hoffa. The man has skills, computer and bloodhound skills."

If there was a possibly that Kitty could be found, I couldn't pass that up. First of all, I wanted to know if she was alive. And if she was, I couldn't spend the rest of my life wondering why she had done what she did. I needed some answers, a whole bunch of them. I had already had too many restless nights.

"You must have been in sales, 'cause you've sold me. I'm looking for two people, but if he finds one, he'll probably find both; if they're alive. Can I meet this guy?"

"Probably not. He's not a social kind of person, if you get my drift.

But I can have him call you. You two can negotiate a contract. Then you can tell him who you're looking for and answer all his questions. He'll want profiles of these people, so be prepared."

After my shift ended, I returned to the condo that Bean and I jointly owned. The condo her parents were now part owners of; and who constantly harassed me about selling. The grieving, now childless parents who confirmed Kitty's lies by telling me Bean had never come to their home after she'd left to visit me in Columbia. They said they'd had called her when she was late and left a message. Bean had called them back and told them she had to get back to her job in Beaufort.

Now I knew why Bean's parents hadn't called me. The kidnapper must have forced Bean to lie to her parents, eliminating their concerns.

I had told the FBI everything; I had to. I don't know what the FBI told Bean's parents. They had lost both their children because of the lottery crimes. Although they never expressed it, I was pretty sure they hated me.

I'm not sure why I came back to the Beaufort condo after the lottery fiasco. I didn't need any reminders of how I had been so easily misled to distrust and even dislike Bean. I rehashed those events every night.

My logic at the time was to stay in the area in case Kitty tried to get in touch with me. Call my actions unsupported hope, wishful thinking, desperation, or whatever. I owned the condo, and it was convenient.

I had tried and tried to push aside the recollections of Bean. I had removed all our pictures, and her mom had taken all of Bean's clothes, jewelry, and personal effects. But this condo, its nick-knacks and original furniture, were haunted by my once little Tinker Bell. Her voice, her wearing only my tee-shirts, her laughter, the good times seemed to always reappear no matter where I looked.

I had grown to accept my guilt. There was nothing I could do about my mistakes but live with them, every night, over and over.

My packed bags sat in the foyer. Yesterday, I had finally given up my useless quest of waiting. The rational side of my brain had decided to list the condo and move on to somewhere new, west, maybe Utah, hopefully where I could sleep all night. I was going to drive until I found it; great plan. But like most of my recent plans, it never reached fruition; it had evaporated after my luncheon meeting with Charles Forrester Townsen.

Somewhere between boredom and hope, I had started unpacking my bags when my phone rang. Over the past many weeks, paranoia dominated me whenever my phone rang. "Hello," I said with concern.

"Is this Brent Layne, Charlie's friend?" a male radio-voice asked.

99

The next day, I had just started to serve lunch at the soup kitchen when Charlie arrived.

"Well, did he call yet, did he?"

I looked up from my chores at the frazzled little old man. He was so excited he couldn't stand still, bouncing from one foot to the other.

"Charlie, settle down before you have a stroke, and 'Good Morning' to you as well." I don't know why I loved to tease him, I just did. So I took my time ladling two scoops of soup into a bowl.

Charlie leaned toward me and grabbed the offered soup. "Okay, good morning. Now, did he call?"

"Yes, he called." People had always made me ask the obvious question, so I guess my silence was my way of getting even. Poor Charlie.

He sat the bowl down and glared at me. "So'd you negotiate a deal? Told you he'd give you a fair price. He's worth every penny, too. You'll see."

I sat the ladle down in an empty bowl and threw my spill towel over my shoulder. "Yes, we settled on a price, and it was more than you said. He'll have to be awfully good to earn it."

"Well, how much did he want?"

"That's between me and him."

"Don't worry, it won't cost you much. It won't take him long. Did he have a bunch of questions like I said?"

"Too many. I can't believe all the things he asked. I never even met one of these people, and he'd asked me questions his family probably couldn't answer."

Charlie nodded. "I don't know nothing 'bout any of this, but I'm bettin' two days tops, and he'll find'em."

I scanned the dirty, bent-over old man. I wondered if a woman could destroy me as badly as he had been decimated. Losing Bean had been horrible; I wasn't sure what I'd do if Kitty were dead as well. I couldn't believe everything she had said was a lie. I had to know. If not, I'd be close to crashing. Hell, I was only a table away from Charlie's world now.

I needed something else to focus on, other than women. I rubbed my chin. "Okay, let's make this interesting," I said.

"How so?" Charlie's eyebrows crowned.

"If your mystery man calls me in two days or less, I'll buy you a new coat." I scanned him again. "Hell, make it an entire outfit, skin out, including a new coat and ... and shoes. You could definitely use new clothing. And if he takes longer than two days, you got to promise me you'll take a job, and not just any job, a position requiring your previous skills and talents, a brain tester. And then you'll get off the street."

He scrunched his face into a mass of wrinkles. "I don't know 'bout this here bet. All I get is a new outfit versus having to go back to work? Doesn't seem quite balanced to me." He held his hands out palms up and moved one up and the other down.

"What more do you want?"

He licked his lips. "Throw in a case of good, single malt scotch with the clothes, and it's a deal."

"So it's street forever or no street?"

He looked up to the side and nodded.

I pointed at him. "You can't talk to him and try to influence him in any way."

He jammed his fists onto his hips. "What do you think I am; a cheater? No, I'd never do that. When do these two days start?"

I glanced at my watch. "How about right after your friend's call to me? So tomorrow night it's over at let's say eight o'clock."

"Let's shake on it." Charlie extended his right hand.

I shook his little hand.

"Regardless, I hope this turns out good for you," Charlie said, releasing my hand.

"Thanks, Charlie, so do I." I surveyed Charlie again. This man on the street, with nothing, wanted things to be good for me. If I wanted good things, I probably should accept my losses and go back to the condo, repack my bags, head west, and start over. I was afraid of what Charlie's mystery man would find.

After making the bet with Charlie, I spent the rest of my day fidgeting. I could not relax even after a long walk, a good meal at my favorite restaurant, and too much wine. If Charlie were right, and I thought he was, the answers to all my questions throughout my involvement with the lottery were hours away. I prayed Kitty was well, but if she was, what did that mean? The FBI had sworn they'd call me if they found out anything. Since they hadn't called, I had ruled out Kitty being kidnapped and held for a ransom. If she were alive, could she be living with Camden Sparks? Could she be that desperate for money? Had she used me so she could live with Camden? My ego wrestled with my heart.

Bored with TV, I went to bed after watching the late news. I should've known better than try to sleep. My mind was too wired. I finally got up and watched an old movie until I dozed off in a chair, a chair Bean had bought and loved.

Morning came too soon. Sleeping in Bean's chair had given me a stiff neck. Bean's chair ... I needed to get out of the condo and move on.

Moving like a lame slug, I conducted my rituals and ambled to the soup kitchen.

Charlie was the conduit between my past and future. My fears combined with my lack of sleep made me dread his arrival at the soup kitchen this morning. Poor Charlie had become the potential bearer of my next nightmare; Kitty was either dead or a horrific self-centered manipulator and maybe a murderer. I didn't want to see Charlie or talk to him.

But like a reliable employee, Charlie arrived at his normal time. In he walked, wearing his dirty blue shirt and soiled blue jeans. His long gray hair stuck out from under his old blue Cubs ball cap like he'd just been shocked. And his old work boots looked like they were steps away from being sole-less.

As if he sensed my mood, or already knew something, he just gave me a half-smile and a nod without uttering a single word. He took his piping bowl of chicken soup, brimming with the extra ladle. He walked to a table, sat down, and ate like all the other zombie-like street people.

His actions made me all the more agitated. What the hell was going on? I slopped soup and shoved bowls at people for another half-hour.

After serving the last person, I busied myself cleaning up the serving area. Then as part of my normal routine, I went into a little room off the kitchen and retrieved a bucket of hot soapy water and some towels to clean off the tables.

When I returned to the hall, everyone was gone but Charlie. He sat at a table. His eyes darted back and forth from me to a wall clock and back again; over and over, like I was volleying with the clock in a tennis match.

If he wanted to talk to me, that was up to him. I wasn't in the mood to engage him.

I was halfway through cleaning my first table when my phone rang. I should've known why Charlie had lingered.

(101)

I stood over a soaped table at the soup kitchen as my phone rang in my pocket. I dried my hands and glanced at Charlie, sitting at a rear table. He was grinning like he had just won a case of scotch.

"Hello," I said, my voice grumbled, expressing my lack of sleep and my fears.

"Mr. Layne, this is Charlie's friend. I've found Senator Camden Sparks and his lady friend and all that money.

My tongue tripped over my anxiety. "How? Where? 'Lady friend'?"

Charlie sat up and pointed at the wall clock. Then he flashed his toothless smile, mouthed the words 'I told you so', and gave me a 'thumbs up'.

"Senator Sparks was easy to find. He takes a rare drug with a short shelf-life for his trimethylamineria. I found the few sources for the drug in the United States and checked on their recent sales to new users and the locations of the shipments. And bam, Senator Sparks, a.k.a. Carter Speck, received his first delivery in Winfield, Kansas last week." He paused and papers shuffled. "After a whole bunch of research," he whistled, "man, those two have a whole bunch of money."

The last thing I wanted to talk about was that damned money. But I could understand his infatuation. "As I told you before, that's Powerball money belonging to over forty states. If we retrieve it, they'll probably give us a sizable reward, which I'll split with you." I rubbed my chin, a trait I must've picked up from Kitty. And Kitty was alive, thank God. The nightmares would finally stop. I would have closure. Though some of the horror was true, Kitty was with Camden, a fact hard to understand; but at least Kitty was alive.

"Winfield, Kansas, where in the hell is that?" I asked, changing the subject.

"It's a small town about sixty or seventy miles south of Wichita, close to Oklahoma. And I mean a small town … you know, like the high school marching band's a trio. A place where a person can hide without concern. I think Baby Face Nelsen hid in the area back in the thirties. A town where no one would know what a US Senator from South Carolina would look like. All they would know is a fat stranger had arrived with a woman."

I couldn't dodge my fears any longer. I took a deep breath and released it. "This woman, is she Catherine Franklin? I emailed you a picture." The papers had been full of Kitty's pictures for at least a week after her disappearance, and I had cut a few of them out, a memory of a love lost and a fool's manipulator.

"I've got your pictures and … well I'd rather not guess over the phone. My experiences have taught me women are much more capable of changing their appearances than men."

It had to be Kitty, Kitty and that fat bastard. I had always tried to push Kitty's story about her and Camden into a dark hole. I didn't want to believe she had fucked that grotesque man. I just couldn't fathom Kitty and Camden being lovers, and me being the fool. The thought defied logic as well as crushed my ego.

"And what are they doing? Are they posing as husband and wife?"

"Ah, I don't know how to tell you this other than just say it. They're dead. They—

"Dead?" That couldn't be; that wasn't fair. Was taking both of these women from me God's way of punishing me for cheating on Bean and not believing in her? Now I'd never know why Kitty used me. I became lightheaded, my knees weren't trustworthy; I had to brace an arm on the wet table for support.

"I'm sorry. They were found yesterday. The police report said they'd been shot to death."

"Police report, how'd you get a police report this quickly?" I was talking to hear myself. My mind was at Kitty's office that first day, watching her glide across the room to greet me. Then my memory jumped to the yellow sweater at Seven Gables Inn, and then to the Full Fishnet Restaurant when I looked up from my meal and saw her in that green dress, so beautiful. She couldn't be dead. I had never felt so empty, so lost.

But I had to know for sure. There could be no doubt. Either Kitty was dead, or I'd continue to search. "Did you get a description of the woman? Are there pictures?"

"I'll send the full report to your phone, with pictures, as soon as we finish talking. The police think the couple had an argument and shot each other. I guess what they say is true."

Why did I always have to grill people to get them to finish a thought? "And what's that?"

"About redheads and their tempers."

"Redheads? Who is a redhead?"

"The woman had cropped red hair. But that don't mean much, woman change their hair color and style all the time."

An injection of hope caused me to straighten. My legs no longer needed my arm braced against the table for support.

"Did the woman wear heavy facial powder, the kind used to hide blemishes?"

"Ah, yeah, she did. Is this Miss Franklin?"

"I don't think so. I think the woman is Nancy Beltner." Who else would have known about the magic Sally Kellerman had discovered? Nancy had to be the one who had switched the video tapes for Andrew. She was a 'techie' and had access.

"So there was another woman involved," Charlie's friend said. "This is all starting to make sense now." He cleared his throat. "The whole thing smelled like a set-up, and the police have swallowed it hook, line, and sinker."

I shook my head. Everyone must think I'm a frigin' mind reader. "And why s that?"

"'Cause the money's moving."

The call from Charlie's buddy was over. As promised, he'd done his job.

I pocketed my cell phone; the piece of shit never brought me any good news. Some day I'd throw the damned thing away. I slipped off the damned hair net and removed the apron and flung them on the wet serving table. I went out the door of the soup kitchen, disregarding Charlie's questioning yell from the back of the room. I wasn't sure if it was noon yet, but I needed to find a bar, I needed a drink.

Lou's Libations was around the corner and open. Although the place had to be a germ-breeding factory, the whiskey would kill what Lou hadn't washed properly.

I sat at a bar stool and ordered a double Jim Beam. Kitty was alive. Who else could be moving the money? Bean was dead; I took a gulp of the whiskey, wincing at the burn sliding down to what seemed to be my toes. Everyone else was dead, Andrew, Sally Kellerman, Jim-Nick Sanders, Jeanette Cummins, Preston Franklin, and now Camden Sparks and Nancy Beltner, and at least a half-dozen others. Kitty was the only one left, at least that I knew about. It had to be Kitty moving the money, had to; I finished the drink and ordered another.

Charlie's friend had provided me with enough information to deduce who and why; Kitty and the money.

I held the second glass in front of my eyes and studied the golden fluid. This drink was for me, the fool. Kitty being alive meant she was involved in the lottery scam up to her deceiving blue eyes, and she had played me. And perhaps she was more than a user, maybe she was a murderer as well.

Maybe she killed Bean. The thought opened the bile valve to my stomach.

Not only had I trusted her, I thought I had fallen in love with her.

I raised the glass in a mock toast to Kitty's fool, and a hand touched my shoulder. Charlie stood next to me, too close. He smelled like sour milk. The soup kitchen had a similar odor. I didn't like it, but I had gotten used to it.

"Ya know what they say about fellas who drink alone, don't ya?" he asked.

"Yeah, yeah, yeah." I shrugged his hand off my shoulder.

"What's wrong? Didn't my friend take care of you?"

"He's got some more work to do, but, yeah, he took care of me." I chugged the warming fluid and set the glass on the bar. "Want to join me? That way I wouldn't be one of those fellas you mentioned."

"I can't remember ever turning down an offer for a drink. Plus I need to give you somethin'." He extended his hand with a folded piece of paper in it.

I ordered two more doubles and took the paper. "What's this?" I scanned his beady brown eyes.

"It's my sizes, including shoes. I figured you'd need it since you done lost our bet. Plus I've listed a few single malts for you to choose from for the case of scotch."

I nodded. "You're on top of your game. I'll fulfill my end of the bargain, but I'd still like to see you put your mind back to work."

The drinks arrived and Charlie raised his glass and smelled it like it was wine.

"Ya know I could do that, and it'd be a good thing. But first we need to get you out of your funk. What's goin' on?"

"Your friend found two of the three missing people, but not Kit- not the governor."

"I'm sorry. Does that mean she's … she's dead?"

"I don't think so. He found the money."

"All that money?"

"Yeah, and it's being moved."

"So she's movin' it."

"You've got a firm grasp on the obvious." Charlie wasn't the bad guy. None of this mess was his fault. I sucked in some air as I rubbed my jaw. "I needed a few drinks. One to celebrate her being alive, and a whole bunch more for being her boy toy, her fool."

"There ain't enough booze in the world to fix being used by a woman," Charlie said. "Believe me, I know."

My first drink had burned. The second had tasted good. I knew if I drank the third one, it would call for more. "I never was very good at listening to advice." I chugged my third double.

Charlie joined me throwing down his drink like a true cowboy.

The booze was working, my gut didn't ache and the tension was gone from my shoulders. I ordered two more drinks.

"I'd like to sit here and drink with you all day, Marine, but you're too big for me to carry home," Charlie said. "Why don't we have one more and call it a day? Trust me, my friend will find the governor. And when he does, you'll need to have a plan, or all of this was a waste of time. And drunks don't plan very well, I know."

"You're a very wise street person, Charlie. What a waste. Here," I slid both drinks in front of him, "you finish these, I'm going home."

I put enough cash on the bar to cover everything plus tip and walked out, buzzed and in need of coffee, but capable of walking home. Charlie was right; I had some thinking to do.

(103)

Two long days later, I still hadn't heard from Charlie's friend. I wasn't sure who was more anxious, Charlie or me.

After wolfing down his soup on the second day, Charlie came back to the serving table.

"More soup, my friend?" I asked.

"No. Do you have a plan yet?"

I looked away, head shaking. "Not really. Whenever I concentrate on developing one, all I come up with is finding her and asking her face-to-face what really happened."

"You're dreaming, aren't you?" Charlie asked. "You're hoping she'll have a legitimate explanation for her actions. And I'm sure she will. But do you really expect her to tell you the truth?" He stepped back and studied me. "My God, you do. What a romantic; you're still in love with her."

My head dropped, I stared at the floor. "I didn't choose to be in love with her; it just happened."

"Is it love or the fear of being a fool that's made you brain-dead?"

I looked him in the eye. I didn't like having my buttons pushed. "Both."

"After you confront her, no matter how believable her story, will you turn her over to the authorities?"

How many times had I thought about that question, over and over? Sure Kitty was a felon. She was guilty of at least rigging the Powerball. I

283

wasn't sure what else she'd done, but based on the recent information, Kitty's Powerball fraud seemed minor.

But my heart said there had to be some reason for her actions other than greed. After all, her gramps had mega-bucks and, per her words, she'd inherit all of it in a few years.

This woman had made me feel like no other woman had ever made me feel. Was I that naïve or was she that good of a con? Kitty and I needed time together. I had to know who she really was.

I didn't know the answer to Charlie's question, and I didn't want to think about it anymore. My head ached from all my thinking.

"Go away, Charlie."

"Go away? I'm the only friend you have."

I nodded as I scanned the dirty, old, toothless tramp; the only person trying to help me. I had tried feeling sorry for myself once when I was a kid, and it didn't fix anything. So I wasn't going to try it again today. "You're right. You are my only friend. So what should I do, friend?"

"Stay out of it. When my buddy finds her, have him turn her in, and let the cops figure it out."

Charlie had tapped my anger button. Didn't he or anyone recognize that I had feelings for this woman?

I spread my arms. "How could I live with myself if I did that?"

"You'll live; maybe sad for a while, but at least free. If you confront her, she'll manipulate you just as she has done before, and you'll end up on the wrong side of the law."

"You're assuming she's guilty." The words slashed from my lips.

He sighed and nodded. "If's it got webbed feet, a bill, and feathers, it's a duck. And your governor has millions of reasons for being guilty. Walk away, lad. You can start over. And you will find love again, I promise you. Let me handle this."

"I can't do that."

"Look at me, damn it! Is this how you want to end up, with your insides eaten away by self-contempt, and your life behind you?"

"No." My words were hollow, placating. I really didn't care about what happened to me. I just wanted to know if Kitty, the woman I loved, was real.

"Then heed my words; walk away."

I looked into his beady, brown, imploring eyes. "You are a friend, Charlie. And I appreciate your concern and everything you've done for me. But I'm asking you to stay out of this. I'll take care of it by myself. This discussion is over."

His head dropped, he turned, and shuffled out the door, seemingly more broken than when he'd entered.

After my confrontation with Charlie, the days crawled by becoming a week, with Charlie and I barely acknowledging each other at the soup kitchen. I spent most of my free time clothes and scotch shopping for Charlie.

During my idle time, Charlie's advice to me about planning chewed at me. But I found planning to be impossible because of my emotions. All the information, as well as my gut, supported Kitty being alive. I wanted her to be alive. And if someday I found her and faced her, I had no clue what I'd do except solicit the truth. And I was pretty sure I already knew what she had done. And the thought of what the truth had to be scared me. I wasn't sure how I'd react to being used and turning my back on the only woman who really did love me. Over and above my emotions, I also wasn't sure what I'd do about Kitty, turn her in, let her go, or ... I didn't know.

After buying all Charlie's stuff, I decided it was time to end our impasse. The next morning, I walked to the soup kitchen and got there early. I put on the stupid hair net and apron and helped the cooks peel potatoes for the soup. I had served most of the soup by the time Charlie arrived.

Charlie seemed more bowed and older than normal. And I could tell by the way he slouched and moved he was grumpy.

"Good morning, sunshine," I said and smiled as I added an extra ladle of soup to his bowl.

"What's up with you, you get laid last night?" he asked in a gravelly voice without making eye contact.

I laughed. "Yeah, right, and I rode a flying cow into work." I handed him the bowl of steaming soup. "I just want to be friends again. What do you say, Colonel?"

Charlie sat his bowl down and looked me in the eyes. "Ya know, I went out of my way to try to help you."

"I know that, and I appreciate all you've done."

"Then why don't you listen to me?" His voice raised in volume.

I studied his wrinkled face for a few seconds. "Because I love her."

He snatched up his bowl of soup. "You're gonna end up just like me." He turned and headed for the tables.

"Save me a seat; I'll join you in a few minutes," I said to his bowed back.

After cleaning off the serving table, I ladled up a bowl of soup for me and joined Charlie at his table. He sat alone as he normally did.

I sat across from him. I wanted to see his face.

"I've got some clothes for you and a case of some very good single malt scotch. I thought when we finished here you could go with me to my condo and pick up your winnings."

He nodded without looking at me.

"Why are you so mad at me? If our roles were reversed, you'd be reacting the same way I am."

"No I wouldn't." His brown eyes fixed on mine. "Knowin' what I know now; I'd walk away, and let her be turned over to the cops. That's what I'd do."

I tilted my head to the side and back. "Okay. I hear you. Let me find her and go from there."

Charlie wagged a forefinger at me. "That's the problem. If you're with her, you'll be thinkin' with the wrong part of your anatomy, and she'll own you. She controlled you before, and she'll do it again. You're a Marine officer, damn it. How can you go into battle without a plan?"

I swallowed my last spoon full of soup. I didn't want to argue with him. "You're right." I stood and picked up my bowl. "Let's clean off this table and get out of here."

We walked out of the kitchen and strolled side-by-side toward my condo. "Tell me, what are you going to do with all these clothes I bought you and a case of scotch? Do you have somewhere to store them?"

He shrugged. "I can rent a small locker at the bus station."

I rubbed my chin. I don't know why I hadn't thought of this earlier, when I first came back to the kitchen. "Why don't you move in with me, today, now?"

He stopped. "What?"

"After this ordeal with Kitty is over, I plan on putting the condo on the market and put this place in my dust. If you promise me you'll keep the place clean and not let anyone else move in, you can stay there until it's sold. Hopefully, that'll give you enough time to get your act together so you'll never return to the street."

His eyes moistened. "Why? You don't really know me, and you're inviting me to share your home. I could kill you in the middle of the night."

"You could. But you've helped me, and you're a Marine. I trust you. And I think you need another chance at life."

Charlie glanced up at the sky. "Ya know it's spose to rain tonight."

Charlie extended his hand and I shook it.

"'Though you're a fool, you're a good man, Brent Layne. Let's go sample that scotch."

My phone rang, a long tone followed by a short one, a new ring tone for strangers. The trumpet had to go. I checked the number, it was Charlie's friend.

My fingers trembled as I accepted the call.

I swallowed the lump in my throat. "Hello."

"I've found the money, and maybe the mover," radio voice said.

(105)

Charlie and I stood on Bay Street in Beaufort, South Carolina, a block or two from the soup kitchen. Although the mid-day April sun was warm, the man's smooth voice on my phone chilled me. This was the moment I had both sought and dreaded. I put Charlie's friend on my speaker phone so Charlie could hear the conversation.

"Where is the money?" I asked.

"The money is in Grand Cayman. It's almost equally divided in a few more than one hundred banks in Georgetown."

"Damn, that's a lot of banks for one town," Charlie said.

"Hey, Charlie, it's good to hear your voice," said the man on the phone. "Actually, there are close to six-hundred banks in Georgetown."

"Wow, Georgetown must have replaced Switzerland for the world's place to hide money," I said.

"Charlie, I thought you told me this guy used to be in the banking business?" Charlie's friend's voice was lathered with sarcasm. "That's been the case for at least the last twenty years, probably more."

I didn't have the time or the patience to sword tap with this stranger. My resume didn't include hiding money in off-shore accounts. My remarks would have to wait until I met him to pay him. "So, who is the mover, and where is she, ah, I mean where is the mover?"

"There are only account numbers, no associated names, typical of Georgetown's banking policies. I don't have an identity. It'll take awhile to cut through the bureaucracy. But I've traced several transactions on one of the smaller accounts to the Tortuga Club. It's a resort on the opposite side of the island from Georgetown. Either the mover has employed someone staying there or the mover is there. Do you want me to go there and identify that person?"

"No," I said and glanced at Charlie, who grimaced and shook his head back and forth. "I'll do that."

(106)

The first flight I could get was the next day. It left Savannah at dawn for Miami and then to Georgetown. I had never been to the Caribbean. Most people would have been excited about the trip, but I wasn't. My anxieties about possibly seeing Kitty again were one issue, and the other was I didn't like flying.

I had only flown a few times, mostly in the service, and I didn't like being out of control of my destiny. Being five or six miles above the ground dependent on thousands of parts working correctly as well as at the mercy of some unknown person at the controls, wasn't my favorite pastime.

The flights were all fine and the approach onto Grand Cayman Island was spectacular. It was a clear day, the ocean was as blue as Kitty's eyes, and the island looked like a floating paradise and a place to land in all the endless water, thank God.

After I cleared immigration and customs, I hired a cab to take me to the Tortuga Club. My baggage consisted of a small carry-on bag with one change of clothing. I didn't plan on being on the island very long. I had reservations for a room for one night at the Tortuga Club and a flight leaving the next day.

The taxicab ride from Georgetown across the island to the Tortuga Club was thirty or forty minutes of nothing. My mind was too occupied with all the 'what ifs' that awaited me.

When we arrived at the club, I had the taxicab driver give me a rolling tour of the grounds. It was always good to know the terrain if you were possibly going into battle. The Tortuga Club was a beach-front condominium-complex of numerous two-story, white stucco buildings with red Spanish-tiled roofs. The multi-unit buildings were well maintained and landscaped with flowering bushes interspersed with mature palms trees. A large pool, with an in-water bar, separated the complex from the beach. The place made me wish I'd brought more clothes. Regardless of whom I found here, this would be a great place to spend a week or two. And I needed a break from my Beaufort condo and all the Bean memories.

A beautiful young brown-skinned girl with black eyes in a white resort uniform was behind the reception desk.

I gave her my name, and she checked her computer.

"I'm here to surprise my girlfriend, ah, it's really more than that … I'm here to ask her to marry me," I said, shifting my weight from foot to foot like a nervous suitor. "And she has no idea about me being here; it's a total surprise. She came here with an old girlfriend I've never met, and, unfortunately, I can't remember her name. Her friend booked the room." I held up a picture of Kitty. "Have you seen her?"

The girl studied the picture for a moment. "I am sorry. No, I have not seen this woman. But she could be here. I only work the day shift. You are lucky, we are currently in between diving groups, and there are only ah … let's see," her fingers tapped the computer keys, "twenty occupants. And if they aren't in the pool at noon, they will be around it for the free lunches. The only time people leave is to go diving or, late in the day, to go to Georgetown for the nightlife." She glanced at her watch. "And it is quarter-past twelve. And since there are no dives scheduled today, everyone should be at the pool."

I filled out the paperwork.

She handed me my condo key and a piece of paper. "This is a map locating your unit, Mr. Layne. And the pool is right out that door." She pointed at a glass double-door. "Good luck." She winked one of her shiny black eyes and smiled.

Could Kitty be just a few steps away? I took a deep breath and walked to the door.

The mid-day sun radiated heat off the concrete surrounding the large Tortuga Club pool. I felt the warmth through the soles of my dress shoes. My wrinkled black pleated pants and blue long-sleeved oxford cloth shirt were not suited for either the climate or the setting.

By my count there were twenty-five people either in the pool or at the umbrella tables surrounding it. Most were either splashing or drinking in the water or sitting along the pool eating, talking, and laughing. Five wore white uniforms composed of tee-shirts with resort logos over a breast, Bermuda shorts, and scandals and worked the tables.

Kitty wasn't there.

Plan-less, I plopped down in a poolside chair at a table shadowed by a large umbrella. One of the servers took my beer order and left.

As I scanned the guests, my eyes fixed on a blonde who was staring at me. She wore sunglasses and little else, reclining in a lounger across the pool. Her tiny white bikini struggled to contain her voluptuous golden-skin assets. She held a phone in her hand and her head tilted toward the cell-phone and then turned to me and back to the cell. After several more checks, she placed her phone on a table. She rotated her long-muscled legs off the lounge chair and slid her tiny feet into a pair of scandals. She stood on bent legs, removed her glasses, and shook out her shoulder-length hair.

In that moment, as she stood, only a few square inches of cloth from being naked, tossing her long hair, I had stopped breathing. I was captivated by her beauty.

This gorgeous she-creature picked up her cell-phone and then struggled to walk on what had to be permanently bent legs. She shifted her body weight just so with each step to be able to balance and support herself on her distorted legs. She limped, jerked, and wobbled around the pool to my table, a Herculean task.

I couldn't take my eyes off this broken beauty.

"Your name wouldn't be Brent, would it?" she asked in a soft southern drawl with her head held high.

I had never met a beautiful woman with a physical handicap who also knew my name. This woman had to be an envoy for Kitty, a Kitty conduit. Kitty had expected me. I should've been at least concerned, if not fearful; but I wasn't. I was excited about seeing Kitty.

I didn't want to hurt this young woman's feelings, so I concentrated on looking into her sparkling green eyes.

"Ah, how do you know my name?"

"Just for assurance, how do spell your last name?" she asked, balancing before me, a damaged Barbie doll.

I eased in a long breath. "L-a-y-n-e."

"Okay, good," she said. "Generally, when I meet someone new, I answer the questions before they are asked." She nodded at her legs. "High school prom, two couples, drinking, car wreck, and I was the only survivor. And there are days when I don't think I was the lucky one."

I had seen worse, much worse, but I had nothing to add. I had other issues on my mind.

She held up her cell. "You mind if I take your picture, Mr. Layne?"

Kitty needed proof. "I, ah, I guess not."

She aimed her lens at me and pushed a button. Then her thumbs tap-danced on her screen as she spoke. "Kitty said you were good-looking, but that picture she gave me … well it doesn't come close to … mind if I sit?"

When she mentioned Kitty's name both her beauty and handicap vanished, poof. "Please," I extended a hand. "Where is Kitty?"

"She ain't here. But she's gonna be glad."

I released a long sigh. "Kitty is alive."

She giggled. "She sure 'nuf is."

"Why is she 'gonna be glad'?" I asked.

"'Cause you're here. You found me." She smiled, exposing small teeth.

"And who are you?" I asked.

"I'm Kitty's cousin, Jamie. She texted me a few days ago, and asked me if I wanted an all-expense paid month-long vacation in the Caribbean. She gave me a bank account number I could draw from and told me all I had to do was look for a man, you." She spread her arms. "So here I am, livin' a dream. And I've done my job. Hope I don't have to leave too soon."

"So, you have actually talked to Kitty?" I asked.

"Talked? No. I haven't actually spoken with her, only texts. Why?"

A barbed chunk of doubt spun in my stomach "Just curious."

The server delivered my beer. His interruption gave me time to ingest Jamie's words. Kitty knew I'd look for her, or at least she'd hoped I would. Maybe she really did love me. More realistically, maybe she was afraid I'd pursue her, and she was using Jamie as a rearguard. Or was someone posing as Kitty? Jamie hadn't talked directly to Kitty. Why wasn't anything simple?

I couldn't stop my eyes from roving over my surroundings. If someone besides Kitty was using this girl to eliminate anyone smart enough to find the money, this was a trap. But who would know Kitty's cousin; if this woman really was Kitty's cousin?

I wondered if I'd completely trust anyone ever again.

"Would you like a drink?" I asked her.

"No, thank you," she patted her flat belly. "I'm watching my weight."

And I was sure she knew every man here was also watching her weight. "And you found me, now what?"

"I just sent her a text with your picture."

I took a drink of beer. "So now we wait."

She canted her head. "Yeah."

Jamie's phone rang, causing both of us to jerk. "Hello," she said, looking at me with raised eyebrows. She listened and her eyebrows eased back to normal. "Yeah, I'm at the Tortuga Club." She fiddled with a bikini strap as she listened. "He's sitting right across from me." She handed me the phone.

Sitting in the mid-day warm Caribbean sun on Grand Cayman across from Kitty's beautiful, but damaged cousin was secondary to my anticipation of talking to Kitty. I took the offered phone from Jamie.

My hair tingled and I got goose bumps on my arms despite the heat. My excitement surprised me. No doubt, innocent or guilty, it didn't matter, I loved Kitty.

"Hello, governor, it's been a while." I tried to make my voice sound light and carefree.

"Mr. Layne, I'm sorry to disappoint you, but this is Joshua Franklin, not Katherine."

Hearing the old man's gruff voice was like being slapped awake from a wonderful dream.

I glared at Jamie and took a deep breath.

"Mr. Layne, are you there?"

"Yes, I'm here." My voice was flat and lifeless.

"We need to talk."

"Where's Kitty?"

"Kitty told me you were trustworthy."

"Where is she? I don't want to talk to you. I want to talk to Kitty."

"I'm in Austin, Texas, I can be there by dinner. Will you have dinner with me, Mr. Layne?"

"Why won't you answer me?" My voice raised.

"I will, tonight, at dinner."

"Answer me now, damn it, where is Kitty?" My hand squeezed the phone.

"You need to listen to me, Mr. Layne. Your life is in danger. Stay with Jamie at the Tortuga Club until I get there and nothing will happen to you." The phone went dead.

109

I needed some time to think. "Would you like some lunch?" I asked Jamie who sat slumped across from me in the shade of the pool-side table's umbrella.

Jamie's green eyes scanned my face. "Are you angry with me?"

Anger wouldn't have been my word choice; more like tired and pissed off. I was tired of being set-up, damned tired.

"Let's talk over lunch." I stood. "Can I get you something?"

"Yes. But could you first get me my cover? It's on the lounger." She pointed.

"Sure." I walked around the pool to retrieve her white, sheer cover. I glanced over my shoulder and Jamie was texting. I needed to find out what Jamie knew before Joshua arrived. I walked back to my table, handed her the garment, and sat down.

She stood on her bent knees and pulled the cover over her head and shoulders. Her skimpy bikini was outlined by her dark skin under the sheer cover.

She sat down. "About lunch—"

"Jamie, I don't know how much you know about Kitty and I, but I care for her a great deal. I think my presence here tells you how much. What's going on? Is Kitty okay? Who were you texting?"

Her chin pulled inward as her eyebrows arched. "Why on earth would you ask me that? Is Kitty in danger? What did Gramps say to you?"

"Who were you texting?" I asked, nodding at her phone.

"I, ah, I texted Kitty, and asked her why Gramps was calling me on her phone."

"Did she answer you?"

"Not yet."

"Do you know about Kitty ... about her disappearance?"

"Well sure, I read the papers and listen to the news. I haven't missed a thing. I love her." She bowed her head. "But I don't believe she's a crook like those reporters say. I don't know what happened or why she left." Her head raised and she looked into my eyes. "I texted her and asked her, and she said she'd tell me later."

If I could believe Jamie, we had a lot in common. We were both being used, by someone.

"Has anyone else called you or texted you, or come up to you since you've been here and asked about either me or Kitty?"

"No."

"Have you noticed anyone watching you? Not gawking at you because you're beautiful, which must happen often; but someone who looks away when you catch them staring."

She smiled. "Do you really think I'm beautiful?"

"Without a doubt." I leaned toward her. "Is someone watching you?"

She turned her head and looked over her shoulder.

"No, no, don't look around, look at me. So there is someone watching you."

Her green eyes fixed on mine. "Yes. But I just thought ... well, you know, I work hard at keeping my figure and—"

"Without looking at this person, are we being watched now?"

"Well I saw him just before you came. And after that I was too busy to care."

"Where is he?"

"He's in one of the pool-side rooms ... on the second floor. Whenever I come to the pool I see the curtain move, and there he is, watching me. And I see him around the complex frequently. He's a big man, you know bulky like one of those wrestlers. And he's maybe older than you. But I just thought he was one of those married men who weren't getting any."

Her weak description sounded like one of Joshua's bookends.

"Have you seen him with a woman?"

She looked away and chewed on her lip. "Ah, no, I haven't. He's always alone."

"Without looking, tell me which room."

"Ah, let's see," her eyes looked up and to the side, "the fourth condo from the left side, second floor."

"What do you want for lunch?" I stood.

"I'm a veggie. Any of the vegetables and a bottle of water please."

I walked to the buffet table and got in line. I didn't want to look at the room. I noticed a silver serving bowl lid lying on the table. I picked it up and tilted it until I could see the room in its reflection. One of Joshua's goons stood in the window watching me.

Jamie, Kitty's cousin, and I sat at the Tortuga Club's pool and picked at our lunches.

I was paranoid. Being watched was like being seen naked by your sister. I wanted to hide somewhere, find cover, and I kept looking over my shoulder to see if I could find Joshua's other bookend.

"Jamie, how are you related to Kitty?" I took a bite of a deviled-egg.

"My mother's sister was Kitty's mom."

I swallowed. "Was?"

"Within months after having Kitty, my Aunt Susie, ah, she left; walked out. Kitty never knew her, only pictures."

I wondered if Joshua had paid Kitty's mother to disappear. But I didn't want to upset Jamie, so I kept my thoughts to myself.

I was worried about Jamie. By finding her and the money, I was afraid I had crossed a line and taken her with me.

"Do you see your gramps often? Are you close?"

"I see him at various family functions, like Christmas and sometimes Kitty's birthdays, stuff like that. But not because he invited me, Kitty was my link to the family, she always invited me. No, Gramps and I aren't close, no way. My mom and I have struggled to survive all our lives. We're poor, the wrong side of the tracks part of the family."

Jamie needed to leave before Joshua got here. Before she became a witness to whatever he had in mind for me.

"Your grandfather is on his way here to meet with me. He and I have a lot to talk about. And, ah, well you've accomplished your job here. You found me. I suggest you cash out the account Kitty assigned to you and go to a place you've always dreamed about. Do you have one of those?"

She clasped her hands together between her thighs and pushed her shoulders up. Her expression morphed to a little girl's look when told she was going to the circus. "I've always wanted to go to Paris."

"Then Paris it is," I said, patting the table for emphasis. "You get dressed. Pack, and check out. Then I want you to go to the bank and get ten thousand dollars in cash and transfer the rest to your home bank account. After you've done that, call me. I'll book you a flight, today, this afternoon if possible. Just go to the airport from the bank."

"'All the money'? That account has over three hundred thousand dollars in it."

"Then take your mother to Paris with you. I'll book the tickets and you can meet her there." I couldn't think of a better use for what was left of Jim Smith's money.

Her green eyes darted from one of my eyes to the other. Then her face erupted into a smile, dimpling her cheeks and pinching her eyes. "Oh my God, you're serious."

"As serious as a walk through Notre Dame."

She stood. "I'll go get dressed."

I stood. "And I'll go make you and your mother's flight reservations." I dug in my pocket and found a pen. I slid it and a napkin to her. "Write down you and your mother's full names and where she lives."

She scribbled on the napkin and then hobbled around the table and gave me a big hug. "No wonder Kitty likes you," she said into my ear.

I couldn't keep from glancing over her shoulder at the bear in the condominium's window. He was watching us while he spoke into a phone.

An hour later, I met Jamie in the lobby and waited for her while she checked out of the Tortuga Club. We weren't alone. One of Joshua's goons sat at a chair nearby. I recognized him. He was part of a bad memory. I had talked to him at Kitty's country home, just before I found Bean.

I handed Jamie the flight reservations for her and her mother. As we walked toward the front door, me with both hands full of her luggage, the big man stepped in our path.

"Where're you goin', Mr. Layne?" said Mr. No-Neck in a voice too high for his size. The man's blue eyes were cold, blank, and void of emotion.

I had seen that look before. Either this man was fearless, or he didn't consider me a threat.

"Mr. Franklin's grand-daughter is leaving, and I'm walking her to that cab waiting by the curb." I nodded at the cab just outside the door.

"Why don't you and I watch her leave, from right here?" He stepped out of the way, next to me, and gripped my arm.

I didn't want to cause a scene in front of Jamie. "Okay, why don't I stay here, and you take her luggage to the cab?" I glanced at his hand squeezing my arm purple. "I think you're strong enough to handle that."

The man tilted his head at Jamie, and another large man dressed in a Tortuga uniform came from nowhere and took the luggage from me.

I leaned down to accept Jamie's kiss on my cheek.

She took my hand and whispered in my ear, "Take the paper in my hand. It's got my number and email address. If you need anything, call me. Do you want me to call the police? I want to see you again … with Kitty."

I took the paper. "I'll be fine. You go and have fun with your mom. And I hope I'll meet you again with Kitty. That'd be great."

I watched her do her wobble-walk to the cab. She turned before getting in and blew me a kiss. Then she was gone, thank God. At least one woman in my life had escaped the insanity.

I jerked my arm from No-Neck's grasp.

"If you ever touch me again, your boss won't like it when you're arrested."

He chuckled. "You think someone here is going to call the police if I kick your ass? Mr. Franklin owns this place."

Maybe Charlie was right, I should've gone to Utah.

(112)

I was in my condo at the Tortuga Club, not by choice. Two of Joshua's 'boys' had taken me to my lodgings and had told me to stay there until Mr. Franklin arrived. They took both my cell phone and the condo's phone.

I've always been able to depend on my hand and foot speed to overwhelm difficult situations. I probably could've gotten away from Joshua's hired help. But I figured I could get away later, after I heard what Joshua had to say. I hoped I was right.

The early morning flight had robbed me of my sleep so I lay down and tried to take a nap. Thoughts of Kitty and possibly seeing her again kept me awake. The only thing I accomplished was mussing the bed.

I spent the next several hours sitting in a chair in my living room watching brain-death television until my eyelids failed.

A phone rang causing me to jump into consciousness. The room was dark as was the outside window except for a nearby streetlight.

I looked around. The second ring pulled my eyes to the end table next to my chair. Someone had entered the room while I slept, turned off the lights and the TV, and put a cell phone on the table next to me.

I snatched up the phone before it rang a third time.

"Hello," I blurted.

"You are a tenacious man. That can be dangerous."

I recognized Joshua's voice.

"Where are you?" I asked.

"Are you ready to talk?" Joshua asked.

"That's my question to you." My disturbed state took control.

"Look outside your door. You'll find a bathrobe, exchange it for the phone. Strip naked, put the robe on, and come barefooted to the second unit left of yours, number forty-two. You'll find the condo unlocked. Sit down and wait in the dark. If you turn the lights on no one will come." The call was disconnected.

Joshua must have some heavy talking to do since he was obviously concerned about me wearing a wire. I had thought about it. But I figured I'd be searched. And I didn't want anything to keep me from the truth.

I did as Joshua had instructed.

Wearing only the robe, I entered condo number forty-two. The place was dark except for the glow through the drawn curtains from the exterior lights on the outside balcony walkway connecting the residences. I found the bathroom and sloshed water on my face. I needed to be fully aware for this meeting. I feared my life depended on it.

When I returned from the bathroom, the front door was open. I froze. Silhouetted in the glow of the outside lights was the figure of a woman standing in the opening.

⑪⑬

The silhouette of a woman in the opening of the door to the dark condo had to be Kitty. Or at least I hoped it was her.

She just stood there, unmoving.

My lips and tongue had momentarily lost their connection to my whirling brain as had my feet.

Two people frozen in the moment.

I found my breath and rushed toward her.

She must have sensed my movement in the darkness. "Brent, stop." Kitty's soft command brought me to a halt.

She stepped inside and closed the door, returning the room to semi-darkness.

Kitty had come back to me. All my anger, my resentment, my disappointment, all the regrets, all Charlie's warnings were swept away by her presence. She had come back for me. My heart skipped several beats and then began pounding at an orgasmic pace. The woman who had lied her way into my heart was here, alive, just steps away. The past was shoved into the darkness by her decision to come here and meet me. I had to hold her, feel her against me, smell her, taste her; I stepped closer.

"Brent. Stay where you are and leave the lights out. I ... I don't want you to see me or touch me ... I'm different. I'm not the woman you knew."

I halted. Her words tumbled my thoughts. I had let my desire to touch her compromise my scruples. Our relationship was void of trust, and she was telling me she was different. What the hell did that mean?

"I knew you'd come," she said. "I knew if anyone could find me, it'd be you. Gramps thought I was crazy to bring Jamie here. But if you came, I wanted to be the one to stop you, not Gramps."

"Stop me?" The vulnerability I felt earlier, sitting almost naked in a darkened room, was nothing compared to how I felt now.

I needed to understand her intentions. We were in the dark. What would a hug hurt? I decided to charge her ambush. I moved toward her.

"No! Stay away, please; please don't touch me."

Her shrill plea left me no choice. I froze. Frustration pushed words from my mouth. "Kitty, I need to hold you. For God's sake, let me hold you. For the past several weeks, I didn't know what had happened to you. I thought you were dead. I'm the fool who still loves you." I sighed. The mystique of the earlier moment, when I saw her in the doorway and knew it was her, faded. Reality regained control of my hormones. I was here, risking my sanity and maybe my life, to find the truth. "I don't understand. What's wrong? I thought you loved me. Was everything I thought we had a lie … like your fictitious FBI admirer Tom Peterson? How could you be that cruel?"

"Brent, I know you won't believe anything I say right now. I came here to … please sit down and let me try to explain … everything."

Reluctantly I fumbled in the dark until I found the couch and plopped down. My gut churned as my curiosity wrestled with my fears.

Kitty sat in an armchair adjacent to the couch. I could barely distinguish her outline in the shielded glow of the outside lights. I don't know if it was her attitude, or the fact that I couldn't see her, but all the past came roaring back, I had only been a puppet to her, someone she could control for her enjoyment. She was going to explain everything to me. How could I believe anything she said, ever? She was a liar. I wanted to stand and scream at her for what her lies had done to Bean. If I'd known the truth, maybe I would've acted differently the night I had Bean and Kitty and their kidnappers cornered in the barn, maybe—I needed to shut off the 'maybes' and listen. That was why I was here.

In the dark I could see her hand go to her chin; her thinking ritual.

"Tom Peterson was Gramps' idea. What was the word you used to describe the lottery scam … oh yeah, magic. Although I fought it, Gramps insisted that you needed a distraction; something to divert your attention. Your snooping around was getting you to close to the truth. He feared that if you discovered what was actually taking place, we'd all go to jail."

A surge of anger erupted from my lips. "How can you adore and be led by a man who schemed to ruin innocent people's lives, killing Bean, for the sake of protecting his wealth?"

Her head bowed. "I understand your anger and saying I'm sorry won't fix anything. Please bear with me. Let me tell you what happened before you judge us."

Kitty blew out a long breath. "What I've told you in the past about Camden and me was true ... just not complete. The reason I continued to sleep with that bastard wasn't just because of the tapes. He showed me evidence he had that could indict my grandfather for insider trading."

She sniffed and I could see her head shake in the semi-darkness.

"The only leverage I had that kept Camden from turning Gramps in was how Andrew and I had rigged the drawings and the answer was safe with me, since I didn't know. Andrew never told me, and I never asked."

Her back stiffened, pushing her taller in the chair. She obviously wasn't comfortable with what she was about to say.

"Unbeknownst to me at the time, not only was Sparks blackmailing me to rig the lottery, he was also blackmailing my Gramps. The fat fucker financially destroyed my grandfather. All those years my grandfather busted his ass for nothing; to make a lazy fat ass richer." Her fist pounded the arm of the chair.

"What made me almost as nauseated as sleeping with the stinking lard ass was that my father," she cleared her throat, "my father was helping Camden. My dad has always hated Gramps. And my dad was broke and too lazy to work. And he knew, after all his failures, my grandfather would never give him another penny. So he provided Camden with the information about his father's insider trading in return for a share of all the lottery winnings and the money they extorted from his own dad." She shook her head and paused as if waiting for me to say something.

But I already knew Preston Franklin was involved after what Joshua had told me and finding Preston shot to death at her home.

"Dad and Camden figured I had to have help to rig the system and deducted I'd used Andrew. They must have threatened him to rig the game again and, knowing Andrew and how much he wanted out, he must have threatened them back. One of them killed him. I can't prove it, but I know it."

She spoke of Andrew's death so casually. Thank God she wasn't there. The vision of Andrew sitting in that chair with half his head blown off was tattooed in my memory. It would always be there, particularly late at night.

"Just be thankful you weren't the one to find him," I said.

In the semi-darkness, I could see her head turn away from me. I would never learn to keep my thoughts to myself.

"I'm sorry," I said. "Please continue."

She cleared her throat. "I don't think my dad ever liked anyone in this world; his own father, or me. On countless occasions, he reminded me he didn't care for me because I loved his father. And I'm sure he loathed a fat, smelly asshole like Camden. But he needed him and used him." Emotion crept into her voice. She spoke faster, emphasizing key words. "Somehow, he and Camden knew Andrew had fixed one more drawing, maybe Andrew told them before they killed him; I don't know. Anyway, my father wanted all of that money for himself. So Dad kidnapped Bean in order to try to coerce you to tell him how the lottery was rigged. I knew it was him, he's suffered with allergies for years, and though he changed his voice, I recognized his cough in the ear piece I was forced to wear when we were in that restaurant."

She leaned back in the chair and shook out the ends of her hair, like it was the tension in the room.

"The person who called me when Andrew was killed, left me a bug to wear the night I came to your bed and breakfast, and you were shot. Damn, I felt so awful about that. They swore to me nothing would happen to you, they just wanted to scare you." She sniffed. "You could've been killed because of me." She partially blocked a sob.

"I'm okay, thanks to you."

She blew her nose.

"Do you remember the teddy, the one I wore when we were at my country home?"

"Sure." I tried to keep my voice flat, non-reactive. How could I forget that transparent teddy? And she knew I'd never forget how she looked. But those were memories of a relationship founded on lies.

She canted her head as if surprised by my response. Then she looked away again as if something was troubling her.

"They told me to wear it. It was bugged. That's why they came and got me and the numbers after you told me about them. They gagged me and dragged me out of my bedroom."

She turned to face me, and I could feel, versus see, her blue eyes docking with mine.

"I was so afraid they were going to kill you." Her words bled concern.

"They tried." Vivid memories flashed in my mind of Sanders bleeding upside down in the four-wheeler.

"Then after you saved me, they tried to kill us at the drawing; Camden, my dad, and Jeanette of all people. That was close. We should've never gone there."

"That was my stupid idea. But at least we found out she was involved."

"And then the bar fight and the car chase and we lost them. But they found us again."

Her words resurrected a dormant thought. I had always wondered how they found us again as we maneuvered through Columbia. Was it just luck?

"Yeah, and then I, ah, I fired that shot at the car chasing us. I … I ka-killed her. I killed Jeanette." She choked back another sob.

I had to restrain myself from going to her and cradling her in my arms. "That couldn't have been helped; it was her or us. Don't beat yourself up over it. It happened. It's over."

"I know you're right, it's just that … I'm almost through."

I clamped my hands together. "Okay."

"While you changed the tire in the alley, Camden and that bitch Beltner and a couple of their thugs took me and Bean on that terrible ride. I was sure I'd never see you again." She sniffed. "Until all that shooting in the woods and then … then the beating they gave us in the barn, trying to draw you in," she moaned, "then my country home, and the God-awful shooting started again. I, I saw Nancy shoot Bean. She just shot her like it was nothing. Then she and Camden forced me into the car and took me away … to another hell."

She wiped her eyes.

I wanted to console her, but she was at the point in the story I knew nothing about. I wanted to hear what happened.

A long awkward moment of silence seemed to make the room darker.

"Then thank God, Gramps found us and saved me."

"And all that money," the words just slipped out.

"It was *his* money." Her indignation was over the top.

"And your Gramps killed both of them to get it."

"It was self-defense."

"If my banking memory serves me correctly, online bank accounts containing that much money are normally protected with at least one password over and above the account number. Did Camden tell your grandfather the passwords before the shooting started?"

"What are you insinuating?" she asked as her body straightened.

"Your account of what happened reminded me of several things I've let slid; things I should've chewed on longer before swallowing."

"Like what?" she asked, scooting to the edge of her seat.

"After Sally was murdered, the kidnapper called me and had Bean make me tell him how the lottery was rigged."

"So? You told me about him, and how he wanted proof of how I rigged the game."

"During that conversation I discovered Bean's kidnapper didn't know who Andrew was or that he was dead. So if you're right; and your father kidnapped Bean, who killed Andrew?"

"Camden or one of his hired thugs." Her words were condescending like any dummy would have known the answer.

"Then I guess you think Camden had Nancy Beltner kill Sally Kellermann? After all Camden and Nancy must have been an item since they ran off together with the money?"

"Of course."

"But if your father and Camden were in a partnership, why wouldn't your father at least have known Andrew was dead? And he didn't know that the drawing manager was a woman or that Sally was also dead. How do you explain that?"

"I can't answer for them. They're all dead. So I guess no one can answer your questions." She leaned toward me. "Anything else bothering you?"

"Yeah. Just before you were abducted from your country home, you asked to borrow my phone. Why did you want my phone?"

"I, ah, I don't remember asking for it."

"Trust me, you did."

"I don't remember. That was a traumatic time for me."

"I'll bet. And how did your bugged teddy end up on the bed? Did your kidnappers stand around while you changed clothes?"

"No!" Her hand smacked the armrest. "I had already changed when they appeared. What's wrong with you? Don't you believe me?" She shrugged. "I didn't think you would."

"There's one other thing. You said you recognized your dad's cough when we were forced to wear the head-sets in the restaurant."

"Yes."

"Then why would your father ask me to kill his daughter? How can a man hate his grown daughter enough to kill her? If he truly hated you that much, why hadn't he killed you long ago?"

A door opened from an adjoining room and the lights came on making me blink.

"The gun was filled with blanks, Mr. Layne," Joshua Franklin said.

I jumped to my feet, not because of the lights or Joshua's words, but because of what I saw. Kitty sat next to me. She had long blonde hair strapped to her head by a bandage covering her face except for her eyes, nostrils, and mouth. And all of her fingers were bandaged

"What the—"

"I told you he wouldn't buy it," Joshua said.

I turned and the old man stood in the doorway of a bedroom with a gun aimed at me.

Two of Joshua Franklin's defensive nose guards came into the condo from the front door, blocking my escape from the gun-wielding Joshua. One of them I recognized from the Full Fishnet Restaurant, the man at the bar. The one who had given me the gun wrapped in a newspaper. The gun I was told to use to kill Kitty and her driver or they would kill Bean. The gun Joshua said was filled with blanks.

I assumed these two mammoth men had been outside the condo all along in case I decided to make a run for it.

Kitty extended her bandaged hands and glared at Joshua. "Why did you come in? I could've convinced him. Damn it." She blew out a long breath.

"He found you. He found us. He could do it again. We need to find out how he did it and then—"

"No!" Kitty leaped to her feet. "No. Brent won't tell anyone. He'll come with us. We'll have his identity changed as well; face, fingerprints." She held out her bandaged hands. "We'll get married." Those blue eyes bore into mine. "He can't testify against his wife. Please, Gramps, do this for me. You've gotten your money back three-fold, and they're all dead; everyone who tried to hurt us."

My knees buckled, and I had to grab the armrest of the couch to steady myself. This whole thing had been a lie, all of it.

I stared into what used to be Kitty's breath-taking blue eyes. "So it was you. You killed Andrew."

Kitty's eyes welled. "He had rigged the numbers one last time, but not for me, for proof. He was going to the police to turn himself in and to tell them everything. I shouldn't have taken the gun. I took it to scare him. He was so belligerent, so fucking righteous. We argued. I couldn't talk him out of confessing. He was sitting in his chair. I pulled the gun to threaten him, he tried to grab it out of my hand, and it went off. It … it was an accident." Tears soaked through her bandages.

"And you had the balls to take me there to tell me you loved me." I looked away from her. Her presence sickened me.

"I do love you, and he was dead. There wasn't any place else to go."

"And Sally Kellerman, did you kill poor innocent Sally too?"

"No," she said.

I looked at her and she nodded in the direction of her grandfather. "He had one of his goons kill her."

"She would've figured out Nancy Beltner's role as the video swapper, and Nancy would've brought us all down," Joshua said.

I turned to Joshua. "So Nancy wouldn't do your dirty work."

"What're you talking about?"

"She wouldn't kill Sally for you."

"Are you kidding me? She was afraid of her own shadow. She became so paranoid she ran off with Camden."

I nodded as I turned slowly to face Kitty. "So it was you." My tone was flat without a hint of emotion. "You killed Bean."

$$\textbf{\large{(115)}}$$

It must have been after midnight. There was an ironic, peaceful stillness in the overcast darkness. I stood in the stern of a thirty-five foot inboard cabin cruiser tethered to the Tortuga dock. My hands were tied behind me and a dish towel had been stuffed in my mouth. My jaws ached and my hands were numb. And nose breathing wasn't my norm. Fun.

It was just me and the two goons. One was outlined in the glow of the bridge's instruments' lights as he fiddled with the engine and the other knelt on the dock untying the bow rope.

In the dim light from a low wattage light bulb at the dock's entrance, I could make out the gigantic man, standing with the freed rope in his hand. "Did you know that just beyond the reef surrounding this island, the ocean plummets to a depth of twenty-seven-thousand feet; damned near five miles deep." He kicked a waist-high stack of concrete blocks by his feet. "Five or six of these babies and some good nylon rope," he kinked and then snapped the rope taunt, "and you'll never be seen again, ever."

I didn't want to die, especially by drowning. The thought sent a shudder through me. I'd rather be shot. I needed a plan.

After sorting though several ideas, I'd decided to slam a shoulder into him when he tried to get back on the boat. Maybe he'd fall into the water. Then I'd jump to the dock and hopefully outrun the one on the bridge.

I watched him, waiting for him to move toward the stern line. He bent and picked up one of the concrete blocks with his enormous hand like it was a brick.

"I've got an idea. I think I'll let you load these. Why should I work? I'm always taking orders; time to give some." He set the block on top of the stack. "Plus you need to get use to these babies; they're gonna take you on a five mile dive." He chuckled as he bent and looped the rope back over dock cleat. He reached into a pants pocket, took out a knife, and opened the blade. Then he pulled out his gun and cocked it. "Step over here and turn around."

Having my hands freed would probably be my only chance. A slug of adrenaline jolted my system. I walked on shaky legs to the side of the boat. At the gunwale, I turned my back to him, and he cut the bindings on my wrists.

I rubbed my wrists and then pulled the towel out of my mouth.

"Did I tell you to take that out?" He sounded like an angry adult admonishing a child.

Pissing him off would get me drowned, but acquiescing could also be a loser. I took the middle ground, stood tall, and looked him in the eyes. "I need to breathe if I'm going to work." My words were soft and non-threatening.

"One peep, one miscue, and I'll make you pray to be drowned."

I nodded and stepped off the boat onto the dock.

⑽

It had been a long time since I'd messed around with concrete blocks. When I was a teenager, and we couldn't afford weights, we used blocks to do curls with both hands on one block. They had to weigh about thirty or forty pounds each.

In the dim light of the Tortuga dock, I grabbed a block in each hand and stepped back onto the boat. Not an easy thing to do when the boat moved under me and my hands were full. I staggered to keep my balance. And an idea was born.

The giant had pocketed his knife and stood on the edge of the dock near the stack of blocks, gun at ready.

I set the blocks on the stern deck and climbed back onto the dock. With a block in each hand, I stepped back onto the boat. When my second foot stepped onto the bobbing boat, I feigned lost of balance and whirled around, arms extended. Spinning like a discus thrower, I flung a block as hard as I could at the big man's chest.

He batted it away like it was a foam rubber ball, skipping it across the dock into the water on the other side.

Fuck.

Gun raised and pointed at my face, he said, "I warned you asshole! Set the block down and turn around."

I was out of options. I needed to think of something, but all I could envision was being tied to the blocks and sinking deeper and deeper, fighting not to gulp the water and end it.

If he tied me up again, I was done. I had no choice. I had to test his shooting skills; anything but drowning.

Facing him, I squatted to put the block on the deck as well as to position myself to lunge at him.

But when his eyebrows arched in surprise, I paused unsure of what he was doing. Then both his hands disappeared behind him. His mouth spread to an oval, and he emitted a grunt. His hands returned to his chest and clutched something protruding near his breastbone. I stepped closer; the giant was grabbing the blood-smeared head of a spear, just before he toppled into the water. His splash was not only loud, it rocked the boat, gaining Neanderthal number two's attention.

I dove off the boat and rolled behind the pile of blocks as a puff of noise seemed to cause a chunk of concrete to explode off one of the blocks.

Soft running footsteps on the dock made me peer out from behind the blocks. A hooded shadow was sprinting towards me.

I looked around and the speared-man's gun lay on the dock about ten feet away. I bolted toward the gun only to withdraw behind the blocks as two puffs splintered the dock's wood between me and the gun.

The second thug, the one I had met at a different time in my life, in the restaurant, back when I believed everything I heard, came out of the enclosed bridge.

The running shadow slid to a stop when the bar goon came onto the rear deck of the boat. The hooded person shouldered a spear gun as Joshua's nose guard fired two flame suppressed silenced rounds.

The mystery person had created just enough of a diversion for me to dive to the gun on the deck. Clasping the gun, I rolled onto my side, aimed, and fired three rounds at the man from the bar. His body jerked as each bullet found its mark. He lurched backwards and toppled over the railing into the water.

I scrambled to my feet. My savior was down and the hood had fallen away exposing long blonde hair fixed by a white bandage.

I ran to Kitty and dropped to my knees. She was bleeding from her shoulder and side.

I cradled her head and her eyes opened.

She sucked in a stuttered breath. "Magic," she said, then she smiled, and passed out.

$$\textbf{(117)}$$

Four weeks later,
Columbia, South Carolina

I stepped down from the witness stand and walked past Joshua Franklin, seated at the defense table, and through the thigh-high gate to the rows of spectator seats.

Sitting on the aisle, Charlie looked up at me and smiled. "Good job, I think your testimony fried him," he said in a hushed tone.

I sat down next to him. "I can't get over how good you look; a new suit, a haircut, and those store-bought teeth. You look like a proper business man."

"How many times do I have to tell you, they're implants, damn it? Or I should say they'll be implants in another few months after my gums heal."

The person in front of us turned and glared at Charlie.

Charlie leaned forward and returned the glare causing the man to turn around and face the court. "When I'm done, I'll have over ten grand invested in my mouth," Charlie whispered. He patted my knee. "If you hadn't shared your reward money with me and Bloodhound, I'd still—"

The judge banged his gavel and ordered a thirty-minute recess, and we mingled with the crowd as it flowed out into the huge hallway of the Columbia courthouse.

Charlie and I retrieved our personal belongings at the security desk and stepped outside into the South Carolina summer heat and humidity. "It won't be long now," I said. "The lawyers will give their closing arguments, and the jury will be sequestered."

Charlie nodded and then checked his iPhone. "Ah-ha, Eric sent a message."

"Eric?" I asked.

"Oh, I forgot to tell you our new partner's proper name. Bloodhound is just a nickname. Eric Troudeau is his God-given name. And by the way, Eric thanks you as well. Like me, he never thought he'd be a multi-millionaire." Charlie's fingers tapped icons. "Here we go." He read.

"Don't tease me, what's it say?" My voice raised an octave. "Read it out loud."

"Miss Kitrina Blavnof left the Geneva hospital yesterday. Both her and the fifty million she had in a Swiss bank are in the wind. Do you want me to find her?"

I glanced away at the traffic rolling by on the heat-simmering street and rubbed my chin with my forefinger and thumb, a gesture befitting the moment. "What did you tell me yesterday our open case load was?"

"Between missing people and stolen valuables, ten."

"And how much do we make if we collect, let say half of it, in round numbers?" I asked.

Charlie scratched his groomed hair-covered head. "Two million plus expenses."

I nodded. "That should keep us busy for a while." I took a deep breath and eased it out. "Tell Eric to forget Kitty for the time being." I threw my arm over Charlie's shoulder. "We'd better get back in there if we want to hear the summations."

Charlie hesitated. "One second, there's something I've been meaning to ask you." He stepped away and faced me.

"Okay."

"What'd you do with your share of that money? I don't see any new clothes. You're still driving that old car. The only change I've seen is you've listed the condo. Are you going to buy or build a mansion, if so, where? Are you planning on leaving here?"

Worry lines creased Charlie's face.

I reached out and patted his shoulder. "If I leave here, I'll tell you."

"Thanks."

I started to walk into the courthouse and Charlie grabbed my arm stopping me.

"I know I'm prying, but I'm curious, what did you do with all that dough?"

Although what I did with my money wasn't any of Charlie's business, he was my friend, and I would never keep secrets from my friends, never. "I kept enough to sustain our business for five to ten years, and I gave the rest away."

His eyebrow arched as his arms extended out from his sides. "You gave all that money away? Who'd you give it to your parents?"

"No, not my parents; they're dead."

"Then who?"

"Somebody else's needy parents who had lost both their son and … and their daughter."

THE END

AUTHOR'S NOTE

Thank you for reading my novel. If you liked "Dead Winners" please tell your friends and write a twenty plus word review in Amazon's 'Comment' section and Goodreads. And please review the descriptions of my other ebooks. Hopefully you'll find another story of mine that peaks your interest.

Respectfully,

Dave McDonald

Dave McDonald's other ebooks:

Kugi's Story

Sam's Folly

Death Insurance

Killing by Numbers

A Common Uprising

FB link:

https://www.facebook.com/RDaveMcDonald?fref=ts

And soon to be published:

Too Many

Nesting on Empty

The Death Chase

The Federation

ABOUT THE AUTHOR

A romanticist at heart, with a deductive mind, I am a graduate engineer who traveled the world keeping commercial jet engines flying safely. I thought I loved my first career until I found my second, writing.

For decades, I traveled abroad. At the time I was performing my job. In retrospect, I was collecting data; sights, smells, emotions, experiences, and stories for my second career.

I've written ten novels, with several more in seed.

I live with my wife, Linda, and dog, Bentley, on Hilton Head Island, South Carolina.

46112653R00183

Made in the USA
Charleston, SC
11 September 2015